W9-AZE-921

THE THIRD HELL

CONNIE DIAL

THE THIRD HELL

The Permanent Press
Sag Harbor, NY 11963

For information, address:
The Permanent Press
4170 Noyac Road
Sag Harbor, NY 11963
www.thepermanentpress.com

Library of Congress Cataloging-in-Publication Data

Dial, Connie, author.
The third hell / Connie Dial.
Sag Harbor, NY: The Permanent Press, [2017]
ISBN: 978-1-57962-494-1

PS3604.I126 T48 2017
813'.6—dc23 2016044268

Printed in the United States of America

Dedicated to men and women in law enforcement,
especially those in the Los Angeles Police Department.

Which way I fly is Hell; myself am Hell;
And, in the lowest depth, a lower deep
Still threat'ning to devour me opens wide,
To which the Hell I suffer seems a Heav'n.

—Milton, "Paradise Lost, IV"

ONE

The desert cactus exploded in a shower of green sticky flesh. The retort echoed like thunder over the wasteland and the boy froze before lowering the 9mm Beretta and grinning confidently. Nino Angelo watched as his son carefully engaged the decocking lever and shoved the semiauto back into the holster.

Matt was short for a twelve-year-old, but his hands were big with long slender pianist's fingers, and he easily manipulated the weapon. His interest in guns seemed to grow as they spent more time together. Anyway, that's what Angelo told himself. Like most retired cops he kept guns stashed in his car and in the house. It was easier to teach his son how to handle them than hope he'd never find the hiding places.

After Angelo left the Los Angeles Police Department, he still wore his service weapon whenever he left home, even to go to the ballpark or Disneyland. Lately, as images of that night faded from his life and memory, and the pain subsided, he felt less compelled to strap on the cumbersome thing. He enjoyed the freedom of dressing in tank tops and Levi's without a jacket or long shirt to hide a gun.

Matt looked up at him. "What now?"

A mangy brown rabbit bolted from the brush twenty feet in front of them. Matt unsnapped the holster and pulled out the gun. Angelo started to say something but hesitated. It would be a nasty but effective way to teach his son a valuable lesson. No decent human being forgets or wants to repeat the gore created by firing a high-powered weapon at an innocent creature. He changed his mind and put his hand over the slide.

"You don't want to do that," he said, lowering the muzzle.

"Why not?" Matt whined. "Wild rabbits are nothing but big rats."

"Don't point a gun at any living thing, unless it's trying to hurt you or your mom. Understand?" He said it more sternly than he had intended.

Matt shrugged; his expression became a sullen mask. It had been a battle all morning to get his brooding offspring in a good mood. With one gesture, he had wiped out the positive effects of a large breakfast and allowing the boy to drive his classic MG on the open road—not to mention two hours of patient instruction on gun handling, but Angelo knew his limitations. Teaching young cops how to do police work was a pleasure, and he'd always been good at it. Trying to tutor an obstinate preteen was seriously stretching his tolerance level.

His son had begun to open up, actually talking about school and his friends. Now Angelo figured he'd ruined whatever progress they'd made that day. In spite of what he told Matt, he didn't care if some stupid rabbit got blown apart. They were big rats, but he already was responsible for more than his share of his kid's bad dreams. He didn't want to notch another ugly memory on one of the few days they got to spend together.

"What can I shoot?" Matt asked, shoving the gun back into the holster.

"That's enough this time. We'll come back in a couple of weeks. You did really good," he said, reaching down to secure the holster strap.

The boy pushed his father's hand away, unbuckled the gun belt, took it off, and practically in one motion shoved it at him. Then without a word, Matt turned and trudged back toward the car. He was slightly overweight and had difficulty navigating the rough terrain. As Angelo watched him, he wondered if he had wasted the last two years attempting to become a better father. Matt didn't like him. Even his ex-wife eventually had to admit the obvious. Sidney kept telling him to try harder until she realized that Matt was resisting any connection. His son wasn't usually disrespectful or unruly, just . . . inaccessible.

There were those moments when the boy seemed to forget his anger and past disappointments concerning his absentee father. He would smile and have a good time, in spite of himself. He would sit beside Angelo on the couch while they watched television or fall asleep against Angelo's shoulder. For those few occasions when he felt what it was like to be a father, he figured it was worth the disappointments.

"You hungry?" he asked once they were on the highway. Food was the one sure thing that appealed to his son.

"No."

"How are the piano lessons coming?" he asked, trying to find a way back in.

"Okay, I guess."

"Your mom says you got picked to do a solo at your school's band recital next Saturday."

"I guess so."

"Would it make you nervous if I came?"

"Maybe, I don't know."

He glanced at the boy who stared out the window at the boring landscape. The endless patches of dried brush were hypnotic, and Matt seemed to prefer their monotony to his father's conversation. Angelo slipped a Mitch Woods CD into the car player. The bluesy piano fit his mood. He had interviewed enough reticent suspects to know when someone wasn't going to talk. Besides, it had been a long day. He was tired. He would take Matt back to Sidney's condo and let her deal with him. She didn't expect them until the next morning, but he'd had enough fathering for one day.

For nearly two years, Angelo had worked on the East Los Angeles home he'd inherited from his father, adding a second story with two bedrooms and another bathroom. It was for his son. Now whenever Matt slept over, he had his own room with a balcony. The original bedroom downstairs was converted into a game room with a pool table and dartboard. There was even a used spinet in the living room so he could practice.

His son treated the house as if it were a prison, never wandering more than ten feet in any direction. But although he had the option, he never refused to visit. Angelo guessed that Matt got some sort of satisfaction out of annoying him. He would readily practice the piano unless his father entered the room. As soon as Angelo stopped to listen, the music would trail off and he would revert to boring exercises. They played pool, but his son wasn't very good so that wasn't much fun for either of them. Matt moped around the backyard, sat on the oak swing his grandfather had carved, and generally avoided his father. Angelo thought their relationship mimicked the one he'd had with his own father. Matt came to the house every Sunday, just as Angelo had done when his father, Sal, was alive. The only things missing were alcohol and the constant arguments. Angelo would have welcomed an occasional argument, anything but silence. He had loved his father in spite of his failings and hoped Matt could find a way to love him in spite of his failings as a father.

He knew his job as a police officer had kept him away from home on too many special occasions. Birthdays, holidays were spent at the police station instead of with his family. His wife complained and eventually left him; Matt withdrew. When they told him he couldn't be a cop any longer with a bullet lodged too close to his heart, he saw that as an opportunity to reconnect with the boy.

The sun was setting on the horizon in a backdrop of dusty rose and light charcoal grays. Angelo smiled at the desert's natural beauty.

"Are you watching this, kid?"

Matt nodded and continued looking at the sterile landscape.

It was still early, but Angelo decided to drive straight to Sidney's place. He wouldn't make the scheduled stop by his house. He was exhausted. A full day of trying to please his son was more work than any double shift in the narcotics squad during the worst tactical alert, but then totally giving up wasn't an option either.

In less than two hours, they were in downtown LA. His ex-wife had moved a few miles from the city center to a leased condominium in the Hollywood Hills. He loved the drive but hated the location. Her building was in one of those death-trap canyons that even the fire department had written off as impossible to defend. Angelo had tried to persuade her to move to a safer location, but Sidney liked her view of rooftops, trees, and the rural landscape. Apparently no-sidewalks-or-curbs was trendy in her world. She didn't even mind the wild dogs and coyotes that howled all night until they cornered or carried off someone's pet.

Sidney was in her element living among the rich and self-centered. She gave Matt everything he wanted, so naturally nothing he had seemed valuable or important to him.

Angelo turned off Sunset onto Laurel Canyon, anxious to test the MG on the narrow, steep curves. His brother-in-law had installed a new engine, radio, CD player, and racing tires on the classic green roadster, and it ran better now than when Angelo bought it new thirty years ago.

Most boys would have enjoyed the wild ride up the hill, but Matt sat impassively as the tires screeched and centrifugal force pulled at their bodies. He looked bored. Angelo slowed as he approached the building, a white, three-story Mediterranean surrounded by banana trees and thick patches of bamboo.

Sidney occupied the top floor. She stood on the balcony looking out over the street like a beautiful queen surveying her kingdom. So tall and slender that he thought a strong breeze might blow her into the canyon. Her auburn hair was trimmed very short, a boy's cut. He liked it. He always wanted her. She was an easy woman to love, impossible to live with. Her last divorce from his successor, Deputy Chief Joe Denby, left her with a large settlement, and Angelo was still paying child support for Matt. The woman lived well thanks to her discarded husbands.

"How did she know we were coming?" Angelo asked as he parked in front of the garage.

"She's probably waiting for Reggie," Matt said, shaking his head.

"Who's Reggie?"

Matt shrugged and wiggled out of the tight passenger seat. "See you next week, Dad," he said, as he opened the side door to the building and disappeared inside the lobby.

"Yeah, I had a good time too," Angelo said to the rearview mirror. He backed the car down the driveway under the balcony. She was still there. "How are you, Sid?" he shouted up to her.

She waved at him. "Good. You?"

"Who is Reggie?" he asked. It was none of his business, but he always worried about the men she brought into Matt's life. He counted himself as one of her questionable choices.

"Reggie Madison. That would be me." The introduction came from the man who stood in the street closing the door to a shiny, new, black Mustang. "You Matt's father?"

Angelo turned off the ignition and got out of his car. He extended his hand to the tall, dark-haired man with narrow blue eyes. "It's Angie. Sorry about prying into your business. It's not about Sidney. I'd never . . ." He decided to stop talking. He didn't owe this guy any explanation.

"Hey, Angie, if Matt were my kid, I'd want to know who was hanging around."

Angelo stared at Reggie's eyes and wondered if he ever blinked. His gaze was cold and fixed on him. He knew the guy was a cop before he saw the bulge of a gun grip under his jacket. All the signs were there—the short hair, the trimmed mustache, the scrutinizing look, and finally the swagger, an arrogance that comes when you've been tested and won.

"Who do you work for?" Angelo asked.

"LA, same as you."

"Uniform?"

"Surveillance."

Angelo nodded and sat in the car again. "Gotta go." He wanted to ask Reggie how he got along with his son, but thinking about it made him angry. His abrupt departure was rude, but he didn't care. The new engine roared and he backed out of the driveway into the street. He glanced at the balcony.

Sidney was gone. His instincts warned him that her choice in men hadn't improved much.

It was a warm, breezy summer evening, so he pulled the car off the narrow street onto a dirt turnaround and removed the black canvas top. He had kept it on all day so Matt wouldn't get sunburned. The boy had delicate, pale skin like his mother's. Angelo couldn't think of anything his son had inherited from his side of the family, except maybe his Sicilian stubbornness and love of music. Unlike Matt, he was tall, thin, and coordinated enough to enjoy playing several sports. With his black curly hair and olive complexion, Angelo invoked some interesting expressions whenever he introduced his chubby, blond son to one of his buddies.

Refurbished neon lights lined Hollywood Boulevard as he drove toward home. At night, the street looked nostalgically clean and glamorous. The drug-dealing gangbangers and prostitutes hid on the side streets or in the less discriminating T-shirt and sex shops. They knew how to avoid both private security and police footbeats who patrolled the touristy area. They popped out of doorways like snakes from a basket, snared their willing prey, sold drugs or their bodies, and disappeared.

Angelo felt at home on this street. He knew every business owner, whore, and drug dealer. He saw a hand-to-hand narcotics sale as he drove slowly in heavy traffic. The urge to jump out of the car and make an arrest was still there. Although he was happy that he could still spot the crime, he was satisfied with just seeing it. He was relieved that someone else would have to catch them, book them, do the paperwork, and go to court. He touched the front of his shirt and could feel the scar tissue so close to his heart. Maybe there was another reason.

He thought about stopping to eat at Musso & Frank on the boulevard, but saw the long line of tourists standing outside and decided to keep driving home to East LA. Besides, he wanted to call Matt and try to talk to him. It would be a one-way conversation, but he felt a need to say something. The day hadn't ended well.

The ride was so pleasant that he drove past the Hollywood Freeway on-ramp and decided to go home on surface streets. Hollywood Division ended at Normandie. As he entered the Rampart area, he took his gun from the glove compartment and put it on the seat beside him. It was precautionary. The barred storefronts and gang graffiti made him feel vulnerable in the open car, but the cool night air blowing in his face and hair gave him a taste of freedom, a temporary touch of abandon that he wasn't willing to forfeit to his fears.

Forty-five minutes later, he reached the hilly section of East LA. The residential street was quiet as he maneuvered the little sports car onto his driveway. He parked it inside the gate and locked the deadbolt. The neighborhood had changed since his father had lived there. The older residents had died or moved to smaller houses and younger families with lots of kids moved in. Most of them did what he had done, remodeled or tore down the old houses to build bigger ones and put in security systems. He leaned on the car and looked at his property. It was worth much more than when he inherited it.

The value of his property and the security system were two more things his older sister, Lucy, had to complain about. Deeply religious, she never forgave him for his divorce and constantly complained about how little she saw of her nephew. His sister also resented his reluctance to include her in his life and give her unfettered access to the old family home. She hadn't minded his inheriting the house because it had been so pathetically run-down when he got it. Their father wasn't wealthy but he had saved nearly every penny of the insurance money after their mother's death. Their mother was a young woman when she died, forty-eight . . . his age. Angelo remembered her black hair and red chapped hands. She worked hard to support the family while his father, a talented cabinetmaker, mostly sat at home, drank wine, and swore he would never work until the perfect job was offered. It rarely was.

He turned on all the lights downstairs. Dark, empty rooms made him feel lonely. His last companion, a rodent-and-bird-eating orange tabby with a bad attitude, had died a few months ago. He suspected someone poisoned the big cat that had guarded the yard like a mountain lion on catnip and had mangled more than one visiting kitty. Most of the neighbors had complained about him, so the list of suspects was endless.

He remembered the cleaning lady had been there, when he noticed every book was on the shelf and there weren't any newspapers or socks on the floor. The house smelled of lemon-scented furniture polish and fresh-baked apple pie. Mrs. Pollard always left him something in the kitchen and a new scratch or nick on the coffee table. She was clumsy, a little farsighted, and didn't clean very well, but she was cheap and he didn't have the heart to fire her.

His father wouldn't have recognized his old home. Angelo had added on to the back of the house too and created a big, open kitchen like the one his mother always talked about having in the old country. He had put nearly every penny of his retirement buyout money, thousands of dollars, back into this house. Without a family, he might as well be living in a studio apartment.

He had done all of it for Matt. When his son was there, even sulking around the house, it was worth the money and effort.

The house looked great. Repairing what was wrong between him and his son wasn't as easy as fixing the house. Angelo wondered who Matt really was and worried about what sort of man he would become.

"Fuck it," Angelo said and slid off the stool. "I'm depressing myself."

He turned on the television in the living room. It didn't matter which channel. The noise was company. He sat at his computer in the den. There was never any e-mail on Sunday, but he had been out with Matt all day and hadn't gone online since the previous night. The Internet was a hotline to his buddies still on the job. They told him all the LAPD gossip. Cops, especially retired cops, live for gossip. What they didn't know, they made up.

The familiar greeting, "You've got mail," surprised him. He started with the first message. It was from an old girlfriend who still kept in touch. She just wanted to say hello. The next one was advertising. He deleted it and quickly clicked onto the last one. He stared at the screen and smiled.

He laughed and hit the print button. He read it several times to himself and then out loud. "Thanks, Dad, it was fun."

TWO

The barnlike garage behind Angelo's house had also undergone a major transformation. His father's dusty, junk-filled space had been converted into a workshop. Like today, Angelo spent most of his mornings there drinking coffee and struggling with his latest project.

It had cost him a fortune to rewire this building. A heavy-duty table saw, thickness and finish planers, a drill press, disc sander, and band saw were just a few of the power tools positioned strategically around the ample space with plenty of room for his workbench in the middle. He had constructed a storage bin for the different types of hardwood he had collected and some boards his father had abandoned when alcohol became more important than making cabinets.

Angelo sat at his drafting bench under the workshop's only window and tried to design a display table. He'd been thinking about it for a couple of weeks. Matt had shown some interest in his knife collection, so he had decided to give his son pieces from the collection for Christmas. The kid couldn't hurt himself or lose any of the expensive, ivory-handled knives if they were sealed under glass.

There was a nice piece of walnut in the bin. He would match that with one of the lighter woods. When he was in his shop, lost in the process of making a simple cabinet or table, he experienced a kind of satisfaction that he had never felt. He could think of nothing, worry about nothing but the moment—the perfect fit of doweling, joining one seam to another. There was a beginning and an end. Every creation was different, special. He'd sold two smaller cabinets to friends and had begun to believe he might have found his real talent.

His retirement was less than two years ago, but he felt as if he hadn't done police work for decades. The edgy nervousness he had felt every day for twenty-five years as a cop was nearly gone and he guessed that the four or five hours he spent in his workshop each day were the primary reason for his peace of mind.

He had begun dragging the eight-foot piece of walnut out of the bin when he heard the telephone ringing in the kitchen and realized he'd forgotten to bring the mobile phone with him. The answering machine would get it. He was tired of racing back to the house to catch a call from his sister and then have her scold him for the next hour over some trivial bullshit. He wasn't expecting anyone else to call. Fifteen minutes later it rang again. The third time, he was near the door and jogged to the kitchen. She must be really upset about something. It was better to answer the phone than have her give up and come to the house.

The prerecorded message on the answering machine was just starting when he picked up the phone.

"Hello, Lucy," he said impatiently. "I'm here."

"Angie?" a man's voice asked.

"Yeah."

"Angie, this is Reggie. You remember me yesterday from Sid's place?"

He did and felt uneasy. This was one guy who had no reason to talk to him. What were they going to do, compare notes on his ex-wife?

"What's up?"

"It's Matt."

A chill cut through Angelo's body; he felt a sharp pain in his chest. He sat on one of the stools near the counter and took a deep breath. "What?" he asked as calmly as he could.

"Sidney can't find him. She got up this morning and he was gone. The school called. He never showed. She thought he might have come to your place."

"He ran away?"

"He didn't take anything. Is he there?"

"She actually believes I wouldn't call her if the kid showed up?"

"She's not thinking too clear."

He hung up and guilt washed over him. Had he said something or done something yesterday that made his son want to run away? He locked the garage and put on a clean shirt. The trip to Hollywood was a blur. The black Mustang was blocking the driveway, so he parked in the street.

Reggie pulled him into the living room. "She's in the bedroom on the phone."

"Did you check with the kids at school?"

"That's what she's doing now. Because of Matt's age, the captain at Hollywood is setting up a command post. We can go down there if you want."

Angelo met Reggie's stare. His first thought was, "Who the hell does this guy think he is? I'm the father." He kept silent, his anger tempered by his concern. He wanted to know where his son was and then he would deal with Sidney's new boyfriend.

"I'm going to check his room," Angelo said. Reggie stepped aside.

The room was tidy but lived in. He thought about Matt's bedroom at his house. It was guest-room clean. This one had cluttered bookshelves, junk on the dresser, and black-and-white posters of Charlie "Bird" Parker and Miles Davis on one wall. He shook his head. Matt would never tell him what kind of music he liked. Jazz was Angelo's favorite too.

The bed hadn't been slept in. An old leather suitcase that his grandfather had given him was still on the closet floor. Matt loved his grandfather in a way Angelo never could. He wouldn't run away without that bag. A worn Levi's wallet, a birthday present from Angelo, was on the dresser with three dollars in it. A three-by-five, black-and-white picture of a young Angelo, Sidney, and five-year-old Matt was stuck to the mirror. Another picture of Angelo in his police uniform was directly below it, his graduation picture from the police academy. His son kept a picture of him in his bedroom. At the worst time in his life, he just felt as if someone had given him a million dollars.

He looked up at Reggie, who was standing in the doorway.

"What do you think?" Reggie asked.

"I don't know," Angelo admitted. He lifted one side of the mattress and Reggie moved the blankets and sheets so they could see between the mattress and the box spring, every kid's favorite hiding place. They looked at each other and Angelo reached in and grabbed a small, plastic, ziplock Baggie, a full nickel bag of marijuana. It was such a small amount that Angelo was relieved. At least his son wasn't selling it.

"Give it to me," Reggie said.

Angelo hesitated and then handed it to him. Reggie went into Matt's bathroom. The toilet flushed, and when he came back his hands were empty.

"Thanks," Angelo whispered, looking down at the carpet. What he did for Angelo's son could get Reggie fired.

"For what? I know oregano when I see it."

"Angie, I'm so sorry." Sidney was standing by the door. Her eyes were red and looked tired, her hair disheveled. Her frumpy, white sweatshirt and pants were wrinkled and soiled with fresh coffee stains.

He put his arms around her and felt her press closer to him. She wasn't crying. "We'll find him, Sid." She clutched the front of his shirt and shook her head. Angelo let her stay that way for a few seconds before pushing her back a little to look at her face. "When did you last see him, Sid? Where was he?"

He felt her body stiffen. "Here, where do you think? He was in his room when I went to bed."

"What time was that?"

"I don't know. Midnight, I guess. At five this morning he was gone. His bed hadn't been slept in."

"Five? Why didn't you call me right away?" Angelo asked.

She stepped away from him and folded her arms. "What difference does that make now? Just find him, Angie."

Reggie coughed and they both turned toward him. "A Sergeant Hill from Hollywood said he already checked Matt's computer. There was nothing helpful on it." Reggie hesitated. "The last message was the one to you."

Angelo instinctively touched the wallet in his back pocket where he had tucked away a folded copy of the message. "Did Matt say anything to you, Sid? Was he upset? Did you fight about something?"

"No," she said, edging closer to Reggie.

"Where do you think he would go?"

"I don't fucking know, Angie. If I knew, I would go there and get him." She sat on the bed, and covered her face with her hands.

Angelo stared at her. It wasn't right. She wasn't telling him everything. Reggie moved toward the door.

"The command post has the name and address of his best friend. We can check Deputy Chief Denby's place too," Reggie said, nodding at Angelo. "You coming?" The suggestion was transparent. Angelo was upsetting Sidney, and Reggie was trying to gently separate them.

She looked up at the mention of her most recent ex-husband's name and said, "He wouldn't go there. Joe never liked Matt."

Angelo knelt by the bed and touched her knee. "It looks like he ran away, Sid. Every kid's gotta run away at least once. We'll track him down. Knowing Matt, he probably stopped at the first McDonald's he found."

She tried to smile. Angelo wrote down his new cell phone number and told her to call him if their son returned or if the police found him. She nodded. Reggie started to follow him out the door. Angelo stopped and blocked his way.

"I'll let you know if I need help," Angelo said as nicely as he could and closed the door in Reggie's face.

Angelo had a bad feeling on the elevator ride down to the lobby. He was trying to decipher the message that Sidney's body language was sending. She seemed on the verge of hysteria, but it was so controlled. Two years away from the job had left him rusty. The one time he really wanted a little intuitive edge and it wasn't there.

Reggie Madison's place in her life was another total mystery to him. Sidney always complained about Angelo's lack of emotion, but the stoic Reggie Madison made him look like an overwrought sorority girl.

He appreciated the fact that possession of marijuana wouldn't be an issue in his son's life right now, but the ease with which Reggie disposed of it made him uncomfortable.

Angelo wasn't a saint and had let a few Baggies of contraband slide during his career. But he had never done it in front of a witness, especially another cop, even a retired one.

The command post was a police van with an attached awning, folding chairs, and a table. It was set up at the end of Sidney's cul-de-sac where the canyon brush began. Sergeant Hill and two uniformed officers were huddled over a map when Angelo approached. He showed them his ID and explained that Matt was his son.

"What do you have?" Angelo asked, not expecting much from this makeshift operation.

"We talked to his best friend at school, an older kid named Jake Bennett. He says he doesn't know anything. Because of your son's age we're going to get the explorers out here to search the canyon." He stopped and thought a second. "It's a formality. There's no indication your son went into the canyon."

Angelo nodded. He doubted Matt would venture into the dense brush on his own. "What about the neighbors, did they see anything?"

"The guy in the house to the north said that at about three or four this morning he thought he heard crying or whining outside. When he looked out the window, there was nothing there. He thought maybe it was coyotes. Sometimes animal cries sound almost human. I checked behind the man's house myself and didn't find anything," Sergeant Hill said.

"You searched that whole area yourself?"

"Most of it is inaccessible," Sergeant Hill said, looking up at him for the first time. He had gray hair but a youngish face. Too cocky, Angelo thought; this guy loves himself. The supervisor could barely move his muscular arms in the skin-tight uniform. "I've done this before, sir," Sergeant Hill said in a tone of voice Angelo thought was far too condescending.

Angelo ignored the comment. "There were no signs of struggle inside the condo or any forced entry, but his mother thinks the only clothes missing are his pajamas. What did the other neighbors say?"

The sergeant looked up at him. Angelo knew that annoyed expression. He'd used it himself. It said, "If you would stop bothering me, I could probably start asking them."

"Sarge, I'll leave you my cell phone number. Call me first if you find anything, and I'll talk to my ex-wife. Okay?"

"You bet," Sergeant Hill said too glibly, exchanging glances with the two officers.

"What's wrong?"

"Nothing. But is it okay to talk to Detective Madison? He said he was a friend of your ex-wife."

"I don't give a fuck what you tell Reggie Madison. Just be clear, I'll talk to Sidney if you find anything." He was anxious and worried and his temper was boiling over like battery acid.

"Roger that," Sergeant Hill said, holding up his hands as if protecting himself from Angelo's anger before returning to his map.

Angelo copied Jake Bennett's home address. He was done trying to deal with this supervisor. When he returned to Sidney's building, Reggie was waiting in the driveway.

"What's wrong?" Angelo asked.

"She took something to calm down. She's exhausted. I need to help try and find him. Did they know anything?" he asked, nodding toward the command post.

"Not yet, but they said some kid Jake Bennett is his friend. I'm going to talk to him."

"Angie, I can help if you let me. I got some time off. Just say what you want me to do."

"You're on vacation?"

"Not exactly. It's more like forced time off."

"Suspension?"

"You're dying to ask, aren't you?"

Angelo did want to know. For a Special Investigations Section detective to get suspended it had to be pretty bad. While Angelo was still on the job, the chief treated the SIS guys differently than the rest of the department. They were an elite, well-trained bunch of surveillance cops who got the tough, dirty jobs done any way they could and everyone including the chief of police knew it.

"No," he lied, "but you're dying to tell me."

"Not really, but you'd find out anyway. You retired guys know everything. I told my lieutenant he was a dangerous, incompetent fuck and the captain told me to go home for three days at my expense."

"It could've been worse."

"Probably will be if the incompetent fuck is still there when I get back."

"What's wrong with him?"

"It's a long story. Let's just find the Bennett kid. You got an address?"

Angelo nodded and knew he was about to make a huge mistake. Every instinct told him to dump this guy, let him hold Sidney's hand or something until he could find Matt on his own. Instead he held open the passenger door to the MG.

"Want me to drive? I still got my city ride."

Angelo understood the advantages of being in a city car with an active cop, even a suspended one. Reggie could go places and do things he couldn't with the word "retired" on his badge and ID.

He waited until Reggie emptied his stuff out of the passenger seat of the Mustang. For surveillance guys, their car was a mobile home. Angelo didn't ask him why he was still driving the car if he'd been suspended. He figured that was between Reggie and the department.

They found the house on La Mirada Avenue in Hollywood. The Bennetts had the front unit of a duplex located on a street that housed mostly South American illegals. Angelo had worked this area nearly every day when he was a detective in the Hollywood narcotics squad. It was only a few blocks from the station, and had a reputation as a street market for marijuana and Mexican brown heroin. If Jake was Matt's best friend, it was no mystery where his son had acquired the Baggie of grass.

"Mrs. Bennett?" Angelo asked the emaciated woman with thinning brown hair who answered the door. She stayed behind the latched screen and stared at the police IDs he and Reggie held against the torn wire mesh. He could barely see her but recognized the ill-fitting secondhand clothes of poverty and wondered how she could afford to send her son to the pricey Saint Mark's Academy.

"What do you want?"

"Mrs. Bennett, I'm Matt Angelo's father. He's missing, and I thought maybe we could talk with Jake a minute."

"Jake didn't do nothing," she said, her voice growing stronger.

"I know that. I thought maybe Jake might give me some ideas where Matt might be. They were friends, right?"

"Jake ain't here. He went to school." She unhooked the latch, opened the screen door, and stood back for them to enter. "Cops already talked to him at school. I sent them there."

The house was cramped but clean. An open sofa bed in the living room was stacked with clothes and blankets. Angelo stepped over a mongrel puppy asleep near the door, while

Reggie moved cautiously around the room looking into the kitchen.

"Your husband home, Mrs. Bennett?" Reggie asked as he peeked into the two back rooms.

"He don't live here no more. Your son's a good boy, Mr. Angelo. I hope he's okay. He never said nothing about wanting to run away . . . always quiet, but real polite," she said, talking as she folded clothes. "Did you punish him for missing school? Maybe that's why he run away. I hit Jake hard; as big as he is, I beat that boy good. Father Daly's letting my kids go there for nothing, and he don't show up."

"When did that happen?" Angelo asked. Sidney had never mentioned that Matt was missing school.

"Best talk to his momma or the nuns about that. Not my place to be butting in their business."

"How many kids you got, Mrs. Bennett?" Reggie asked.

"Four, and three are doing real good at that school. Jake's like his daddy. He ain't into books."

"What is he into?" Reggie asked.

"Jake will be here at four. If you want, you come back," she said to Angelo.

"Can we take a look in Jake's room?" Reggie asked, edging toward the back rooms again.

"What for?"

"It might help, Mrs. Bennett," Angelo said. "Matt might have written something to your son or left something here that would give us a clue." He tried to distract her as Reggie stepped inside the nearest bedroom.

"That's mine and the girls'. The boys, they got the other one," she shouted, looking around Angelo.

Angelo gently grasped Mrs. Bennett's arm and escorted her to the messy sofa bed where he cleared a corner so they could sit.

"Is Mr. Bennett dead?" he asked, hoping she wouldn't think about Reggie rummaging through her dresser drawers.

"I ain't that lucky." She laughed, revealing her yellow neglected teeth. Just as quickly her smile faded. "He's in prison. I don't tell the kids. Just let them think the shit run off."

"What'd he do?" Angelo asked, glancing at the bedroom door behind her.

"Killed a man outside some bar in skid row. Never would tell why. I think maybe drugs but don't much care."

Angelo looked into her sad, dull, brown eyes. Hope and joy weren't a part of this woman's existence. But when she talked about her kids it was different, as if she recognized her only shot at happiness was that little piece of herself in each of them. She had to protect her brood for her own sake.

"Did he have much to do with the kids?"

"Nah, 'cept maybe Jake, a little. He's the oldest, the only one my old man ever liked."

"You think Jake still has contact with him?"

"Can't say. Told him not to. Boy don't listen good."

"How old is Jake?"

"Just turned sixteen last month."

Angelo's jaw tightened and he felt his back teeth grinding. Why was a sixteen-year-old hanging around his twelve-year-old son? They wouldn't have anything in common, except the things Matt shouldn't be doing. He was thinking about the bag of marijuana when Reggie returned to the living room and motioned for Angelo to meet with him inside Jake's bedroom.

"The mother's room is clean except empty vodka bottles. But little Jake's got a few issues," Reggie said when they were alone in a messy space filled with two single beds, boys clothes, and toys.

"He's not so little. The kid's sixteen."

"He's also a pervert. Got more porn than the Hollywood vice locker. It's practically the only reason he uses his computer. Some of his stuff is pretty raunchy too."

"Could it belong to the other son?"

"The other boy can't be more than seven or eight years old. This is definitely Jake's corner of the pit. He doesn't try to hide it either." Reggie pulled at his trim mustache. "We might want children's services to come out here and talk to his sisters."

"What'd you find?"

"He's got some pictures he took in the living room," he said, hitting the enter key. "I'm guessing these are his practically naked sisters in very suggestive poses. There's a little marijuana and a couple of pipes too, but no other drugs."

"What's the matter, Mr. Angelo? Did you find something?" Mrs. Bennett was standing behind them. She looked worried, maybe a little guilty.

"Why was Jake in trouble with the police?" he asked. Angelo had been a detective long enough to know you never ask if. Always ask why and when. With kids like Jake, there had to be at least one major screwup.

She started to deny it, but didn't. Her eyes filled with tears and she shook her head. She pulled a dirty tissue from her robe pocket and wiped her nose and eyes. "He hurt a little boy. Beat him up bad. Court sent him to the psychiatrist. He's been good for a long time."

"Have you seen these pictures?" Angelo asked. Somehow he knew she had.

"I don't pay no attention. I don't like to look at that stuff."

"He's a minor," Reggie said, adding, "Are those your daughters?"

"They're just playing around. There ain't no harm in it."

As they stepped out into the hallway, the front door flew open and banged against the coat closet. A teenage boy stood in the entryway and stared at them. He was skinny and nervous like his mother, tall with stringy brown hair and a bad acne-scarred complexion. The Saint Mark's green uniform pants were about an inch too short for him. He had loosened the tie and pulled out the white shirt so it hung over his hips.

"Come on in, Jake. This is Matt's father." She took a deep breath and seemed relieved the detectives' attention had been diverted elsewhere. "How come you're home so early?" she asked, glancing at the kitchen clock. It was barely lunchtime.

"Did he come back?" the boy asked politely but indifferently. He put his backpack on the kitchen table and pushed his mother's hand away as she tried to straighten his frayed collar. "Running away is stupid. I told him it was."

"He told you he was running away?" Angelo asked, watching Jake shove past Mrs. Bennett and take a can of Pepsi from the refrigerator before sitting on the edge of the table.

"Sure. He was always talking about going someplace. Nobody believed him," Jake said and laughed. "Guess he meant it."

"When did you last see Matt or talk to him?" The boy's cockiness was irritating him.

"Friday at school. He didn't say nothing about leaving or I would've told," he said too earnestly.

"Who would you have told, Jake?" Reggie asked with a touch of sarcasm.

"Father Daly, the principal."

"Did Matt ever say where he wanted to go if he ran away?"

"Didn't say."

"Was he afraid of something? Could he be running away from something or somebody at school?"

Jake sighed. "He was a little kid. I let him hang around, but we didn't really talk about stuff."

"He was a lot younger than you. Why did you let him hang around?" Reggie asked, leaning over the table inches from Jake's face.

The boy pulled back. "He played piano in my band."

"What band?" Angelo asked, continually having to admit to himself how little he knew about his son's life.

"Mine. I play guitar, Matt's on piano. Stevie was drums, but he quit last week. So I'm looking for some drums and another steel guitar."

"Why Matt? He's so young."

"Hey dude, you're his old man; you must of heard him play. The little kid's real good . . . does arrangements too." Jake leaned his head back. "Shit, now I ain't got nobody."

"Is there anyone Matt hung out with who might know something?"

"There's that fat girl in my sister's class. She's always sniffing around . . . Jennifer or something."

Angelo glanced at Reggie who seemed to know what he was thinking and shook his head. No naked little fat girls were in Jake's collection of photos and computer printouts. They huddled in a corner away from Jake and his mother and decided to call the Department of Children and Family Services before they left. He was afraid Mrs. Bennett might be clever enough to clean up Jake's room if they waited and called later.

As always, it took hours for someone from DCFS to arrive at the Bennett home. They sat and stared at each other until the caseworker got there. Reggie briefed the woman outside and then gave her a tour of the bedroom. Jake didn't seem to notice or care. He closed his eyes and fingered the chords on an imaginary guitar, humming some bizarre tune that was totally unpleasant to Angelo.

When Angelo and Reggie were going to leave, Mrs. Bennett ignored them. She sat patiently in the kitchen with her arms folded. Her attitude suggested that Jake's behavior had resulted in more than one public agency's intrusion into her home. She knew the routine and her designated role—be concerned, don't interfere, and shut up until they tell her where Jake will be taken and when she can pick him up.

During the next few days, she'd most likely sit quietly through court hearings, petitions, and probation reports and eventually Jake would come home and nothing, especially Jake, would have changed.

"I don't think he knows anything," Reggie said as he started the Mustang. "He's too stupid to tell a convincing lie."

Angelo had been thinking much the same thing. He doubted that Sidney's second ex-husband would contribute anything relevant either. Deputy Chief Joe Denby never spent time with Matt. Sidney had told Angelo that Denby always remembered to send the boy something for his birthday and Christmas, but as far as she knew, they hadn't talked since the divorce. Denby was a spoiled rich guy with expensive toys, a pretty new wife, and baby son. Sidney said he remembered Matt like a business obligation or a bad debt that had to be reckoned with twice a year. Matt took his unopened presents and dumped them at Goodwill.

"Let's forget about Denby for now," Angelo said.

Reggie slowed the car. "Then where to?"

"Back to the command post. Maybe Sergeant Hill's heard something. Denby's a waste of time." Angelo was feeling anxious. It would be dark soon and he didn't like the idea of Matt out on the streets alone. In spite of recent revelations, he still believed the boy was an immature twelve-year-old.

Reggie made a U-turn on Santa Monica Boulevard and drove back in the direction of Sidney's condo. "Maybe they'll let us look at Matt's computer again."

"What do you mean? Sidney won't care," Angelo said.

"I know, but she doesn't have it."

"Who does?"

"Some detective from downtown."

"Why would they take his computer? Did they find something on it?" Angelo kicked at the floorboard. "I hate those prima donnas in the building. He's my kid, and they probably won't tell me anything."

Reggie turned onto Sidney's cul-de-sac, passed her building, and followed the dead-end curve stopping on the dark, empty street. The van was gone. Sergeant Hill and the officers were gone. The searchlights and frantic activity that Angelo expected weren't there. They sat silently for a few seconds.

"They moved it," Reggie said, trying to understand what had happened.

"Go back to Sid's. Somebody must have told her something."

She opened the door and was the composed woman Angelo had always seen in stressful times. Her hair was washed and combed and she wore clean jeans and a long sweater.

"Did you find anything?" she asked. Her voice was thin, but hopeful. Angelo recognized the symptoms of a heavy downer, drowsy eyes and slurred speech. He wondered how much she was overmedicating but wouldn't say anything. She was sensitive about her drugs.

"Where's the command post?" he asked instead.

"Jake Bennett didn't know anything," Reggie said, putting his arm around her shoulder and leading her inside to the living room.

"Sid, where's the command post?" Angelo asked again, louder this time.

"It's gone."

"Have they stopped looking for him?"

"Sergeant Hill said they would keep looking. Captain Davis from the Hollywood police station called too. He was very nice."

"Did he say why they shut down the command post?"

"They said because there was credible information he ran away. Why would he run away, Angie?" Sidney looked confused. She hadn't slept well. Her bloodshot eyes were still sunk in dark shadows.

Angelo remembered the number for the captain's office at Hollywood station. Captain Davis was getting ready to leave for the night, but he took Angelo's call. He explained that one of Matt's classmates, Jennifer Goldberg, told the officers that Angelo's son had run away. The boy had confided in her a few days ago that he would try to hitchhike to Arizona.

"Why the hell would he go there? He's never been out of LA. None of his clothes are missing." Angelo realized he was shouting. It didn't make any sense.

Captain Davis hesitated a moment. "Well, none of the clothes you know about are missing. These kids have money. They buy what they like and they hide it. Most parents would have a stroke if they knew what their kids wore once they left the house."

"Why did you take his computer? What do you think is going on here?" Angelo asked and waited. There was a long silence. "Captain Davis?"

"I'll have to check that for you, Angie. I didn't know we still had the computer. Let me speak to the detectives, and I'll get back to you."

They talked for several minutes. Captain Davis tried to reassure him that everything that needed to be done had been done. Angelo gave him his home and cell phone numbers and hung up. He had a difficult time believing that Matt had a wardrobe of black leathers or any other secret life. The boy was childlike in many ways, and never rebellious.

"One of his friends told the detectives Matt was hitchhiking to Arizona," Angelo said when he looked up and saw Reggie and Sidney staring at him.

"Matt?" they said nearly in unison.

"This is not a kid I figure to stand on the side of the road with his thumb up," Reggie added. "And why Arizona?"

"I didn't think he smoked grass, or missed school, or played in some dope band with a sixteen-year-old moron either," Angelo said. "My kid is full of surprises."

"No, it's not true," Sidney whispered, turned, and walked back into the kitchen.

Angelo followed her, with Reggie a step behind. "Sid, he told some girl in his class named Jennifer. You know her?"

"He's hitchhiking in his pajamas? They must think I'm an idiot," she said, pacing in front of the refrigerator. "I don't know her. Where is she? Go talk to her, Angie."

"Captain Davis thinks maybe Matt had clothes stashed," Angelo said and tried to stand in front of her. "Think about it, Sid. It's possible."

"No, it's not. He's my kid too. There's no way. You talk to that girl, Angie. Find out why she's lying."

She was so angry her body was trembling. He wanted to comfort her, but she turned to Reggie, put her arms around him, nearly disappearing inside his bulky jacket. Reggie was whispering something to her and Angelo felt like a voyeur. They seemed to forget he was there. Speaking, even to say good night, would be an intrusion so he left.

SITTING IN his convertible at the end of the cul-de-sac, he stared into the blackness of the canyon. It was too late to talk to the Goldberg girl tonight. He would confront her at Saint Mark's in the morning.

He had never been this unhinged in his life, one minute wanting to believe everything would be okay, the next fearing the most terrible evil had taken his son. After so many years as a cop, he didn't need much imagination to picture the horrors an unsuspecting, sheltered kid like Matt could encounter. Not knowing, not being able to do anything was gnawing at him. Matt was gone. He might be cold or hungry, scared or in pain somewhere alone or worse. The vulnerable boy was no match for the cruelty Angelo had seen in this world, and he couldn't bear the thought that anyone might hurt his son.

He rested his aching head against the steering wheel for a minute. A sharp pain in his side woke him several hours later. He was lying across the bucket seats with the emergency brake poking his ribs. His muscles were stiff and his clothes were damp from the morning mist that had settled in the canyon. It was nearly sunrise. Adjusting the rearview mirror, he caught a glimpse of his unshaven face and the dark lines under his eyes. He checked his cell phone, no messages. A sharp pain in his chest forced him to sit up straight for a moment, but it passed as quickly as it came. He pulled up his shirt and checked the ugly scar. The brake handle had left a temporary indentation over it but he knew that wasn't the real source of his discomfort. The gunshot wound had healed long ago. Guilt, he thought, was gnawing at his insides. There was no good reason to have taken Matt back to his mother's house Sunday night.

Angelo drove around the cul-de-sac and back down Sidney's street. The dew-covered Mustang was parked in the driveway. He needed Reggie's help but couldn't make himself stop at the condo. His anger at Sidney was unreasonable but festering nonetheless. It wasn't her fault. He knew that, but how could she have been so irresponsible? He trusted her to protect their son. No, he didn't. He couldn't lie to himself about how little he expected from his ex-wife. The failure and the blame were his.

THREE

Saint Mark's was a pricey kindergarten-through-high-school Catholic academy in the West Wilshire area. Its students had very respectable test scores but, according to Sidney, families with money who were willing to make large donations were appreciated as much as any student's GPA.

Angelo pulled the MG inside the front gate left open every morning for arriving parents. A line of limousines and expensive sports cars queued up on the circular driveway to deposit uniformed children in front of the premises. The four-story, brick building looked similar to many of the huge estates lining Highland Avenue south of the Hollywood area. No signs or markers told the outside world that this was a parochial school.

He parked near a small office building sitting between the school and a mission-style chapel. A stocky, middle-aged woman dressed in a dark brown nun's habit immediately stepped from the door of the building and approached his car. He climbed out of the MG and waited. He guessed she was a Franciscan with the white starched winged headpiece covered by the brown veil. It had been a long time since his Catholic school days, but he still felt a nervous twinge whenever a nun zeroed in on him. He could remember the wrath of a Dominican nun, Mother Ann Marie, whenever she caught him doing something wrong—which was most of the time. By reputation, the Dominicans were a sterner group than these Franciscans but it didn't seem to matter.

"I'm Sister Domenic. May I help you?" she asked, standing a few feet away, looking up at him. She had pale, beautiful skin and large blue eyes magnified by thick lenses.

"Sister, I'm Matt Angelo's father. Do you mind if I talk to you for a moment?"

Her expression softened, and he exhaled. She motioned for him to follow her back inside the office building.

"So you've heard nothing from the boy yet?" she asked as she closed the door behind them. She led him through what looked like a living room to a small office. Books were piled on the floor and covered the chairs. The top of a mahogany desk was hidden by a snowstorm of papers. "Sit, Mr. Angelo," she ordered. He did by carefully relocating several volumes of history. Sister Domenic sat behind the desk and stared at him. She tapped nervously on a pile of papers with a well-chewed pencil. "Please excuse my workplace. I'm running the school and arranging a fund-raiser for new textbooks, but I'm also in the process of editing a book on the church pre-World War II," she said, pointing at the biggest stack of papers on her desk. "God blessed me with a lot of energy but few organizing skills. Now, what about your Matthew?"

He had her attention, but her fingers tapped nervously on the desk as he said, "I was hoping you could help me. His mother and I don't believe he would run away."

"Frankly, I don't either. He missed school several mornings, but that was dealt with long ago. His music was more important than his studies. He insisted on spending time with that Bennett boy, but I've taken care of that too."

"What do you mean?"

"Jake Bennett has been expelled and won't be returning."

"Can I ask why?" Angelo thought it was too soon for the DCFS to have notified the school.

"He was disruptive and had unsupervised, unlicensed access to his mother's car. He was a menace and a bad influence on the other children." She blushed slightly. Angelo could see Jake was a sore subject with her.

"He drove the other kids around . . . Matt?" he asked, surprised she had revealed so much about somebody else's kid, but he would keep probing.

"I don't know. Mrs. Bennett promised to stop him." Sister Domenic shook her head. "Of course, she didn't."

"Is there anyone else Matt hung around with who might know something?"

"I believe his closest friend was, excuse me, is Jennifer Goldberg. She's an odd little thing, somewhat intelligent, but different . . . if you know what I mean." Her hands disappeared into the sleeves of her habit. "Jewish father, Catholic mother," she mumbled to herself.

"She told the police that Matt said he was running away. Do you think she was lying?"

"Probably."

"Did you mention that to the police?"

"I believe my opinion was, how did they put it, 'discounted.' It seems little Miss Alice in Wonderland with her influential daddy was deemed more credible." Sister Domenic looked up at the ceiling and closed her eyes for a moment. He figured the young girl was another burden for the busy nun. "Would you like to talk to Jennifer? You can form your own opinion."

Angelo stood and she waved him back to his chair. "Sorry, I thought . . ."

"She's in her homeroom. We'll catch her in twenty minutes between classes, less nasty chatter among the girls that way. Poor Jennifer doesn't need any more gossip. She's withdrawn and isn't very popular. How is Mrs. Angelo doing?"

"We're divorced. She's not doing very well. She doesn't believe Matt ran away and the alternatives are frightening."

Sister Domenic's eyes narrowed slightly when he mentioned divorce and she stood. "Your son's homeroom is already empty. Let me show you his desk. Maybe there's something in there that might help."

Sister Domenic led him into the four-story building to a classroom on the second floor. Matt's desk was near the back of the room by the windows, the wrong place to put a kid who daydreamed. Angelo lifted the top and wasn't surprised to find a clutter of notebooks, papers, and half-eaten pencils. He removed each item and examined it as Sister Domenic stood quietly watching. He thumbed through a music book, pages filled with symbols and notations in Matt's handwriting.

She took the book from him. "I wonder did he do all this?" she asked.

Angelo shrugged and she returned the book. Apparently he wasn't the only one who had underestimated his son.

At the bottom of the desk drawer, he found four photos. One was Matt and a young girl about his age. He held it up to Sister Domenic.

"Hmm, that's Jennifer Goldberg. I don't know where it was taken."

The second one was Matt, Jennifer, and another girl who looked familiar. "Do you know her?" Angelo asked.

"That's Caitlin, Cate Bennett, Jake's sister. She's in Jennifer's homeroom. She's the only reason any of the Bennett children are here."

"I don't understand," he said, finally realizing this was one of the girls in Jake's collection of photos, just a little older.

"Cate has a very high IQ. Father Daly offered her a place at Saint Mark's, but Mrs. Bennett wouldn't allow her to come alone. It was all four of her kids or nothing. So we took them without tuition, of course. Surprisingly, only Jake has been a disappointment. The others are quite bright, but Cate is special. Father Daly wanted to give Jake another chance for her sake, but I put my foot down. I won't have him back."

"Did she spend much time with Matt?"

"Not really. I don't think she liked him very much."

"Why do you say that?" Angelo asked, but he could think of a few reasons why a pretty, preteen girl might shy away from his son. He remembered some introverted kids from his school days. They were usually alone.

"You know how children are. Their hates and loves are so dramatic and so transient. The few times I've seen them together she treated him very badly. Oh, don't look so stricken, Mr. Angelo, she acted like a stuck-up little girl, that's all."

The last two photos were landscapes with a small lake he didn't recognize. "Can I keep these?" he asked.

"Certainly. Everything in there is Matt's. There's nothing else?"

"Not that I can see. It's mostly trash."

"Typical. Come on. We'll catch Jennifer coming out of homeroom." They trotted up to the third floor as a bell rang. He was surprised by the nun's agility and speed.

He immediately recognized Jennifer from the photo. She sat in the back of the room with a pretty girl he knew was Caitlin Bennett. Jennifer was short for a twelve-year-old and overweight like Matt. Her white uniform blouse was too tight, pulling at the buttons. The pleated, green plaid skirt wasn't flattering to her plump figure.

Cate was a dark-haired, green-eyed beauty who resembled Jake without the acne. She seemed taller than Jennifer with a slender figure. She had shortened her skirt to show off her long, shapely legs. The girlfriends were an unlikely pair, Angelo thought. Cate looked up when they walked in. She froze and Jennifer turned to the door and then jumped out of her desk, dropping her glasses on the floor.

"It's all right. Calm down, Jenny. You've not done anything wrong," Sister Domenic said and whispered just loud enough for Angelo to hear, "that I know about anyway." Jennifer reached down and picked up her glasses, pulled at her skirt, and tucked in her blouse. "Sit down, Jenny," Sister Domenic said impatiently.

Jennifer sat at her desk again. Cate remained standing and stared at Angelo. Now the prettier girl seemed unconcerned about Sister Domenic and had focused on him. He thought she showed a lot of Jake's attitude, but it worked for her.

"Jennifer, I'm Matt's father," he said when she mustered the courage to look at him. "I wonder, would you mind talking to me for a few minutes?"

Jennifer turned to Cate, who smiled at her. "Would you like me to leave, Sister?" Cate asked with the poise of a forty-year-old woman.

"Thank you, dear. Just wait outside. We won't be long."

The girl picked up her book bag from the floor. She leaned over and gave Jennifer a quick kiss on the top of her head, a motherly peck. It struck Angelo as an odd gesture from one little girl to another. Cate smiled too sweetly at Sister Domenic and left.

As soon as the classroom door closed, the nun's smile faded. "Now Jenny, tell Mr. Angelo what Matt said to you," she ordered.

Angelo saw tears well up in the girl's eyes. He knelt down beside her and put his hand over hers. She was trembling; her skin was clammy. "I'm sorry to ask you to do this again, Jenny. Maybe something you know will help me find Matt. Please, don't be frightened. You're not in any trouble."

It was too late. Tears trickled down her cheeks. "I don't know anything," she said. "He ran away."

"Did he tell you that?" Angelo asked as gently as he could.

"Yes," she said, avoiding his eyes.

"When?"

"All the time."

"But did he say he was going for sure this time?"

"I think so."

"You told the police you were certain," Sister Domenic said sternly and leaned over to look at the little girl's face. "Isn't that what you told them?"

Jennifer's lower lip quivered. "Yes, Sister."

"Did he tell you why?" Angelo asked. She shook her head. "Did he tell Cate too?" She shook her head again. "Just you?" She nodded. "Did he say where he was going?"

"Arizona," she said without hesitating.

"Are you sure? Why would he go there?" he asked. She nodded quickly and then shrugged.

"He just wanted to, I guess."

"Was he alone, Jennifer?" Angelo wasn't certain why he asked that question. She seemed surprised and looked up at him and then at Sister Domenic.

"I don't know," she answered. "Is somebody else missing?" she added with genuine concern.

Angelo stood and stretched his back. "No, honey, only Matt. You can leave if you want."

Sister Domenic lifted Jennifer's heavy black book bag from the floor and shoved it at the girl. Jennifer grabbed it with both arms and shuffled out of the room. Cate met her outside the door and the two friends scurried away.

"I don't know," Angelo said to Sister Domenic when the door closed. "She's so timid. It's hard to say if she's being truthful."

"Jennifer lies. I've caught her myself. Her family is very wealthy. They travel and work and the girl practically raises herself. She has no real friends except Cate and maybe Matt. She lives in a fantasy world most of the time."

"Cate seems to treat her like a little sister."

Sister Domenic laughed. "Caitlin is a year younger. She's been moved up a grade because she's so far ahead of her peers in every way—intellectually, socially, physically. I'll never understand what she sees in that Goldberg girl. They're complete opposites."

"Maybe," Angelo mumbled, glancing out the window. He noticed Cate and Jennifer huddled near the brick, perimeter wall. Jennifer had stopped crying and appeared to be scolding Cate, who stood quietly listening. He was surprised when he realized that Jennifer was actually the taller of the two. Her poor posture made her seem shorter. The bell rang and the bigger girl put her arm around Cate as they walked back toward the school. "Can you give me a little more background on Jennifer's family, Sister?"

"Hmm, her father is a lawyer. Her mother is Catholic and on the boards of several charitable foundations. I'm sorry I don't recall which ones."

"What's the father's first name?"

"David? Yes, David and Susan, a very nice couple."

Angelo guessed that "very nice" probably meant David and Susan Goldberg had given large sums of money to the school, enough for Sister Domenic to overlook the academic and social shortcomings of their daughter.

"No siblings?"

"I don't know. None that attend Saint Mark's."

Sister Domenic escorted him back to his car and stood outside her office until he drove away from the school. He was tired but needed to stop at Hollywood station and talk to Captain Davis. Matt's computer was still somewhere in the police department labyrinth. He wanted it back for a lot of reasons and was certain a captain would have better luck retrieving it than either he or Reggie.

He hadn't been home since yesterday morning and needed to brush his teeth, shave, and take a shower. Luckily, his hair was thick and curly and never looked unkempt, but his clothes were beginning to smell since he'd worn them for two days.

He was closer to the police station than his house and didn't want to drive back. Sidney's condo was a few minutes away. He could shower there but had seen enough of his ex-wife and Reggie Madison for a while.

The front desk at Hollywood station was as busy as he remembered it. He flashed his ID and the baby-faced officer who looked up nodded at him without bothering to read it. Many of the officers he knew in Hollywood had left. He felt like a man who comes home after a few years and finds a new family living in his house.

He walked past the jail and cut through the watch commander's area to reach Captain Davis's office. The little blonde records clerk they called The Wrecker because of all the marriages she'd destroyed was still working there. She always hung around the new officers looking for any cop who didn't know her reputation. As Angelo passed the watch commander's desk, she was wiggling in front of a young lieutenant.

"Hi, Kerri," Angelo said as she turned to inspect him. "How's Ted and all the kids?" Angelo saw the lieutenant's smile fade and he knew he had just yanked a fly from the web.

The door to Captain Davis's office was closed. His secretary was digging in her desk drawer and didn't see him. Angelo tapped on her shoulder.

"Hello, Diane."

"Angie," she screamed and jumped from her chair. She threw her arms around his neck and kissed him. Several uniformed officers loitering in the hallway clapped and whistled. "Why haven't you been back to see us? Are you okay?" she asked, gently touching his chest then stepping away from him, seeming a little embarrassed.

"I'm terrific," he said, giving her another reassuring hug. "Doc says I'm healthy enough to do whatever I want as long as it's not police work."

Several of the office staff moved closer to greet him. He was glad to see them, but this was the reason he never visited. He hated being the center of attention. That might've been another explanation why he and Sidney couldn't live together. She thrived on being noticed and admired.

Before Angelo could tell her his reason for being there, the door to the captain's office opened, and Davis stepped out shaking the hand of Deputy Chief Joe Denby. Denby stopped midsentence when he saw Angelo. Davis turned to follow Denby's stare. Both men stood quietly for a second or two. Captain Davis was the first to recover and walked over to greet Angelo.

"Angie, we were just talking about you," Davis said, looking back at Denby.

"Joe," Angelo said, offering his hand to Denby before the man could put his arm around Angelo's shoulder. Joe Denby had an irritating habit of grabbing people. Sidney confided in Angelo that Denby had learned the gesture in one of the department's leadership courses. He was taught to do it as a demonstration of strength and character. It annoyed Angelo because he knew Joe Denby had neither.

"There's still nothing much coming up on Matt," Denby said, as his gaze followed the blonde records clerk sashaying seductively away from the watch commander's office.

"What are you doing to find him?" Angelo asked.

"Why don't we go back in my office and talk," Captain Davis said, leading the way.

Angelo followed a step behind Denby and waited until the door was closed. "Where's Matt's computer, Bill?" he asked Davis.

"Sit down, Angie. That's what I wanted to tell you. My guys didn't take it."

"I know, but it's your investigation, isn't it?"

"They think John Delong from Juvenile booked it, but they haven't been able to confirm."

"Have they called and asked him? What the hell takes you people so long?" There was no attempt to hide his disgust. Fatigue and worry weren't improving his disposition.

"No need to get testy, Angie. Bill is trying to help," Denby said. "I asked Juvenile to get involved in this. It was my suggestion that they look at the computer."

Angelo ignored him. "Did your guys ask if he still had it?" he repeated.

"They asked," Davis said curtly. "Delong told them he had it but wouldn't release it yet."

"Because?"

"Because he thinks it may contain evidence."

"Of what?" Angelo asked. He was talking to a commanding officer and tried to maintain some level of respect, but was losing control of his temper. This piecemeal rationing of information was wearing on him.

"I can't tell you." Captain Davis took a deep breath. "It's not my place to talk about Juvenile's investigation. Ask Lieutenant Delong. That's all I can say."

"How's Sidney doing?" Denby asked. Apparently he had stopped listening and didn't realize how offtrack his question was.

"How do you think she's doing, Joe?" Angelo said after a few seconds. He was irritated and upset by Davis's runaround, but more so by anything Joe Denby said or did. The deputy chief had dumped Sidney and abandoned Matt before the warranty on their family's SUV had expired. The poor kid wasn't even a teenager and had already been abandoned by two fathers.

Denby fidgeted with his watch and looked at his silent cell phone. "I have to go. Let me know if there's anything I can do, Angie."

"When did you last see my son or talk to him, Joe?" Angie asked before Denby could reach the door.

The deputy chief looked surprised by the question and then amused that someone would consider him a suspect. "I don't really know. It's been months. Matt and I . . . you know. I have the baby and a new wife. The law practice is going good, and I'm handling more civil cases off-duty now. We never really got along. You know that." Denby mumbled something more but he was outside the office and the door swung closed.

Captain Davis sat behind his desk. Both men stared at the door for several seconds.

"They think I had something to do with this, don't they?" Angelo asked. The picture was finally taking shape in his tired brain.

"Family's always the first look when a kid's missing. You know that. If they're divorced, then Daddy's suspect number one," Davis said matter-of-factly. He was a black man in a white man's profession and had fought the system and his own shortcomings to be promoted to captain. His struggles had made him philosophical about life's whims. "Let them go through the motions, Angie. It doesn't matter as long as they get your boy back."

"They're wasting time looking at me. Why would I take him? Sidney and I don't have a problem sharing. Ask her."

"She insists the boy didn't run away. That means somebody took him. The best motive is usually the father's."

"She doesn't think I took him, does she?"

"She's not accusing you."

"But?" He could hear it in Davis's voice. Something was about to happen he wasn't going to like.

"But Delong might ask to take a look around your place, strictly with your permission, no warrants. He still thinks Matt ran away . . . maybe with your help."

"Is that what you and Denby were talking about? Never mind." Angelo was furious. Matt was gone and he had trusted these people, Davis and Denby and the arrogant, overrated Lieutenant Delong, to find him. It was already the second day and they had nothing to show for their combined efforts except some asinine suspicion of him. He knew once the trail went cold, his son might be gone forever.

"You know they've got to eliminate you," Davis said, attempting to appease him.

"Why don't I help. I'm fucking eliminated. Now, what are you doing to find him?"

"You know the routine. They hit all the agencies, hospitals, shelters, national data banks, and put out the bulletins. Pretty much have to treat this like a runaway, no matter what his momma thinks. Right now, despite Delong's suspicions, there's nothing to indicate it was anything else."

"I want to talk to your detectives." Angelo was tired of the bullshit. Maybe he could get a straight answer and some action from another cop.

"There's only one, Charlene Harper. I'll get her in here."

"No, I'll go back to the squad room," he said as he waved off Davis and left the office. He didn't want the captain hovering and contaminating their conversation.

Hollywood detectives' squad room was a huge warehouse of desks and file cabinets sectioned off with cheap room dividers. It hadn't changed since the day they moved from the old station decades ago. No one who worked there really wanted it to be anything but what it was, an environment that timid souls avoided. Homicide and robbery investigators claimed the largest territory. The juvenile detectives were pushed into a cluttered corner near the interrogation rooms.

A woman with short curly brown hair was standing over a young uniformed officer sitting at the juvenile table. She was teaching him how to fill out the numerous forms for a juvenile detention. He looked confused. She patiently instructed for a few minutes, but finally did what the young officer was probably hoping she'd do. She took the forms, quickly filled them out, and dismissed him.

"Detective Harper?" Angelo asked. She glanced up at him. She wore trifocals and was a pleasing few pounds overweight. He thought she looked more like a pretty librarian than a cop.

"That's me. You Angelo? Captain Davis buzzed me as soon as you left his office. I pulled the file so you could see it."

"It's Angie. Is everything still in it?"

"Charley," she said, holding out her hand. They shook hands. "Where the fuck do you think it would be?" she asked, smiling and staring at him with big brown cocker spaniel eyes.

"Sorry, guess I'm getting a little paranoid."

"If my kid were missing, I'd be King Kong on steroids. You have a right to be an asshole."

She took off her glasses. Thick, natural curls fell softly around her face. Her coarse language didn't fit her gentle appearance. Angelo thought she was attractive but maybe trying too hard to be a tough detective.

"Is it still your investigation or did Delong take it?"

Dry laugh. "Mine, of course. Detective Delong can't find his ass with both hands."

"Do you know why he's keeping Matt's computer?"

"I can tell you what he told me. He thinks Matt might have been corresponding with someone in one of those chat rooms. He thinks your son voluntarily left to meet someone."

"Who?"

"You or some pervert he met online."

"Well, it wasn't me, and he's not the chat room kind of kid." Angelo remembered the marijuana under Matt's mattress and his relationship with Jake Bennett. He couldn't admit that he didn't really know what kind of kid his son was.

"Delong is following up on the computer stuff. When he tells me, I'll let you know what he found."

"So you don't think I had anything to do with his disappearance?"

"How the hell should I know? Until I find something that says differently, you're his father, not a suspect."

"What will you do next?"

"Nothing. We've done it. Now we sit back and wait for someone to respond to one of our alerts. If he's a runaway, we usually get a call pretty quick. Most kids want to be found after a few nights on the street."

Angelo leaned against the file cabinet. He was exhausted and felt dizzy. The rage and fatigue had consumed his last bit of energy. "None of this makes any sense," he mumbled to himself.

"It usually doesn't. From what I understand your son has a good home. He's doing okay in school. The nuns tell me he's a talented musician. But he's almost thirteen. You have to believe there're some outta-whack hormones."

"Maybe," he said, but he wasn't thinking clearly. His back was stiff and his head was throbbing from lack of sleep. He had a hard time picturing the young man with baby fat dealing with any kind of hormones. He excused himself, and knew he'd better get home before he fell asleep in the car again.

The fastest way to East LA was on the freeway, but he drove west on Sunset from the police station. He would search the Strip and come back east on Hollywood Boulevard. Santa Monica Boulevard would have to wait until later, after he slept a little. All those streets were hangouts for runaways. For years, he had seen the abused and neglected children who gathered at teen centers and safe houses in Hollywood. He never knew their names. Mostly he and other cops ignored them or worked around them, dead or alive. Their stories were numbingly similar—incest, cruelty, indifference. Desperate for security and love, they found disappointment or worse.

He didn't want his son to look at him with that empty, hardened stare of a child who'd crawled through the garbage and settled on leftover scraps as all life had to offer.

FOUR

Angelo's mother haunted his dreams. Everyone in them knew she was dead rotting flesh walking through the routine moments that had been her life. He and Lucy were children again. It was good; no, it was pathetic. After all these years, he still needed comfort and protection. From what or who, he wondered.

Awake he was left with the memory of all those years without her. It was different with his father. The old man, a bit player, a silent, brooding face at the kitchen table, was after all where he belonged and wanted to be—dead. The possibility of becoming his father was Angelo's Sword of Damocles. Being a real father for Matt would've proved he was different and was after all his mother's son.

For too many minutes, he lingered in bed trying to hold onto an image, keep her with him. He wondered if Matt's disappearance drew her spirit back in the night. More likely it was his weakness, the feeling of helplessness that was slowly, certainly dragging him to paralyzing inertia. He couldn't stay there, but couldn't make himself get out of bed again to face the cruel possibilities that today and tomorrow and the next day might bring.

He tried to calculate how long his son had been gone—it had been days, no weeks. Matt had turned thirteen a few days ago. No cause for celebration, time had become his enemy. Every passing minute stole hope and any possibility that Matt would be found. There hadn't been a trace of his son since the night he disappeared.

Angelo's expertise and training warned him that could only mean one thing—the boy was dead. But his heart refused to accept that. He rolled out of bed without thinking. Do the routine things first, shower, dress, and eat. Then try to find a direction he hadn't already taken, a corner of the city he hadn't already searched, eventually go back and do it again. Regardless of the outcome, he needed answers.

The phone rang. Charley Harper called nearly every day. He had stopped answering. The Hollywood detective was concerned about him. She should be. He wasn't happy with her or the LAPD. The machine took her message like it did yesterday. He didn't listen but would call back eventually. It was pointless. The police had given up.

Before he could drink his first cup of coffee, Lucy and Tony were knocking on his front door. His sister was annoying, but to his surprise, he was starting to look forward to her daily visits. She filled the house with empty conversation.

Over the years, Tony had become a real friend to Angelo. He was ten years older than Lucy. Arthritis and a bad heart kept him from working in the garage, but he still managed the business and a dozen employees. Having emigrated from an uncomplicated life in Italy, he put little value on the material things that obsessed Lucy. Angelo never realized how much he trusted Tony's opinion until the last few weeks.

"I'm not an educated man," Tony would say, and then quote Milton or Dante to make his point. Unlike Angelo's father, Tony came to America and refused to be defeated by the prejudice against Italians or the false pride that had crippled his friend Salvatore, Angelo's father. He couldn't find work so he taught himself how to fix cars and opened his own shop.

"There's nothing, Tony. I've looked everywhere for him," Angelo said when Lucy had left them alone.

"Then start again. You missed something."

Angelo shook his head. "I don't think so . . . I'm afraid . . ." He didn't finish. They both knew what he feared.

"What about your wife's boyfriend? He don't have no new ideas?"

"Reggie? He's helped a lot. Some of his buddies and him drove to Arizona and back on the I-10. They stopped at every off-ramp, every rest area. I never could have done that by myself, but if nothing new comes up I might have to do it again."

The phone rang and Tony waited for Angelo to pick it up. When the answering machine started, Tony reached for the receiver. Angelo caught his arm.

"No, let it go. There's people I don't want to talk to."

It was Detective Harper's voice. She needed to see him. Could he meet her at the Goldberg home? Angelo grabbed the phone.

"Charley, what's going on?" he asked.

"Angie, I thought you might be there. David Goldberg's gardener found something on his property. I want you and Sidney to look at it."

"What is it?"

"A schoolbag. All the kids at Saint Mark's are given one. Sidney never found Matt's."

"Where . . . when did he find it? It's been weeks." Finally, maybe they had something, a place to start. He was anxious but had questions.

She interrupted, and gave him the Goldberg address. "It's a big place. You'll see." Charley said she'd meet him there. She didn't want to talk now.

"What happened?" Lucy asked. His sister had returned to the kitchen while Angelo was on the phone. "Did they find him?"

"No, maybe his schoolbag. I gotta go."

"I should drive," Tony said. "You stay, honey, in case they call again," he added as Lucy reached for her purse while pulling off the apron from around her waist. Tony was the only one he knew who could make his sister do anything without an argument.

THE GOLDBERGS lived on an impressive estate in Canyon Country northwest of Los Angeles, on acreage protected by a towering wall. When Tony drove past the open front gate, Angelo immediately recognized the setting. It was the unforgettable landscape he had seen on one of the photographs from Matt's school desk. Extreme opulence is memorable. The house was larger than Matt's school, with riding stables, a tennis court, and an Olympic-sized swimming pool backed by a forest of juniper pines and scrub oak. A portion of the front lawn was a putting green. Angelo couldn't avoid comparing it to his house in East LA. Even with the add-ons, his home was smaller than David Goldberg's stables.

Charley Harper appeared as soon as Tony parked in front of the house. She led them inside where they found Sidney, Reggie, and David Goldberg sitting in the den sifting through the contents of a large black bag. Angelo hadn't seen Sidney for weeks. They got on each other's nerves and couldn't seem to talk without arguing. They had been communicating through Reggie. She looked pale and sickly. Reggie sat quietly on the arm of her overstuffed leather chair with his hand on her shoulder. He stood up when he saw Angelo.

"Sid thinks it's his," Reggie whispered as he nudged Angelo into the room. The contents of the bag had been dumped on a sheet in the middle of the room to protect the cream-colored Berber carpet from the dirt and debris. As Angelo stood staring at the pile on the floor, Charley introduced him to David Goldberg. Angelo heard the introduction but didn't look up. He couldn't take his eyes off the black bag. The canvas was dirty and torn.

"The elements have damaged a lot of it, but there are a few things." Charley's voice trailed off. "You tell me. Do you recognize anything?"

Angelo knelt on the floor. Charley handed him a pair of latex gloves, which he quickly slipped on. He picked up a small flashlight caked with dirt. It was still working. There were several candy bars. Something had eaten through the wrappers. The scribbling in notebooks had faded. Pages were covered with dirt and water stains. It could be any kid's bag. He pushed aside what looked like the remains of sandwiches and held his breath. Two live, 9mm, controlled-expansion rounds rolled toward him.

"These were in the bag?" he asked Charley. She nodded. "Shit," he said and looked at Sidney. They both knew. It was his ammo. Matt had probably kept them when they went shooting.

"That's his music book," Sidney said, pointing at the remains of a yellow notebook stuffed with discolored pages. She opened her hand and showed Angelo a rusted pocketknife. It resembled the one he had given Matt last Christmas.

"Where did you find this?" he asked, finally looking at David Goldberg.

Goldberg unfolded his arms and pushed a strand of gray hair away from his face. Angelo stared at his hands. They looked soft and delicate. His long nails were manicured with natural polish. Funeral director was the first thought that crossed his mind.

"Actually, I didn't." The short, skinny man had a deep, braying voice. "The groundskeeper was mulching or some such thing and dug it up. He told my wife and she called you people."

Charley offered to show them the spot where the bag had been found. It was a ten-minute walk from the house on a dirt path through the forest. Angelo walked slowly, helping Tony navigate the holes and fallen tree limbs. The older man's breathing was labored when they reached the clearing.

Angelo saw that a perimeter had been established for a thorough search. The yellow tape tied around trees kept them from getting too close. Tony and Reggie stood shoulder-to-shoulder with him staring at little red flags surrounding an area near a large pine tree nearly one hundred yards away. It was a peaceful, wooded place with a small lake barely visible behind it. Sidney had opted not to make the hike from the house. She stayed with Goldberg. He didn't know why, but Angelo wished she had come.

He wanted to step over the tape and search the area himself. This was the first hint of evidence they'd found since Matt disappeared. The possibility of answers, of a new direction, was too important to leave to someone else. Charley must have read his mind.

"You can't go in there. It may be the only opportunity we'll have to find anything. Let the team from Scientific Investigations do what they do. If there's something, SID will find it." She started to walk back in the direction of the house but stopped, turned toward Angelo. "If you step on a piece of fiber or partial print and fuck this up, you'll never forgive yourself."

The three men watched as she followed the trail that led away from the trees and back to the Goldberg mansion. Tony knelt on one knee. He coughed and pulled his belt away from his large gut. He was still sweating from the short hike.

"You want to go back with her, Tony? We'll be right behind you."

"Sure, Nino. I'll take it nice and easy. You catch up." Tony put out his hand and Angelo helped him to his feet. He groaned as his weight shifted back to his arthritic legs. "It don't do no good to stand out here and worry."

When Tony and Charley were out of sight, Angelo exchanged a quick look with Reggie. They didn't speak. He ducked under the tape, and Reggie followed. They stepped around the flags and stood over the spot where the bag had been found. He could see where Goldberg's man had pushed aside the fresh pine needles and sifted through the dirt. The bag hadn't been buried but abandoned near the tree. It had been there all along.

"Try not to step on any fibers," Reggie said sarcastically as he walked around the tree, removing the top layer of pine needles with his foot.

"Fucking morons," Angelo said. He knew the best chance he had to find Matt was to do it himself. This might be his only chance. He wasn't going to sit at home and wait for so-called experts to try to do what he did better than anyone. He was still a good detective, a smart investigator. He knew how to use Reggie or Charley or any of them to get what he needed. A fucking piece of fiber wasn't going to get his son back; he was.

"There's nothing, Angie. No footprints, nothing . . . just a shit pot full of pine needles."

"Keep looking. There's always something."

The sun peeked through the trees and as it peppered the carpet of dead needles a faint reflection caught his eye. He carefully picked through the debris until he found the source, a diamond earring. It was a tiny stud, maybe a third of a carat, but it looked real. Reggie was standing over him.

"You know that Bennett kid had an empty hole in his left earlobe. I saw it when I got in his face at his mother's house. I didn't think anything of it. A lot of kids wear them now. Did Matt?" Reggie asked and Angelo shook his head.

Angelo held the stone in his hand. "It's something. Keep looking," he ordered and Reggie saluted, but Angelo ignored him. He didn't have time to say please. It wouldn't take long for them to make their way back to the house and for Charley to figure out that, despite her warning, he was desecrating her crime scene.

They crawled around the tree and searched out to the red flags treading softly inside the perimeter looking for signs of anything unusual. There was nothing. The trail ended on the other side of the trees with a large open field surrounding the lake.

"Want to walk down to the lake? It looks like there's a path through the grass."

"Go ahead," Angelo said. "I want to see what's over here," he said pointing to the dense brush away from the path. Reggie nodded and moved toward the lake, checking both sides of the narrow trail. It was a respectable trek from the trees to the water and there was no indication Matt had gone in that direction.

It was difficult to penetrate the thick growth and after a couple of attempts, Angelo decided it was too overgrown for anyone to break through. He would get Reggie and go back to the house before Charley sent someone to find them.

Reggie was returning from the lake as Angelo reached the clearing. The sun was low enough to reflect off the water. He could make out Reggie's long strides, but the tall figure seemed to have a shadowy movement behind him. It was only when the path jogged slightly to the west that Angelo could see a woman. He squinted, then closed his eyes. When he opened them, they were both a few feet away. She smiled at him.

"Angie, this is Magdalene," Reggie said, and after a slight pause added, "Goldberg."

Angelo stared at the young woman who resembled Jennifer but was prettier. She was probably midtwenties, but dressed the way a child might, imitating some storybook character. She wore a white, wide-brimmed hat, a thin white fur scarf around her neck, white sweater, and long white skirt. Short blonde hairs sprung from under her hat like dirty, bleached fringe.

Angelo held out his hand and said, "Nice to meet you, Magdalene." She didn't respond but smiled at him again. Angelo looked at Reggie. He didn't know where Reggie had found the strange woman or why he brought her back. "We'd better get going," he said.

"Magdalene lives out here by the lake," Reggie said and nudged her gently toward Angelo. She looked scared.

"Magdalene," Angelo said softly. He understood what Reggie was doing now.

"The children don't come here anymore," she said in a young girl's voice. "I've forbidden them."

"They played here?" Angelo asked. "Near the water?"

"Never near my pond. They did things here," she said pointing at the ground. "Nasty things."

"Which children?"

"All of them."

"Do you know their names?"

"Of course I do," she said, squatting on the ground. She held up her index finger and pointed to it with her other hand. "The first certainly is Jennifer, my spoiled, ugly sister." The baby finger. "Caitlin, my wood nymph." The thumb. "Ah, the frog, Matthew and me . . ." she said, touching her ring finger. "Who did I forget?" She jumped up and put her hands on her hips. "The evil one," she said and snorted, holding up her middle finger.

"Who's the evil one, Magdalene?"

"You know," she whispered.

"No, who?" Reggie asked.

"Jake, the serpent."

"Jake Bennett?"

"No, the serpent," she insisted. She dusted off her skirt and tightened her fur scarf. "Hi, Daddy."

Angelo turned and saw David Goldberg marching toward them, a Wall Street soldier advancing among the trees. His expensive suit threw the rustic landscape out of kilter. He looked down at the ground and took long, deliberate strides until he reached the clearing.

"Are you all right, Maggie?" he asked in a voice meant not to frighten a child.

"Yes, Daddy. Are you all right?"

"Go back to the cottage, Maggie. Harriet has your lunch ready." Without another word, she ran away toward the lake. David Goldberg watched silently until she was halfway around the large body of water. "Leave her alone," he said, pausing after every word in a deep baritone warning, then turned and walked in the direction he'd come.

"Goldberg, wait," Angelo shouted. "Why didn't you tell us the kids played up here?"

Goldberg stopped and came back.

"I didn't know."

"Magdalene is here all the time. She knows," Reggie said.

"I don't want you to upset her. You can see she's a child."

"What's wrong with her?" Reggie asked. Angelo cringed at the direct question.

Goldberg closed his eyes. "Nothing is wrong with her," he said. "She had a breakdown. She can't cope with stress. I won't allow you to harass her."

"So you keep her hidden up here," Reggie said. Angelo knew what Reggie was doing, but it didn't make it any less painful to hear.

"I love her. People are cruel."

"Sorry, David. I apologize," Angelo said, stepping in front of Reggie. It was time to be the good guy. "I promise we won't disturb her. I just need to ask if she knows what happened to Matt."

He was the kind, understanding one. Reggie had intentionally made himself the asshole, the common enemy. It usually worked, but David Goldberg wasn't an uneducated drug dealer with a heroin-soaked brain. He shook his head and returned to the path.

"Leave her alone or I'll take you to court," Goldberg ordered.

"What's going on out here?" Charley Harper shouted as she approached them. David Goldberg pushed past her, ignoring the question.

Angelo and Reggie met her before she reached the clearing.

"Did you know he had another daughter?" Angelo asked, trying to distract her and keep her from examining the taped-off area. She pivoted and followed them back toward the house.

"She's incompetent . . . lives in a fantasy world. Nothing she says is reliable," Charley said, nearly stumbling in a deep rut as she tried to keep up.

"Even crazy people have eyes. She might have seen something." A good detective would have questioned her, Angelo thought. "Will you ask Goldberg if I can talk to her, again?"

"No. I need his cooperation. I am not going to piss off David Goldberg so you can interrogate his crazy daughter."

By the time they reached the house, Angelo had made up his mind. He wasn't going to argue. He had seen the cottage on the other side of the lake. Reggie was quiet too. Angelo was beginning to understand the man. His smirk told Angelo he understood what had to be done. Angelo wouldn't be alone when he came back to question Magdalene.

Tony was sitting behind the wheel of his Buick Regal talking on a cell phone when Angelo reached the front of the house. His brother-in-law waved and motioned for them to come closer. His expression was grim. His lips pressed tightly together, he tapped his fist gently on his knee. A clinky rendition of "Für Elise" and Charley was on her cell phone too. She listened quietly. Tony got out of the car and threw his phone on the seat.

"Some sergeant called looking for you and talked to Lucy," Tony said.

"Sergeant Hill from Hollywood?" Angelo asked.

"She didn't remember his name. He told her he found some guy who's talking to them about Matt." He handed Angelo a piece of paper with Lieutenant Delong's name and Juvenile Division's number. "This is where the sergeant said they're gonna take him."

Charley got out of her car as she folded the phone. She went to Sidney, who was standing near the house beside Goldberg, pulled her aside, and whispered something. Sidney shook her head and glanced across the driveway at him. Maybe it was Reggie she was looking at. He couldn't tell. But it was Reggie who went to her.

FIVE

Charley reluctantly offered to take Angelo and Reggie to Parker Center. Tony was tired but agreed to drive Sidney home. Angelo wasn't surprised. Sidney wouldn't be anxious to hear raw, uncensored data.

They found Lieutenant Delong in his office with the Reverend Steven Hellman. It wasn't difficult. A rancid smell filled the hallway. After the introductions, Delong turned up the speed on his portable fan. The reverend, a wiry, middle-aged man with tan, leathery skin and a shaved head, wore a black suit dipped in dry cleaning fluid, stale sweat, and cheap cologne. The pungent odor barely trumped his sour, alcoholic breath. Angelo guessed the man preached and slept outdoors amongst the bums downtown where hygiene wasn't an issue.

Hellman sat on a folding chair near the open office door. Angelo moved as far from him as he could but was still irritated. When he was working, he never interviewed a bum or allowed him in the same room until the guy accepted a meal and a jail shower. The offer was never negotiable. Delong didn't have much field experience, or he would have known that this decaying human smell never dissipated in a room.

"Tell them what you told me, Hellman," Delong said, keeping his hand strategically placed over his nose and mouth.

"There's a picture of this kid. It's stuck to the wall at the food center on Fifth and Wall, and I seen him."

Angelo sat forward. He had tacked those posters all over downtown, anywhere a hungry boy might stop for a handout. He did it praying Matt would never be found in one of those places. Today, he just wanted to find him alive and didn't care what he'd had to do to stay that way.

Hellman rubbed his face. He had made some effort to scrub from his chin to his forehead, but dirt was lodged under his long cracked nails and caked in the crevices of his neck, embedded in his weathered skin.

"Where? When?" Angelo asked.

"I seen him there, standing right under that picture maybe two weeks ago."

"Was he alone? What was he wearing?" Reggie sounded skeptical.

The reverend looked confused. He turned to Charley. "You his momma?"

"I'm Detective Harper. Was the boy by himself?"

"There was a guy with him, I think. A big guy like him," he said, pointing at Reggie.

"Can you describe the man?" Charley moved closer. They all felt it. She was the one Hellman would talk to.

"Don't think so. Kinda ordinary."

"Hair color?"

"Brownish, I think. It was shaved," he said, touching the top of his head.

"Eye color?"

"Brownish."

"Skin color?"

"White."

"Fat? Skinny?"

"Average."

Charley sighed. "Was there anything unusual about him?"

"He didn't have no finger." Hellman held up his left hand and wiggled his ring finger.

"Tattoos?"

"Didn't see none. Do I get some kind of reward for coming here?"

"Maybe, if we find him."

"Shouldn't be hard. He's always at the river."

"Take us." Angelo stood.

Hellman pushed his chair back, nearly falling. "No way. I love Jesus, but I ain't plannin' on seein' him today."

"You can stay in the car. If that man is there, he'll never see you," Charley said. She gave Angelo a look that said sit down and shut up.

"I told you everything I know. How bad can it be to find a little fat boy and man with his finger chopped off?"

"Come with us or I'll tell everybody on the street that you snitched on this guy," Reggie said, glaring at Hellman.

"Why you wanna do me that way? I'm the good guy here." Hellman bounced up and slammed his fists on the door.

"I think you're full of shit, and you made up this story." Reggie didn't move. He kept staring at Hellman, who did a nervous dance between the hallway and Delong's office.

"Miss Detective, you and the chief know I ain't lying." He looked from Charley to Delong, but Reggie's verbal assault was working and they backed off. "Why you messing with me? Go to the LA River. Him and the boy's there," Hellman whined.

"You got any warrants, Reverend?" Reggie's cold stare fixed on Hellman.

Hellman pounded his chest. "Threatenin' to put me in jail? This is bullshit." Angelo thought the little man in black would shake himself into the floor but he stopped, put his hands on his hips, and took a deep breath. "Let's go. Then amen, give me my money and we is done."

Reggie winked at Angelo. "I know where we can grab a utility car, unless Detective Harper wants to take the reverend in her ride." Charley didn't respond. She sat staring at her notebook. Angelo knew she was unhappy. Reggie had given her a lesson in interrogation technique. Informants were manipulators. Hellman took kindness as a sign of weakness. What he feared and responded to was the threat of jail time or a snitch jacket. He wouldn't want his buddies thinking he ratted out another bum.

The air conditioner was on full blast and all the windows of the old Crown Victoria police cruiser were open, but it didn't matter. The Hellman stench persisted even though he sat behind them on the yellow, plastic drunk seat. Angelo and Reggie were cramped in front trying not to breathe deeply. Charley sat between them. She rummaged in the glove compartment and found a crumpled paper towel to hold over her nose.

Angelo had heard stories about the homeless camps near the LA River but had never seen them. As he drove along the access road, he thought the LA wash was probably a better name for the muddy, concrete mess that bordered the industrial areas east of downtown.

Angelo located the Fourth Street Bridge. Central Division cops had told him it marked the entrance to the biggest camp. On the other side, piles of cardboard boxes, blankets, and grocery carts were a clear warning to any stranger to enter at his own risk. The encampment, a human landfill, sat between the railroad tracks and the river. Angelo drove as close as he could, and Hellman slid to the floor.

"Get up. Nobody's going to see you," Angelo said. There were less than a dozen people milling around the debris. Feet poked out from beneath a few of the cardboard-box condos. "Is he there?" Angelo asked. The reverend peeked over the seat and shook his head.

"We'll get the rest where you can see them," Reggie said and opened his door. "Come on, Angie. Hellman, you stay here and tell Detective Harper if you recognize anyone."

Angelo followed him, stepping over broken bottles and discarded crates. Empty food cartons, trash, and human waste were piled like Celtic stones around the camp. The smell was Reverend Hellman times one hundred. A woman in layers of dirty rags tied around her body and a knit cap pulled over her eyes stepped in front of him.

"I'm a pretty angel," she said, spitting on him through broken, yellow teeth. She tried to touch his face, but Angelo pulled back, nearly stumbling over a stack of metal weather stripping.

"Watch it, shithead." A hairy giant in tan overalls and sleeveless undershirt charged toward him. "That's my shit," he shouted.

Reggie pulled his jacket back so his badge and gun were clearly visible. Angelo realized he wasn't wearing his Berretta. He felt stupid and vulnerable and tried not to imagine his boy in this world.

"We aren't interested in your stolen metal. Don't make me get interested," Reggie said. The big man folded his arms.

"You want to make twenty bucks?" Angelo asked.

The man stepped closer. "I ain't no snitch."

Except for twenty bucks, thought Angelo.

"Get everybody out here where I can see them," Reggie said, pointing to the cardboard shanties.

The bum was a natural bully, and he had the foul-smelling bodies standing in front of them in less than ten minutes. They crawled coughing and spitting from their tombs, some half naked. None protested. Judgment day or another cop roust, it didn't matter. They were conditioned to do what they were told.

The possibility of Matt living among them made it difficult for Angelo to dehumanize these lost souls. He glanced back at the car. Charley stepped out and shook her head. He ordered the men to hold out their left hands. No one had the missing finger Hellman had described, although a black man with wild, matted braids had two severed digits. He picked at red open sores on his crusted hands and arms as Angelo checked him. The smell and filth were overwhelming. Angelo's stomach felt queasy, and he thought he might vomit.

"Let's go. He's not here," he said.

"Who you looking for?" the bully asked, taking the twenty-dollar bill Angelo held out to him.

Angelo glanced at Reggie and shrugged. "Why not?" he said.

He described Hellman's suspect. "He should be with this boy." Angelo pulled a picture of Matt from his wallet.

The big man shook his head. "Neither one been here. Never seen that kid. Guy sounds like a dead ringer for Gopher Bob, but he's dead. Got run over by a train last year."

"What was his real name?"

"Bob. She with you?" the man asked, pointing over Angelo's shoulder at Charley, who was running away from the car toward the river. "Not real good for a woman like that one to be alone down there."

Angelo jogged to where Charley had disappeared down the embankment and saw her standing in the mud looking in both directions. Her shoes were buried and large patches of dirt were caked on her legs.

Angelo looked down and realized his own boots were covered in the black, sticky sludge. "What the hell are you doing?" he yelled at her.

"He's gone," she said. Angelo could hear the frustration in her voice. "He had to piss. Like an idiot, I let him go alone."

He put out his hand to help her. "I'm stuck," she said, lifting her bare left foot out of the slush. He stared at the embankment as Charley struggled to retrieve her shoes. Graffiti covered the concrete, but he spotted something odd among the mindless scribbles. An angry, talented artist had fallen into this wasteland. Battling green demons, monsters with large heads and sharp fangs shared space with pornography worthy of the Greeks. The largest figure was a muscular, naked man with wild blue hair and red eyes. Terrible gothic wings sprang from his shoulders, his mouth smeared with the blood of his victim who lay headless, writhing on the ground in front of him. Angelo wondered what sort of mind conjured up this awful image. Charley tugged on his arm, and he pulled her toward the top of the embankment.

He glanced across the concrete riverbed as he waited for her to knock the mud off her shoes. The monster was laughing at him. This artist had revealed the weakness in God's universe. His fallen angels were left to live and hunt among the innocents.

SIX

Why was he here in this house in Burbank? She invited him home, and he didn't say no. A woman hadn't wanted him for anything in so long, maybe he felt compelled to go. Besides, he'd been wearing his favorite boots when he followed her down to the riverbank, and she promised she had a way to get them clean without ruining the leather.

While she telephoned her father, he waited in the living room and stared at his dirty feet. She had taken his boots, socks, and Levi's and left him with a pair of baggy sweatpants. Her stubby-tailed, black rottweiler loitered near his chair. The animal never barked, never blinked. Finally she came back wearing a white terrycloth bathrobe, her wet hair in tight ringlets.

"Sammy, go outside," she ordered. The dog obeyed. "You're welcome to use the shower," she said.

"Maybe," he said and thought she looked different, nicer without her glasses.

Charley's father arrived a few minutes after she tossed their clothes into her washer. Angelo stood when he was introduced, feeling childish without his shoes.

"I know you, don't I?" he asked, holding onto the older man's handshake.

"You should. I shined shoes at Parker Center for thirty years."

"Rizzo? That beard hides your ugly face. You're Charley's father?"

"That's what her mother claims."

"So, Harper's not your real name," Angelo said, turning to Charley. "You married? Divorced?" Angelo asked without thinking. Someday he might learn a little tact but he doubted it.

She smiled at him but didn't answer. Her father nodded. "Good riddance too," he whispered loud enough for her to hear.

Charley led them to the kitchen table where she'd left his boots and her shoes on sheets of newspaper. She told Angelo to carry them outside. He lifted the newspaper at the corners and took the bundle out the back door. He was surprised by the size of her backyard. There was a small swimming pool and behind that two stalls and a turn-out area for her horses. She pointed to the tack room near the garage.

"You can work in there, Dad. I put your cleaning kit on the bench." Rizzo took the shoes from Angelo and disappeared. "The shoe doctor is in. Let's get comfortable. He'll be there forever," she said.

Angelo asked, pointing at the horses, "Yours?"

"My babies. You ride?"

"Matt did. I took him to the Griffith Park equestrian center a few times." Just that quickly, the sadness came. Even the good memories were painful jabs. He followed her to the first stall where two horses poked their heads out through the top half of a Dutch door. He reached up to touch the nose of a big, red quarter horse. The animal avoided his hand and pushed against his arm, shoving him away from the stall.

Charley laughed. "Sarge is a little jealous of other men." She took carrots from a bin outside the stalls and fed both horses. Angelo watched her caress their thick, muscular necks and thought she looked happy there, much happier than she did behind a detective desk at Hollywood station. The front of her bathrobe was covered with streaks of dirt and horse snot, but she didn't seem to care. Sammy jumped on her as they returned to the house and left paw prints on her shoulders. She examined her robe as she closed the back door and excused herself again.

He sat at the kitchen table and looked around the small, comfortable house. The wood floors and paneled walls gave it the appearance of an old bunkhouse. The scratched, worn furniture told him Sammy had the run of the place. He liked that. Most women he knew were too fussy. Sidney never liked his cat because it shed and scratched the furniture. He never understood why it mattered. Something furry touched his bare foot and he pushed back from the table. A black kitten held its front paw in the air as it limped toward the living room.

"You met Tiny Tim," Charley said as she carefully nudged the frightened cat out of the way with her foot. She was wearing clean Levi's and a sweater. "My car accidentally ran over him so I felt responsible. I don't actually like cats, but Sammy's crazy about him."

"Your house is nice," he said and she laughed. "I mean it." And he did. It was small and messy, but it was clearly a home. His house was cold and barren. No wonder his son never relaxed. "Matt would like it here. He's always bored at my place."

"I've been thinking," she said. "Tomorrow I'll get the captain at Central to send his guys into every one of those homeless camps along the river and in the downtown area."

“The reverend lied,” Angelo said. He didn’t like saying it out loud, but he knew one of them had to admit what they both knew. Hellman had lied to them and escaped before they could confront him. It was just a scheme to get money or attention. Charley didn’t argue, but started pulling out pots from cupboards under the counter.

“The schoolbag is a dead end too.” She didn’t look at him. “No prints, nothing.”

“Did you talk to Magdalene?”

“She won’t talk to me.”

“Let me try.”

“Goldberg would never allow it. He doesn’t like you.”

“Don’t tell him.”

She slammed a frying pan on the stove. It sounded like a hammer hitting an oil drum. “I don’t work that way.” She mumbled to herself as she pulled different spices off a rack. “I’m making dinner for the three of us. Is that okay?” she asked. Her voice was angry.

“Can I help?” He didn’t need to discuss Magdalene with her. He didn’t need her permission or Goldberg’s. But it would be better if she helped him. For some reason he didn’t like sneaking behind her back.

“You cook?” she asked.

“Ever since I learned a twelve-year-old will eat anything you can put catsup on.”

She held up a box of spaghetti and a jar of homemade sauce. “Won’t need the catsup. It’s my mom’s recipe.”

“I knew there was something I liked about you. You’re Italian.”

“Sicilian.”

“Better.”

He sat at the table and watched her. She made meatballs, fried, and tossed them into the sauce. He found the smell of sautéed garlic and onions irresistible. When his mother was alive, their house always had that aroma. Charley lowered the heat to simmer, filled a big pot with water, and lifted it onto the back burner.

"As soon as it boils, I'll dump in the pasta and we eat. Until then . . ." She reached under the sink and pulled out a gallon jug of what looked like homemade red wine. "We drink."

He smiled. When he was a boy, his mother kept a bottle of cheap cooking wine in the same place. She would take one of her best wine glasses before dinner and have one drink. "To honor the cook," she'd say and then give him and his sister each a glass with just a sip. He hated the heavy, musty taste but drank anyway when she held up her glass and made the same stupid toast: "To Saint Michael, the blessed virgin, your papa and mama, *e tutti*." Their mother was a delicate woman, but she threw her head back and drank it all in one gulp. He did it the same way because it made her laugh. He loved her laugh.

"What are you grinning at?" Charley asked, handing him a water glass half full of wine.

"Nothing." He took a sip. It burned his throat. "Do you hate your stomach or what?" he asked, holding up the glass.

"Be grateful it's mine and not her grandpa's batch," Rizzo said as he came in through the back door and dropped Angelo's boots on the table. They were magnificent. The mud was gone, the leather supple, its bright natural color restored.

"I've got to pay you," Angelo said, touching the clean, dry leather.

"Bullshit. Charley must owe you big time or she never would of asked me." Rizzo poured himself a full glass of wine and sat at the table. "She told me about your boy. I'm sorry."

Rizzo resembled Angelo's father. He was short and muscular with a thin craggy face and large black eyes. He stared at the table when he talked.

Angelo nodded. He took a long swallow and felt the heavy alcohol burn his throat and insides. After a few seconds, he was warm and the burning sensation had subsided. He drank again, finishing it. Rizzo refilled his glass. Charley tried to take the jug, but her father pushed her hand away. Angelo drank, emptied the glass, and Rizzo poured another and then another. He stopped counting. It was good. He wasn't thinking. They weren't talking. He didn't know if Charley was still in the room, but Rizzo sat across the table, silent, comforting. For a few hours, Angelo enjoyed that numbing condition his alcoholic father had experienced most of his life. The old man drank to forget his failures as a husband and a father. For the first time in his life, Angelo envied his father.

Barking woke him. Wrong bed, wrong room.

He tried to remember. The bunkhouse was familiar. He smelled coffee and sat up, expecting his head to throb, but there wasn't any pain. He felt groggy but rested, with very little memory of last night except that Rizzo had helped him into the spare room and onto the sofa bed. He had tried to walk by himself, but his legs refused to cooperate.

He was still wearing the sweatpants and his T-shirt. The bathroom door was open. Towels were stacked on the counter, so he took a shower and shaved with one of those throwaway plastic razors he found in a drawer. He came out of the bathroom and his clean clothes and boots were on the sofa bed.

"You hungry?" Rizzo shouted from the kitchen.

"Starving," he said truthfully. He felt as if the wine had eaten away the lining of his stomach, leaving a big empty hole. He was embarrassed about last night, but felt calm for the first time in weeks.

He sat at the kitchen table, avoiding eye contact with Rizzo.

"You feel better, right?" Rizzo asked and put a mug of black coffee in front of him. "Last night you looked like crap. Sorry I got you drunk, but you didn't need food. You needed sleep."

"Good wine."

"Shitty wine. But you can't drink it and stay awake. This morning you eat." He placed a large plate of reheated spaghetti and meatballs in front of Angelo.

"My favorite breakfast. I usually eat it cold."

"Not here you don't," Rizzo said and put a loaf of bread and butter in the middle of the table.

"You live here?" Angelo asked, with a mouthful of great meat sauce.

"No. I promised Charley I'd make sure you get breakfast and get off okay."

"She lives here alone?"

Rizzo stared at him, sizing him up. How much of his little girl's life would he share with this stranger?

"Divorced. No husband, no babies. She has horses, a dog, and a crippled cat."

Angelo ate quietly. Rizzo wasn't going to tell him more. He saw it in the old man's face. The veins in his wrinkled neck were bulging. Rizzo was remembering and reliving something that angered him. Angelo finished and handed the plate to him.

"I'm sure Charley could have any guy she wanted, but after the first marriage didn't work, maybe she thinks it's better to be alone," Angelo said, trying to make Charley's father feel better.

"Bullshit," Rizzo said, angrily scraping what little food remained on the plate into the garbage disposal. He cleaned it so hard Angelo thought it would shatter.

"What's your first name anyway?" Angelo asked. It was time to change the subject before the old guy threw something at him.

"Tom. Sorry, what's yours?"

"Nino."

"I'm not mad at you, Nino. Sad story. Save it for another time. You got enough to worry about."

He didn't pursue it and helped Rizzo wash the dishes and straighten up. He couldn't help thinking he had opened a door that wouldn't close. Maybe he didn't want it to.

SEVEN

As Angelo suspected, Reggie didn't turn down his invitation to trespass onto attorney Goldberg's property. It was dark, and they had to hide in the shadows for several hours before someone opened the electronic gate. He heard a dull beep, a cranking whirl, and the wrought iron retreated from the driveway. They crept behind a silver Lexus SUV as it drove slowly over gravel toward the mansion, but jumped away before the car reached an umbrella of security lights and hid behind a large patch of birds of paradise.

Goldberg parked and walked quickly toward the house. His daughter Jennifer stood by the open passenger door, crying and mumbling something Angelo couldn't understand. Her father didn't respond. He held open the front door until she relented and went inside. It reminded him of many similar scenes he'd had with Matt. It was easy when you possessed the power and made the rules. He wished now he had given the boy a few more wins.

When the door was closed, he and Reggie followed the trail again down to the cluster of trees and the small manmade lake. It was a full moon, but the thick brush and tree branches created a natural cover that made it difficult to see more than a few feet in front of them. He told Reggie to turn off his flashlight. The white beam would look like a beacon to anyone who happened to be looking from the Goldberg mansion.

He tried to stay on the path but tripped on rocks and deep crevices in the dirt. He could smell a stagnant odor mixed with the scent of tree moss and moldy leaves long before he saw the lake. Lights from the cottage reflected an image of shimmering twin cones on the water. Somehow Reggie found the narrow path that led around the lake, and they followed it to the door of Magdalene's home.

He looked in the front window, motioning for Reggie to stay crouched behind the overgrown shrubbery. A large, pulpy woman in a white nurse's uniform sat slumped on an uncomfortable-looking wooden rocker. Angelo could hear her snoring. A magazine and reading glasses were on the floor beside her. He tiptoed by the front door and stood outside the window of an adjoining room.

Magdalene was lying on top of the bed, her tall slender figure covered in a white silky tunic. She was reading and laughing as she turned the pages. A tap on his shoulder startled him and he jumped before quickly crouching down, hidden by the shadows. It was Reggie. He pointed to the side of the cottage.

They moved cautiously around the corner. Reggie showed him the unlocked french doors to her bedroom. Angelo hesitated. He wasn't certain how to get Magdalene's attention without frightening her, and a knock might wake the nurse. Just opening the door would certainly scare the unstable girl. In the few seconds it took for him to ponder the situation, Reggie was inside Magdalene's bedroom.

She sat up and dropped her book but didn't make a sound. She stared at Reggie and swung her legs over the side of the bed. Reggie leaned on the pillow, put his index finger over her lips, and pointed toward the door where the nurse was stationed on the other side. Magdalene nodded. Angelo watched from the shadows as Reggie took her hand and led her to the french doors. As they stepped outside, Reggie told her that Matt Angelo's father was waiting and wanted to talk to her. She didn't speak but squinted trying to locate him in the familiar landscape. He slowly stepped into view and walked with them down the path.

When they were thirty yards or so from the cottage, Angelo started to ask a question, but she put her hand over his mouth and guided them back to the spot where the groundskeeper had uncovered Matt's schoolbag.

Magdalene squatted and then sat cross-legged on the damp ground in front of a juniper tree. Pieces of yellow police tape still clung to the bark. It was chilly. She wrapped her arms close to her chest. Reggie took off his jacket and draped it over her shoulders. She pulled it tight around her neck, tucked under her chin, and sat quietly.

"Do you know what happened to my son?" Angelo asked, sitting on the dirt and moldy leaves in front of her. He didn't recognize his timid, cautious voice. Now that he was here and could possibly learn the truth, he was terrified. In a peculiar way, uncertainty had sustained him, given him a tiny bit of hope.

"Did my father tell you about me?" Magdalene asked.

"A little," Reggie said and put his hand on Angelo's shoulder and sat beside him. "You seem okay to me," he added.

Angelo understood. He had forgotten the first rule of interrogation. Earn her trust.

"I'm not crazy. It's mathematics—how much to give or take, how much to get back, plus and minus, what's enough, what's not." She drew the coat closer. "Or, as father says, it's a question of what's appropriate, Maggie."

"What is appropriate, Maggie?" Reggie asked.

"Don't call me that. I hate that name." Suddenly she was angry.

It was a small misstep. Please keep talking, Angelo thought. He waited, tugged at his watchband, afraid to speak and upset her further.

"I can tell you what's not appropriate," she said in her childlike voice, and looking directly at Angelo. He shifted his weight. He was uncomfortable but couldn't turn away.

"What?" he whispered.

"Being so miserably abused that you run away from home," she said and his watchband snapped. "Giving yourself to a man old enough to be your father, having his baby, and letting it die . . . killing it."

Angelo leaned back on his elbows. His emotions were spent. He was frightened, then angry, and finally relieved she wasn't talking about his boy. Why did she look at him? Matt wasn't miserably abused.

He was becoming weary of her theatrics. "I'm sorry about what happened to whoever you're talking about, but I need to find my son," he said, pushing Reggie's hand away from his arm. He wasn't going to stop. Either she had something to say or she didn't.

"All right, Matt's father," she said in a stronger voice, bringing her knees up to rest under her chin. "They were here that night."

He waited for more. Nothing. "Who? When?" She would tell him. None of them would leave until she did.

"My ugly sister, Jake, and Cate. Almost daybreak, they left with your Matthew."

"Why the hell didn't you tell someone?" Reggie asked. He was on his knees now, crawling closer toward her. "What were they doing?"

She let the jacket fall to the ground and stood. "Like always, they came here to tell their secrets and plot."

Angelo felt a sharp twinge in his legs. "I don't understand," he said. His calf muscles were tightening from the cold ground. He tried to stand and clear his thoughts. His mind was cramping too. Charley was right. The woman was crazy. What was he doing here in the middle of the night? Desperation had made him foolish.

She offered her hand to help him. "The little frog was kissed by the princess and he fought to protect her honor," she whispered.

Her thumb, the frog, was Matt, Angelo remembered, and wouldn't allow her to pull away. "Matt fought? Who did he fight?" He recalled the earring and took a tissue out of his pants pocket, opened it carefully, and showed her. "Who did this belong to?" he asked, shining the beam from his penlight on the chip of white stone. "Was it Jake's?"

"Yes and no," she said. Reggie groaned. "It was the lovely Cate's. That night, Jake's." She turned and walked back toward the lake and her cottage. "I'm tired. Talk to the children."

"Will you tell the detectives you saw Matt?" Reggie shouted after her. She didn't answer and faded into the darkness. "Nobody's going to believe her anyway," Reggie said when she was out of sight.

"I believe her. Matt was here that night," Angelo said.

"She's nuts."

"They were here. We need to talk to Jake, again, to all of them," Angelo said.

Reggie didn't argue. He picked up his jacket, switched on his flashlight for a second to find the trail, and led them groping and stumbling on the path back to the Goldberg house. Once they reached the gravel driveway, Angelo wasn't certain how they'd leave the estate. It was late, almost two A.M. The gate might not open again for hours.

They sat in the dark near the exit. The wall was too high to climb and had spear-shaped rods along the top. Angelo studied the elaborate security and wondered if it was intended to keep the world out or to incarcerate the mad daughter. It didn't matter. He talked to stay awake and tried to think of a way to tell Charley what Magdalene had seen.

It would be light in a few hours and too difficult to sneak out the way they had come in. Reggie must have been thinking the same thing. He paced along the wall for several minutes until he was out of sight. Angelo fought the need to sleep, but lost. When Reggie woke him, he had rolled onto his side in a fetal position. He rubbed his eyes, took his watch with the broken strap out of his pocket, and tried to focus on the time. He had slept for more than an hour.

A garden hose hung from the wall in front of him. It was looped around one of the rods that lined the top of the wall. Reggie grinned and grabbed both ends of the hose.

"Watch me and do what I do, sleeping beauty."

Angelo stood and tried to stretch the stiffness out of his back. Aside from the bullet the doctors had left in his chest, he was in fairly good shape, but he hadn't scaled a wall since the police academy. Besides, the hose looked too flimsy to support their weight.

"Watch you do what? Fall and break your neck?"

"Couldn't find a rope," Reggie said, pulling on the anchored hose and planting both feet on the wall. He moved his hands a few inches and then his legs, creeping up the wall like a spider. He balanced on top, squatted, and held onto the rods. "Your turn."

Angelo looked at the hose and at the grayish light around him. Night's shadows were lifting quickly. He had no choice but to wrap his hands around the hose and climb. It was cold, but when he got to the top his shirt was damp with nervous perspiration. Reggie helped him stand, and they repeated the maneuver down the other side to the sidewalk, where Reggie yanked on one end of the hose until it fell to the ground. Angelo watched while he rolled it up and carried it to his car.

"You're taking their hose?" he asked. The precaution seemed extreme. Their minor trespass wouldn't warrant any investigation. Goldberg probably never even would know they were there.

"It's best," Reggie said as he tossed the hose into the car trunk. "I had to kill the dog."

EIGHT

Charley's phone call woke him. He tried to focus on the clock radio. It was seven A.M., so he'd slept for less than an hour. She was unhappy. How could he be so "fucking stupid"? Bad enough to break into Magdalene's "fucking cottage," but why did he kill the "fucking dog"?

There was more, but he wasn't getting all of it, something about Goldberg sending Magdalene away and threatening to sue the police department.

"Why sue the department?" Angelo asked when she took a breath.

"Because you're a distraught parent and I obviously put you up to your stupid midnight excursion to do what I couldn't do."

"Sorry." He really was. His memory was clearing. Reggie shouldn't have killed the dog. He didn't care if the department got sued, but he didn't want Charley to be angry with him. "It was dumb, but I learned something."

"I don't care."

"Yes, you do," he said and told her Magdalene's story. Angelo sat up in bed to stay awake. His eyelids felt like anchors. He really wanted to sleep.

"The woman's crazy, Angie. She made it all up."

"Do me a favor. Talk to Jake and Caitlin again."

"No. You stay away from them too." She went on about how bizarre his behavior was becoming. The children had nothing to do with Matt's disappearance. She had talked to them. Mrs. Bennett was awake until two the morning Matt disappeared. "None of her kids left the house. Let me do my job, Angie."

He liked Charley but wasn't impressed with the way she did her job. Besides, getting his son back was his problem. He had a headache from lack of sleep and promised to call later. She kept asking if he was okay. Should she come over? Should she call Tony or Sidney? He insisted he was just tired and hung up after promising he would call back after he got a few hours' rest. Charley didn't mention Reggie, so he guessed Magdalene only remembered that he had been there. Great, now everyone thought he was a dog killer.

Sleep was impossible. He lay in bed thinking about what he should be doing. Reggie had to work this morning. He would have to talk to Jake Bennett alone. Since the boy had been expelled from Saint Mark's, Angelo wouldn't need to deal with Sister Domenic again and he was relieved. He showered and dressed and tried to decide how he would approach the moody teenager. Intimidation wasn't an option. Jake had been through the criminal justice system too many times to be afraid. He was certain that appealing to the boy's sense of decency would be a waste of time. There was one tactic that never failed. He would offer Jake money.

His bank statement showed $4,785.53. He withdrew all of it and put $1,000 in an envelope with Jake's name on it, but was ready to spend it all for the right information. If he needed more money, he could always borrow from Tony. His brother-in-law kept cash hidden at the garage. Lucy didn't know about Tony's disaster fund, so she couldn't object to the loan.

By the time he reached the Bennett house, Angelo was nervous. He had convinced himself he was about to take an important step in finding his son. He rang the doorbell several times and pounded on the screen. Mrs. Bennett opened the door, leaned against the frame, and stuck her hands into her apron pocket. Warm, musty air and the stale odor of alcohol wafted through the rusted screen.

She didn't speak, but stared at him. He could see her expression harden as she remembered who he was. He thought she would slam the door, but she didn't.

"He's gone," she said.

"School?" Angelo asked, knowing that probably wasn't the answer.

"No, hell . . . the devil's got him," she said and grunted a laugh. "Thanks to you." She wrinkled her forehead as if struck with pain. "Whatcha call it . . . Eeemanstapay . . . livin' on his own, don't wanna be with me or the other kids no more."

"Where did he go?" Angelo was anxious again.

"Don't know. Don't care. Just like his old man." She pulled a dirty dishcloth out of her apron pocket and wiped her nose. Tears rolled down her cheeks and she moaned quietly. "But Caitlin, my sweet Cate . . ."

He didn't understand. He watched her blow her nose in the cloth, and she whimpered how life had cheated her, taken her husband and now her children. "Where's Cate?" he asked when she was quiet.

"The nuns got her." She stopped crying and wiped her eyes on her sleeve. "Least you can't bother her no more." She stepped back, nearly falling, grabbed the door, and slammed it shut.

Angelo stood there. He guessed all her children had been taken but didn't feel sorry for Mrs. Bennett. Any foster home had to be better than this place. He did the mental checklist—alcoholic mother, drug-dealing, murdering father, and pornography or worse from big brother Jake. If they were taken away, Cate and Mrs. Bennett's two younger kids got a break, but now if he wanted to talk with Cate, apparently he'd be forced to deal with the Franciscan nun again.

But first he wanted to find Jake. It shouldn't be difficult. No discernible skills, no money, and a nasty disposition left Mrs. Bennett's older son few options. Angelo guessed the boy would be on the street or in one of the teen shelters in Hollywood. He still had contacts a few blocks away on La Brea at the Haven House, a place that allowed any kid to stay overnight if a bed was available. Drugs weren't permitted on the property, but he knew most of the counselors ignored that rule. Jake would feel comfortable there.

WHEN ANGELO got to the Haven House an assortment of odd-looking teenagers were sitting on the front steps or on rusted chairs and tables around the courtyard. He passed them, glancing at each face hoping to see Jake, wishing one of them might be his son and a second later knowing he wouldn't be there. They watched as he climbed the stairs. So many of those beautiful young bodies mutilated with tattoos or tiny metal studs forced through lips, tongues, and noses, children who were too thin, too pale, with hair dyed bizarre colors. They met his stare, and he turned away.

The Haven's decor was greatly influenced by its patrons. The walls were covered with dark, confusing drawings. Therapy had uncovered monsters worthy of the LA River's concrete gallery. Misty Taylor touched his arm as he studied a black crayon picture of what looked like a dead baby. She was the administrator of the shelter. Young and pretty with black hair pulled back into a single, long braid, Misty was pale and wore no makeup.

"Sad," Angelo said, unable to look away from the drawing.

"Lori, she was fifteen when her pimp forced her to abort her baby. She couldn't forget." Misty reached up and carefully removed the drawing from the wall.

"Couldn't?"

"Lori killed herself . . . overdose. I've been meaning to take this down."

She led Angelo through a hallway maze to her office. The building was basic with concrete floors, brick walls, and donated furniture. Nothing matched, but there were plenty of chairs and tables. The dormitories were upstairs.

Her office was at the end of the hallway. It was cramped, but had a small, round conference table and a worn couch. Her desk was clean, but the table was covered with papers and telephone messages. She offered him coffee, but he refused so she poured herself a cup and sat beside him on the couch.

"He hasn't been here, Angie. I've been watching for him. So have some of my kids."

He hadn't asked about Matt. Of course she would assume that's why he was there. Her unsolicited news was just as disappointing as the last time he had begged her to help and she failed. He had met Misty on one of his narcotic investigations just before he retired and liked her no-nonsense approach to dealing with the kids. When Matt disappeared, Angelo went to her. He couldn't tolerate most social workers, but Misty was different. She never whined about the world's unfairness. A young girl had killed herself over an abortion. Misty efficiently removed any reminders. Screwed-up, abused lives could be worked with or altered, but she wouldn't dwell on the fact that with Lori, death had taken her out of the game.

"I'm looking for this kid," he said, showing her a small booking photo of Jake Bennett that Reggie had given him.

"I don't remember his name . . . no big surprise it's a jail photo. He stayed overnight, stole my petty cash box, and split."

"Was he with anyone?"

"Kids tell me he's been staying with some older guy at the Carlton."

"That dive near Western on the boulevard?" he asked. She nodded. "Want me to get your money back?" He felt he owed her something.

"No."

Of course she wouldn't. He liked her, but Misty would make excuses for Charles Manson. Her mothering instincts were a mess. He figured she had never raised any kids of her own or she wouldn't be so quick to forgive. He thanked her and left feeling guilty. Who was he to judge anyone's parenting skills?

Reggie wasn't answering his cell phone, so SIS was probably in the middle of surveillance. Angelo left a message and told him where he was going and why. The Carlton Hotel wasn't the sort of place a cop should go alone, but Angelo wasn't a real cop anymore and he wanted to find Jake before the kid robbed someone else and had to run again.

He flashed his badge at the desk clerk fast enough that the old guy couldn't see his thumb was covering the small, retired banner that flew over City Hall. Angelo wasn't certain the man could even read but knew he'd recognized the silver LAPD calling card. With a shaky hand, he pushed the register book in front of Angelo. Jake had signed for the room, and no one else had registered with him.

The room was on the third floor. Using the elevator in a dilapidated fire hazard like the Carlton never crossed Angelo's mind. He headed for the staircase and prepared for the sickening odors of dried vomit and urine that he remembered permeated each unventilated landing. The carpet hadn't been cleaned for decades, but occasionally he would see an unsoiled spot where a piece of furniture had protected a rich tapestry of black flowers on deep Venetian-red wool. The artistry was violated by those unwilling to give the building any more respect than they gave each other. Another perfect environment for Jake, he thought.

He knocked on the door to room 305. No answer. He did it again, louder. Silence. The door across the hall opened and a young Mexican woman with pencil-thin eyebrows and thick pink lipstick stood in the hallway. She frowned and shook her head. She didn't say anything but moved quickly, angrily toward the elevator. She disapproved of him. His Spanish wasn't good enough to ask why, but the odds were that any middle-class white guy in this hotel had to be buying drugs. She probably had a dozen siblings or cousins living in her room, so a drug dealer doing business across the hall had to be bad news.

Instinctively Angelo tried the doorknob. It was unlocked. Jake wasn't the cautious type, not too bright either to leave the door unsecured in a place like the Carlton. Angelo wasn't wearing his gun but didn't expect any trouble from the scrawny teenager that couldn't be easily handled. He never hit Matt and wouldn't consider using any kind of corporal punishment with his son. Jake was a different matter.

He pushed the door open with his foot and let it swing into the room before stepping inside. The clutter of dirty clothes, leftover food containers, and empty Jack Daniel's bottles made the room seem similar to others he had seen in the Carlton. Both the kitchen and bathroom had an odor of backed-up sewer pipes. Angelo opened a cupboard above the stove and jumped back as a herd of cockroaches stampeded to darker quarters. A triple balance-beam scale with marijuana and white-powder residue and a pack of ziplock Baggies were on the shelf. He had expected to find some drug paraphernalia since Jake didn't have many ways to pay the rent and selling dope seemed to be his talent.

Angelo left the scale where he found it. He didn't want Jake to go to jail. He wanted to talk to him, make him tell the truth. The junk he found in the room didn't give him any indication of who the older man might be, if he even existed.

He waited in his car outside the hotel for more than an hour, but Jake never returned. Angelo hadn't disturbed anything so the boy wouldn't suspect anyone was looking for him. It was hot and uncomfortable in the MG. He decided to come back later, try to catch Jake that evening. If he sat on the street much longer, the locals would think he was a cop, a parole agent, INS, or someone else none of them wanted to see. Word might get back to Jake and chances were good he'd run again.

Angelo didn't want to drive back to East LA. He thought maybe he should call Charley, ask if she wanted to have lunch. She'd question why he was in Hollywood; he'd have to lie. He called. Charley was in the squad room and didn't mention Magdalene Goldberg or the dead dog. He broached the subject of lunch and to his surprise, she agreed to meet him at the Wine Cellar, his favorite cheap restaurant, or as she described it, "that drafty little diner on Las Palmas." She agreed because the Cellar served big portions and comped for cops. He hated half-priced meals, but liked their food. Besides, the waitress always got a hefty guilt tip whenever he ate there. Being a retired cop was a little like being an ex-president. Some of the perks were there for life. He figured that was okay since some of the nightmares lingered as well.

Charley couldn't get away for another half hour. He parked around the corner from the Cellar on Sunset Boulevard. There was a space in front of a busy store window, a location where burglars and car thieves would be less likely to steal the MG or cut the canvas top and remove the radio. He walked by a parked Lexus with a briefcase left on the front seat and wondered if ignorance was healthier than his jaded view of the world. He didn't think so. If you didn't trust anyone then no one could disappoint you.

A bored parking attendant gave him a dirty look as he sat on an uncomfortable ornate iron bench outside the restaurant. Angelo stared at graffiti across the street. Hollywood had deteriorated further in the last couple of years or maybe he didn't mind as much when he worked there every day. The garbage man syndrome—what smell?

A black-and-white drove slowly down the street. The passenger, a young female officer in a clean new uniform, watched him through designer sunglasses, looking but not seeing. In a few years she would notice the subtle clues, a furtive move, averted eyes, suspicious bulge under the shirt. For now her training officer told her to look so she looked. Angelo smiled at her and she grinned back. An innocent, he thought, and it made him sad to think about the process her partner would deploy to make her tough enough to survive. He would find someone small that she could fight. If she lost, he would do it again and again until she won without his help. He would drag her to every dead body call, suicides, murders, tortured babies, until her eyes didn't fill with tears and she didn't turn away. He would test her in a hundred different ways until they were real partners. She would hate him until she made probation and then thank him for the rest of her career. Angelo wondered if anyone else would miss that sweet smile.

"All you need's a bag of peanuts and a few pigeons." Charley was standing over him, laughing. "I'm jealous of you retired guys sitting around on benches daydreaming."

"Waiting to get mugged by one of your Hollywood gang-bangers," he said and was surprised by her good mood. She seemed relaxed and happy.

She led the way into the Cellar. The hostess, Edie, a little Jewish girl working her way through art school, remembered him. She should. He flirted with her for a year before he retired. She gave them the best table, the one by the window. It was safe from trays coming in and out of the kitchen. Edie took their orders and made certain to rub her arm against Angelo's shoulder when he returned the menus. Charley noticed and rolled her eyes back. Angelo shrugged. It was a game. Edie was twenty years too young and much too smart for him.

"Likes to tease older men," he said. Charley nodded. He didn't need to explain. "How's your dad?" he asked, wanting to change the subject.

She studied him. "Why are we having lunch?"

"I owe you for the bed and breakfast."

She looked disappointed. They talked about Matt, and she explained why she thought the case had reached a dead end, no new clues or reliable witnesses. Even Sidney had stopped calling and gone back to work. Charley mentioned how well his ex-wife was adjusting, and even Chief Denby had stopped asking for follow-ups. "They're convinced Matt ran away," she said and then apologized, explaining that other, fresher cases had priority. He had stopped listening and was staring at the strand of hair curled softly around her left ear. He didn't believe Matt was a runaway, but he had to find out what happened and didn't need her or Denby to do it. Angelo wanted to be with her, but it had nothing to do with his missing son.

Edie delivered the food and made certain Angelo had everything he needed. Charley ignored the snub and concentrated on devouring her sandwich.

"Do you think we could go riding Saturday?" he asked after a few bites of his cheeseburger. She didn't answer for a second and seemed surprised by the sudden change of subject. "I need some exercise and fresh air," he lied. He didn't really like horses. They were stupid and smelly. He jogged every other morning but wanted to spend time with her. Choosing something she loved might make it difficult to refuse. She agreed and turned her full attention to finishing her tuna on rye. He ordered another Budweiser and pushed the remains of the burger plate out of his way. It was easy talking with her. She calmed him, pumped oxygen back into his brain.

Charley stuffed the last french fry in her mouth and grabbed her purse. "I've got to meet with some kid's mother in a few minutes. I'll just give you a five to pay my part."

"Forget it. My treat."

She didn't argue but said, "Come by early Saturday, seven or eight. It's better riding in the morning." She was gone. The Cellar seemed crowded and lonely.

NINE

Angelo didn't see the police cars parked on the sidewalk until he turned the corner from Western onto Hollywood Boulevard. With overhead lights flashing, the black-and-whites blocked access to the Carlton as well as the curb lane. The cheeseburger grumbled in his stomach. His digestive tract worked like an arthritic knee predicting bad news instead of thunderstorms. The hotel was a cesspool of parolees and drug addicts, prime territory for cops, but somehow he knew it was Jake's trouble.

The intelligent move would have been to keep driving, but he parked a block away on Garfield Place and walked back to the hotel. He clipped his badge on his belt and flashed his ID card at the young officer guarding the front door. He still knew most of the homicide detectives in Hollywood and hoped they wouldn't ask too many questions when he got upstairs.

It was eerie how twenty-five years of police work made a man clairvoyant. The door to Jake's room was ajar, and the dead body lay on the floor. The young man could have been sleeping except his eyes were open and blood trickled from his mouth. Angelo pushed the door back another foot and stepped inside the room.

Jake's right hand was on his chest. His dirt-caked fingernails were broken, with jagged, torn edges. The body smelled, not of death but of poor hygiene. The teenager's acne had flared, an indication that he might have been a speed freak along with all his other not-so-important-anymore problems.

"Who the hell are you?"

Angelo turned and saw a tall, well-dressed young man wearing a detective badge on his belt and standing in the doorway.

"That's the guy," the desk clerk said, half hiding behind the detective as he pointed at Angelo. "He's the one come up here."

Angelo introduced himself and held up his ID. He explained his reason for being in Jake's room and then asked, "How long has he been dead?"

"Why don't you let me ask the questions," the detective said.

Angelo forced himself to stop grinding his back teeth. The guy looked like a male model in expensive shoes and a tight, tailored, starched shirt. The new LAPD detective, he thought, all puff no stuff. "Sure, fire away," he said.

"You got a piece?" the detective asked.

"Nope."

"In your car?"

"Nope," he lied, not wanting to give Mr. *GQ* an excuse to rummage through his car.

"What the fuck are you doing here, Angelo?" Maxwell Casey asked, coming in from the kitchen. "Fishing too boring?"

Angelo relaxed and shook hands with the big detective, a friend at last. He repeated his story.

"I'm sorry about Matt," Casey said. "That's a hell of a thing, poor kid. Did dirt bag here tell you anything?" he asked, looking disdainfully at Jake's body.

"He wasn't here. That's why I came back."

Casey studied him for a second and then revealed what they had found. Jake was shot in the mouth with a small gun, maybe .22 caliber. Casey figured it was a drug deal gone sour. There was a scale and residue from a bag of meth in the kitchen. The desk clerk had seen Angelo and another man go up to the room at different times. Not much of a description on the other man. He wore a cap, hid his face pretty well, gray hair, and heavy build.

Angelo gave them Mrs. Bennett's address. The young detective avoided talking to him and continued taking measurements and sketching the murder scene. Angelo didn't mind arrogance, but this guy was too young to be so cocky. He remembered how he hated retired cops coming back to the station and chatting for hours about the good old days. But this was different. He could help. His gut told him that Jake's death was connected to Matt's disappearance, and he trusted his instincts more than Casey's smug partner.

Casey seemed to know what he was thinking and said, "Don't let Georgie bother you. He's a good kid, hell of a homicide detective. Got an ego the size of a gorilla turd, but he doesn't miss much at a crime scene." Angelo hoped that was true.

It surprised him that he didn't feel worse about Jake's death. For that matter, from what he knew about Jake's life, it was pretty pathetic. All Angelo felt was disappointment. He wanted to talk to the boy, find out what had happened that night. Now the only two witnesses who could tell him anything were Cate and Jennifer. Jennifer Goldberg's father would make it impossible for him to question her again. He'd have to corner the girl at school. Anyway, how much would she be willing to say about her father? Caitlin was his best, maybe his only chance. If her mother was telling the truth, she was living with the Franciscans. He had gone to Catholic schools and knew there was always a back door into the convent. As a teenage altar boy, he'd been invited to the room of a novice who'd decided celibacy wasn't one of those critical vows. However, in this case, he thought it would be prudent to ask Sister Domenic's permission.

He had made mental notes at the homicide scene. The empty bag of meth wasn't a type he had seen in Hollywood. It was like a kid's party favor, pink and cellophane and unique enough to be traced. Reggie worked all over the city, so if he wanted to, he would be able to track its point of origin. Every dope dealer had his own method of packaging. This one was odd even by street standards.

Contacting Reggie had been difficult the last few days. Even if the surveillance detective was working a case, he seemed reluctant to return Angelo's phone calls. Angelo guessed Sidney had convinced him Matt was a runaway. For some reason everyone thought it less critical if a twelve-year-old boy put himself on the street.

From the Carlton, it would be easy to drive to Sidney's place. If Reggie's black Mustang was in the driveway, he would knock on the door. He had no desire to see his ex-wife, which surprised him. Sidney usually had a strange hold on him. But since Matt's disappearance, Angelo didn't like or trust her. He was convinced she had lied about being home that night. He saw it in the nervous way her eyes avoided his. She had probably left Matt alone and had no idea when the boy walked out or was taken from her condo. He didn't want to know who the guy was or what was important enough to leave their son alone. Reggie swore it wasn't him. He'd only stayed a few minutes after Angelo saw him that Sunday. Knowing wouldn't change anything. She'd have to live with the guilt. The world might forgive her, but he wouldn't.

The car was there. Reggie answered the door. He was alone. After some small talk that neither of them needed, Angelo described the meth packaging he had seen in Jake's condo.

"Venice," Reggie said without hesitation. "I've seen it all over Oceanfront Walk."

"Who's selling it?" Angelo asked.

"Kids sell it to other kids at the pavilion or in the weight pit." Before Angelo could ask, Reggie volunteered to show Jake's picture on the boardwalk.

"If it's that easy to get, nobody's going to kill him for an eight track."

"That's all he had?" Reggie asked. "A couple hundred bucks worth, I don't think so. Somebody just wanted him dead." He took two Budweisers out of Sidney's refrigerator and handed one to Angelo. Reggie sat on a stool in front of the breakfast counter and gulped for several seconds like a man who had done some hard, dusty work. "She doesn't really believe your boy ran away. She thinks he's dead," he said when he finally put the empty can on the counter. "She won't talk about it, but I can tell from the way she's been acting."

"What do you think?"

Reggie nodded. "Maybe."

"You'll help me?" Angelo asked.

"I don't know where she was that night, but it's eating her up. All I know is she wasn't with me. I'll help, but don't tell her. It would make her nuts again."

So Reggie had figured it out too, Angelo thought. Sidney wasn't a good liar. She wasn't home with Matt but, if she wasn't with Reggie, it meant there was a new man in her life.

It didn't matter to him. He was done with her, but Reggie was acting as if the new man wasn't important to him either.

"Did you ask her where she was?" It was the obvious question, but Reggie glared at him as if he'd just requested details of their sex life. "Forget it. It won't change anything," Angelo added quickly and finished the last few drops in the beer can before tossing it into Sidney's recycle crate. It hit a pile of empty cans and wine bottles. Unless no one was throwing out the garbage, Sidney or Reggie or both were doing some heavy drinking. "You okay, Reg?" he asked, finally recognizing the man's bloodshot eyes and unshaven face as something more than fatigue.

"Fucking wonderful," he said and got them each another beer.

Angelo was aching to warn this guy about Sidney. Reggie wasn't exactly a friend but Angelo would push a stranger away from the front of a speeding train. Before Matt's disappearance, even before their divorce, Sidney had always been complicated. Maybe that's what drew him to her. He discovered the hard way that she was beautiful but greedy and confused. He had learned a painful lesson when she walked out on him and took his son—Sidney will always do what's best for Sidney. If he didn't say anything to Reggie, it was because he knew the guy wouldn't listen. A moth's got to feel a little heat from the flame before he'll believe he can get burned.

Reggie had a few days off and agreed to pick him up in the morning so they could face Sister Domenic together.

Something was nagging at Angelo as he drove home on the Hollywood freeway. He'd recognized the signs of terminal friction between Reggie and Sidney, but that wasn't it. Sidney would survive with or without her latest lover. Most likely, she already had found someone to replace the surveillance cop. Angelo hated himself for thinking it, but he believed Sidney could handle the loss of Matt better than the prospect of not having a new man in her life.

It was the image of Jake on the dirty floor at the Carlton that kept swirling around his head. He hadn't done detective work in so long that maybe he was missing something among the flashes of the dirty fingernails, a single trickle of blood, and the smell.

That was it. The smell reminded him of something. It was a common odor among the street people in Hollywood. They seldom bathed and covered the stench with mothballs or room deodorizers. The combination of stink-on-stink would choke a shit-eating horsefly, but each of these bums had a uniquely obnoxious aroma, and Jake's room had the distinct smell of Reverend Hellman. Angelo was certain. The ride to the LA River with Hellman in the backseat had embedded it in his memory forever.

Jake Bennett and Reverend Hellman . . . what was that connection? He called Maxwell Casey from his cell phone and gave him all the identifying information on Reverend Hellman. Casey promised to compare Hellman's prints to any they found in Jake's room.

"You know anything about a large amount of money Jake Bennett had on him?" Casey asked. "We found it when the coroner turned him over."

Angelo let go of the steering wheel with his right hand and touched the envelope with Jake's name on it in his jacket pocket. It was still there.

"No. How much money?

"Looks like a few thousand. If baby dirtbag got ripped off, why didn't they take the cash?"

"You're the detective, Max." Angelo laughed, but it was forced and he knew Casey would hear that. "What do you think?"

"I think drugs had nothing to do with his untimely demise. What d'you think?"

The car behind him tapped on his horn. The light had changed. Angelo drove to the other side of the intersection and parked. "I don't think anything. I just wanted him to help find my son."

"Guess that's not gonna happen," Casey said coldly. The tone of his voice, one cop talking to another cop, had changed. Angelo was on the outside. "Want to tell me why you took all your money out of the bank today, Angie?"

He was grateful Casey couldn't see his face. How and why did they access his account so quickly? Maybe he had underestimated Georgie. Although he hadn't done anything wrong, he felt guilty.

"The money was supposed to bribe him. He wasn't there. I still have it." No response from Casey. "Fuck you," Angelo mumbled. He was angry. Casey had a right to be suspicious, but they had worked together, watched each other's back for years. The veteran detective should've known Angelo couldn't shoot a kid, even a pathetic slimeball like Jake. "You got more to say to me?" Angelo asked. Casey didn't. He ended the call, tossed the cell phone on the passenger seat, and immediately felt sad as if he'd just been drummed out of the clubhouse.

TEN

Charley was leaning against his front gate when he arrived home. It was strange because he'd been thinking about her. From her stern expression, he guessed it wasn't a social visit. She didn't say anything but stared at the ground and kicked at a stubborn blade of grass that had pushed through the asphalt. He unlocked the gate and held it open.

She glanced up and shoved past him. Her body language was easy to interpret; she was pissed. She spoke and removed any doubt. Casey had told her about Jake. Hadn't she warned Angelo not to do anything stupid? Why couldn't he trust her and let her do her job? She breathed deeply and didn't speak again until he ushered her into his living room.

"You don't believe I hurt that boy?" He had to ask.

"Of course not," she said. "I'm angry because you put yourself in a position to be a suspect. It was stupid." She ran her hand over the built-in, oak bookcases. The smooth texture seemed to calm her, better yet, distract her. "These are nice. Expensive?"

"I built them."

She took a step back and made a closer inspection of the workmanship, nodding her approval. Finally somebody appreciated the effort he had made in this house.

"So if you can do this kind of work, why don't you do it and let me do my job?" She stepped closer to him, her face inches from his. "I'm a good cop. Trust me. I'll find Matt."

Angelo backed away. He wasn't going to lie to her again. He couldn't make a promise he knew would be broken by tomorrow morning. "Let me show you the rest of the house," he said, moving toward the kitchen. She mumbled something. The words were unintelligible, but the frustration was loud and clear.

Granite countertops, tile floors, and his large laundry room distracted her temporarily. It was enjoyable to show her what he had accomplished. She didn't say much, but followed him through the poolroom and upstairs to the bedrooms, occasionally stopping for a second to touch one of his cabinets or the wooden fireplace mantel he had designed and installed.

He led her outside to the garage. The workshop looked abandoned. He hadn't been in there since Matt's disappearance. The design for the knife cabinet was still on his desk, the large sheet of walnut propped against the wall where he'd left it that morning. Charley blew a layer of powder off the desk.

"Make more sawdust. You're good at it. It'll keep you out of my business."

He picked up a piece of oak, ran his thumb over the rough edge. "Ever notice when you're sick, how the things you usually love to eat taste terrible."

"No. I'm Italian. Remember? I can eat during major surgery." She didn't smile, but slid her arm through his and pulled him out of the workshop back toward the house. "As a matter of fact, I'm hungry now. Do you have food in this wonderful palace?" She wasn't shy about searching his cupboards and the refrigerator. "You really do cook," she said, examining the pantry.

"I can make something," he said, opening the freezer, knowing he hadn't shopped for weeks.

"I'll cook. You find some wine," she said.

The basement and the attic were the only rooms he hadn't shown her. The attic was a tomb of family memories, still too painful to revisit, trunks full of his childhood disappointments, things that reminded him of the mother he loved and lost too soon and the father he loved whose grief and discontent killed their relationship. The basement was Angelo's wine cellar and personal memorial. He had cleaned and painted the room, laid carpeting, and installed track lighting and floor-to-ceiling wine racks.

His life as a cop covered the walls, a shadow box filled with silver-plated mementos of police service—his shooting medals, a gamewell key, his first gun, handcuffs, and the policeman insignia off his uniform hat. There were candid pictures taken during his career, a newspaper article about the day he'd been shot, awards, even his medal of valor. It was twenty-five years of some good and some awful memories, but it was private, intended as his refuge, a place he drank and remembered. A few of the faces that stared back at him from black-and-white moments were gone now. One was a traffic accident, another, his last partner, died in the shootout that ended his career. Cancer almost got one but he chose a self-inflicted bullet wound to his head, and two more also were suicides.

In an eight-by-ten glossy, Tommy Lamada, his first partner, stood laughing with his arm around Angelo at Wilshire's divisional picnic. Tommy died on the street in front of him, shot to death. Angelo still remembered that day in South Central LA as the rain carelessly washed his best friend's lifeblood down a storm drain.

Too many nights, Angelo sat alone in the room, finished a bottle of his best wine, and remembered moments he wanted desperately to forget. But he was alive and he owed them. Maybe Charley would understand why he needed this place because he wasn't certain he did. His biggest fear was that one day he would put a picture of himself with Matt on that wall.

He chose two bottles of his best pinot and climbed the stairs back to the kitchen. The powerful smell of sautéed onions and fried potatoes engulfed him as he opened the cellar door. She called it the Rizzo frittata with eggs, potatoes, onions, bacon, and some fresh asparagus he'd forgotten was wilting in the vegetable bin.

Charley had set the table with place mats, cloth napkins, and wine glasses. He liked the homey look. Lately, the breakfast bar was his usual place to gulp a bowl of canned soup or a meal from Burger King. When Matt visited, he didn't like to eat at the table, so they had always planted themselves in the living room in front of the television. Without that distraction, they might have been forced to talk to each other.

The kitchen was warm. The oven and all four burners were lighted. She had messed up the counters with eggshells and dirty utensils. Paper towels were crumpled and thrown in the dish drainer. Water spots decorated the tile floor. He had been living in the house for almost two years and for the first time felt as if his kitchen had been legitimately and properly baptized.

Angelo poured two glasses of wine and gave her one. They clinked the rims.

"Matt," she said, and took a long swallow. He nodded and did the same. They drank quietly for a few minutes. She pulled garlic bread out of the broiler and the odor blended with the frittata to fill the kitchen. Suddenly he was starving. She served the main course and bread and a dessert dish with canned pear halves she'd found in the back of his pantry. They ate and drank silently until all the food and one bottle of wine were gone. He sat back, embarrassed, realizing he had consumed most of it. Charley was laughing at him.

"Don't you ever cook for yourself?" she asked.

"My cooking is more survival food. When Matt was here he always wanted pizza or tacos."

"You're not supposed to feed them what they want," she said and immediately blushed. "Sorry, I've got a big mouth." She stood and started clearing dishes from the table. When he tried to help, she took the dirty forks out of his hand. "Sit down, have another drink. I made the mess. I'll clean it." Something told him arguing with her would be futile so he sat and filled their glasses again.

Watching Charley work in the kitchen, he thought about Sidney's total lack of culinary interest or talent. Sidney wanted to eat out at every meal. If Angelo complained, she'd pout until he relented, an act skillfully mimicked by their son. She was a talented legal secretary but a disaster as a wife and mother.

"How come you don't have any kids?" Angelo asked and was glad Rizzo wasn't there to smack him down for his curiosity. In the mix of his alcohol-laden thoughts, the question didn't sound as prying as it did out loud. She didn't answer and kept wiping the counter. "Never mind. It's none of my business."

"I can't," she said without turning to look at him. She was finished, grabbed her glass of wine, and left him sitting at the table. "You coming?" she asked from the living room. "Bring the rest of the wine." She waited until he sat on the couch beside her. "I lost my baby at eight months. My ex was drunk and ran our car into a tree. It did some bad things to my insides. Doctor said I couldn't get pregnant again." He filled her glass.

"Too bad. You'd be a good mother."

"Maybe, if the kid had four legs and hoofs. Otherwise I don't desire that aggravation or responsibility anymore."

He searched her face for signs of self-pity. There weren't any. She wasn't wearing her glasses probably because of steam in the kitchen. The warm moisture tightened the curls around her face, brought a soft blush to her cheeks. She'd become the lovely Botticelli cherub of his kitchen. He laughed at the thought.

"Do I have something on my face?" she asked, sliding her finger along the side of her nose.

"No. You look great. For a second, you reminded me of a painting I saw once of a chubby, little, naked angel," he said. Charley spit her wine, choking and coughing at the same time. He snatched her glass to keep it from spilling on her jeans.

When she could talk again, she sat back on the couch and stared at him. "I've been called a lot of fucking things in my life, but that has to be an original." He returned her wine glass. When she leaned forward, Angelo kissed her, tasted sweet pear syrup on her breath. She didn't try to pull away, but put her glass on the coffee table and inched closer to the edge of the couch. They stayed that way, their lips barely touching for several seconds until she slid back. He wanted to say something but didn't want to ruin it. She grinned.

Always so certain about everything in his life, Angelo didn't know what to do now. He wanted her as much as he had ever wanted a woman, but Rizzo would kill him, and what would she think about him wanting sex when Matt should be his primary concern?

"Are you ready to be with someone?" he asked, and thought the question, although well-intentioned, sounded stupid. He meant to be sensitive but it was a line better suited to daytime soap operas.

Charley stood without answering. She left the living room and walked upstairs to his bedroom. The light was still on from their tour a few hours earlier. She leaned over the railing and called down to him, "Don't forget the wine."

He locked the doors, set the alarm, and turned off the lights. Nothing he was doing was wrong or concerned Matt, but as he climbed the stairs he still felt the guilt. Somehow it seemed immoral to love, to live when his son might be suffering or dead . . . thoughts that disappeared when he saw her.

She sat on the bed, clothes thrown sloppily on the floor. He stared at her full pink breasts and rounded hips, so unlike Sidney's body.

She opened her arms and said, "Come get your naked, chubby angel."

Angelo helped her stand, slowly caressed her warm body, and touched drops of perspiration in the hollow of her back. He felt the softness of her fleshy thighs and knew there would be time tomorrow for remorse, an eternity for repentance . . . but not tonight.

ELEVEN

He woke rested. No nightmares, no consequences sprang from his pleasant diversion of the night before except the faint odor of jasmine on his pillow. That would have to be enough for now. She was gone. A wet towel hung neatly over the tub. A new toothbrush lay on the sink. Simple reminders she had actually been there.

There was nothing uncomplicated about it, but that wasn't today's business.

Reggie arrived early. His pale blue eyes were streaked with red thunderbolts. Dark furrows were etched under each eye. Angelo didn't have to ask. He recognized the symptoms of Sidney withdrawal.

"You look like shit. Sleep in your clothes last night?" He tried to make light of a situation he figured was anything but amusing to Reggie, but he also knew cops thrived on irreverence. They could deal with disappointment or even tragedy if no one behaved as if it mattered. Reggie didn't answer. He grunted and poured himself a cup of coffee. "Hungry?" Angelo asked.

"I need a couple of cheeseburgers and fries. You got some?"

They made a pit stop at Denny's on the way to Saint Mark's Academy. Reggie ate, donned his sunglasses, and seemed ready to reconcile his battered ego with reality.

"You need a place to stay?" Angelo heard himself ask and prayed Reggie would say no. It was the right thing to do but he didn't especially like the guy and would rather share his house with Charley.

"I kept my duplex," Reggie said. "But feel free to invite me to dinner," he added, seeming to sense Angelo's reluctant hospitality. "I checked Venice Beach this morning."

"Anything?"

"West Bureau did a sweep couple of days ago. They claim cops got a lot of meth. Ray Hill, that sergeant from Hollywood, was the OIC," Reggie said, leaving a large tip for their pretty waitress who tried unsuccessfully to make him pay attention to her.

The man never smiled, never showed emotion. It was difficult to know what he was thinking or when he was serious or angry. Reggie Madison was the prototypical cop: no betrayal of emotion or his personal feelings. For years, Angelo had tried unsuccessfully to correct a similar condition. He finally had to admit his coldness was like being left-handed. If you're inclined to be introverted and a loner, only severe training will succeed in changing you. Maybe he didn't want to change and that's why, despite his misgivings, he respected and felt a bond with Reggie—or maybe it was because now they were both lifetime members of the Sidney rejection club.

Sister Domenic was expecting them. Angelo had called ahead while he waited for Reggie to consume his burger and breakfast fries. When they arrived, the gate was open and she stood like an archangel guarding the entrance to the convent. Saint Mark's Academy was across the courtyard and she directed them to park in front of her office. Angelo had briefed Reggie, but somehow he knew the nun would dislike his partner regardless of his affected good manners.

The convent was spacious and, unlike Sister Domenic's office, clean and orderly. The rooms were small, but there were a lot of them. Most of the doors were closed. The few rooms that remained open suggested that dark colors, heavy, old furniture, and musty odors were the basic decor. They followed Sister Domenic into the parlor. This space was different. There was a large bay window with lace curtains and the couch and chairs were covered in light blue material. A woman, probably the housekeeper, in a white starched apron stood by a side table arranging a tray with coffee. She nodded at them. Angelo wasn't certain at first until he glanced at Reggie and saw that instant of recognition on his partner's face. The housekeeper was the same woman in the white uniform who'd slept outside Magdalene's bedroom. Her stern angular face and unusually large hands and feet were unmistakable.

She offered Angelo a cup of coffee and he let her hold it a second or two until she looked up. He was positive; it was her. He took the cup and her lip curled in a tight smile, the practiced expression of someone who has served others all her life but knows she is and always will be the superior being.

Angelo hesitated to talk in front of the woman and waited until she picked up the coffee tray and closed the door behind her. His thoughts were confusing. He wanted to ask Sister Domenic what her housekeeper was doing at the Goldberg cottage, but didn't. No one except Magdalene knew he and Reggie had seen her that night.

"Is Cate here?" he asked instead. His rusty instincts warned him the mystery of the housekeeper should wait.

"We need to chat first," Sister Domenic said. She pointed to the couch and she sat on the chair facing it. She waited until they were seated. "Why do you want to talk to her?"

"She knows what happened to Matt."

"That's very unlikely. I've asked her. She said she doesn't know."

"Magdalene says she does," Reggie said. The little nun glared at him, but his blue eyes didn't blink. His voice was low and controlled. Reggie's demeanor should've told Sister Domenic she was just another witness with a bad attitude and a funny costume. Angelo debated for a second whether or not he should restrain Reggie's impertinence and decided against it. The tactic might work for them.

"I've been told Magdalene's father has committed her to an institution. I hardly think her input would be relevant," the nun said.

"You're probably right," Angelo said. "That's why Cate's recollection is so important." He didn't mind acting the sniveling suck-up if she would help.

"I'm reluctant to allow Caitlin to be questioned again," she said and interrupted Angelo before he could protest. "She's lost her brother and, in effect, her mother too. For the present, I'm responsible for the Bennett children and frankly, as their guardian, I don't think what you're asking is in Caitlin's best interest."

"How can it harm her?" he asked with a touch of pleading in his voice, and looked to Reggie for support. But Reggie seemed distracted, staring out the window. "She could make the difference in finding my son."

"I don't think so, Mr. Angelo." Her tone was condescending, a mother correcting her misguided son.

"Why doesn't Goldberg want us to talk to Cate Bennett?" Reggie asked, leaning back on the couch and folding his arms. His question was a challenge. Sister Domenic's face flushed and her eyes narrowed, disappearing behind her thick glasses. This was a woman who didn't expect or like confrontation.

"The Goldbergs have nothing to do with this." She stood and waited until they were standing. "I'm afraid that's all the time I have this morning. If I change my mind, I'll give you a call, Mr. Angelo. Until then I'm telling both of you to stay away from Caitlin and the other Bennett children." As she left the room she said, "Mrs. Pike will see you out."

Reggie shrugged. "Did I say something wrong?"

"Touched a nerve is more like it." He was angry and disappointed. What sort of people would interfere with finding a boy? He was having some increasingly bad vibes about not only David Goldberg but this authoritative nun as well.

The housekeeper stood in the doorway. She didn't speak but turned slightly to allow them to leave the room. The heavy mahogany furniture and dark walls of the other rooms in the Franciscan convent suited the Gothic aura of Mrs. Pike. They silently followed her lumbering gait through the hallway to the front door. Angelo detected a trace of incense lingering in the air.

Reggie waited for Angelo to go first, then turned to face her as he stepped onto the porch and asked, "How long have you worked for the Goldbergs, Mrs. Pike?" He was blocking the door with his body.

She released her grip and moved back. "Sister Domenic doesn't want me talking to you." Her voice was small for her hulking body. The question seemed to unsettle her and when Reggie moved back a little, she quickly reached out and closed the door.

Angelo's frustration was growing. Each turn was another dead end, but he was increasingly certain of one thing. Something terrible had happened to his son at the lake that night. Jake was dead and apparently Magdalene was locked up in some psycho ward. Cate and Jennifer were the only remaining witnesses and he needed to talk to them even if it meant breaking into the convent and the Goldberg mansion.

Reggie was quiet until they sat in his car. And then he mumbled, “This stinks.”

A layer of gray clouds blocked the sun and cast a shadowy blanket over the school and the convent. Two uniformed boys ran from the small chapel behind the convent where a frail priest with thinning gray hair and a soprano voice stood on the steps shouting after them. They stopped running and pulled their sweaters closer around their necks to keep out the sudden chilly wind. Shoulder to shoulder, they bumped and walked quickly, a tangle of gangly arms and legs, until they reached the shelter of the school's front porch. The boys were Matt's age. One of them was chubby and uncoordinated.

“It stinks,” Angelo repeated.

TWELVE

Because he was desperate, Angelo believed there was an advantage in having a man with Reggie's sense of justice working on his behalf. Ordinarily he might have cringed at the man's tactics and his tendency toward expediency, but as an anxious father he welcomed this avenging angel who didn't seem to be intimidated or constrained by rules or legalities.

Reggie drove them to Wilshire station and Angelo followed him into the records section. He told Angelo he had picked this particular location because the records clerks were never at their desks but they left their computers signed on so officers could get report numbers without bothering them. They intended to do an unauthorized search and this was the best place not to get caught.

Reggie sat at the computer farthest from the door and entered David Goldberg's name for a local and national criminal records search. The computer accepted the request without asking for a password. Angelo looked around the empty room expecting someone to walk in and question their unauthorized access, but Reggie was right. No one challenged them and, better yet, the inquiry couldn't be traced.

There were several David Goldbergs in the system, so Reggie first found Goldberg's driver's license using his home address, and with the birth date from that document, he was able to identify the right person.

The wealthy Valley man had an interesting rap sheet. There were two, decades-old arrests for soliciting prostitution. His other problems with the law occurred as a juvenile and were hidden under court seal. Reggie located the prostitution arrest reports. Both incidents had occurred in Hollywood with undercover policewomen. Angelo knew one of them. Jackie Dennis was a burglary detective still assigned to the Hollywood area.

They made copies of the rap sheet and arrest reports and were out of the station without encountering a single suspicious records clerk. Angelo wondered how any business got done in that place. Actually the excursion reaffirmed what he'd suspected during the span of his career: Civil service was a haven for the unskilled and uninspired, but for a change, it worked in his favor.

Hollywood was a ten-minute drive from the Wilshire area. Angelo felt a twinge of anxiety. He was infringing on Charley's workplace. Yesterday it wouldn't have mattered, but after last night he felt as if he might be crowding her. A room divider hid her juvenile table from the rest of the squad room and Angelo turned his back hoping she wouldn't see him. There was another reason he preferred that she didn't know he was there. She'd made it clear she wanted him to stay away from investigating his son's disappearance. He couldn't do that but didn't want to lose her. If he got lucky, she'd be out in the field.

Jackie Dennis was buried in stacks of burglary follow-up reports and having a late lunch at her desk. Jackie had been one of the first women to work patrol in the early eighties.

She had a rough time at the beginning, but despite her small stature she gradually earned the respect and support of her male partners. Tommy Lamada was crazy about her. They dated and probably would have married. After Tommy got killed, she avoided Angelo. He thought she blamed him, but he couldn't fault her. Some nights, sitting alone in the basement staring at Tommy's picture, he felt the same way. After a few minutes of polite war stories and catching up on mutual friends, she read the prostitution reports while she ate.

"I do remember this guy. He was one of the stranger ones," she said, wiping mayonnaise from her upper lip.

"Strange?"

"Trick task force wasn't my thing, but the department made us work that week. They were looking for some weirdo who was killing whores."

"So why do you remember Goldberg?" Reggie asked.

"I remember his red Porsche 911 Carrera. We impounded it. He was pissed and came back to get me after they processed him."

"Didn't he figure out you were a cop?" Angelo asked.

"That's the strange thing. I'm sure he did, but he was furious, a crazy little man in a three-piece suit."

"Did they book him again?"

"No. He calmed down when his wife came back."

"Came back? She bailed him out after he tried to fuck some diseased hooker?" Reggie asked and laughed. "No offense, Detective Dennis. I wasn't talking about you, but that's one understanding little woman."

Jackie Dennis returned the reports to Angelo. "I remember she was cold as ice . . . acted like she was picking her hubby up from his Sunday golf game at the country club."

"Can you recall anything else that's not here in the reports, Jackie?" Angelo asked. He didn't know what he was looking for, but had an uneasy feeling about this guy. There was a lot of sleaziness under that million-dollar veneer.

"He talked about taking me back to his lake house, whatever that meant. I didn't put it in the report because I figured it was just another come-on line to get me into his car."

She was done eating and gathered the remains of what appeared to be a substantial meal. Jackie was still attractive but had gained a few pounds during the last couple decades. Angelo doubted many johns would be tempted to hit on the plump little woman these days but he remembered her in her prime, the way she looked when Tommy loved her. In those days, she was a tiny, coltish girl with a pixie haircut, endless legs, and a baby doll face that screamed jailbait. Tommy's youth and good looks were fixed in time. Jackie's extra pounds and wrinkles were a small price to pay for life.

The little hairs on the back of his neck told him someone was watching, and he turned to see Charley with her arms folded standing across the room staring at him. He smiled, but her expression didn't change. His mind scrolled through a series of plausible lies to explain his presence as she approached. Nothing except the truth, which she probably already guessed, made any sense. He was a better liar when it didn't matter.

"Hi," he said, touching her arm. "I was just coming back to see you. Reggie and I had lunch. He had some stuff to do here and I wanted to say hello to you." She didn't speak or smile. "Sorry, I didn't mean to upset you. I can go if this is embarrassing."

"I'm not fucking embarrassed. I'm not stupid either. What are you doing here?"

"Hey, Detective Harper," Reggie said as he joined them, putting his hand on Angelo's back. "I'm done here, Angie. Let me know when you're ready." He nodded at Charley and walked back to the burglary table. Although a nicely performed gesture, it was only a temporary fix. Charley would talk to Jackie Dennis and she'd know he and Reggie were lying to her.

"Did you know Goldberg has a rap sheet?" Angelo asked. He was already in the water; he might as well swim.

She looked down at the floor and breathed out hard. "I can't fucking believe you. You trespass on the guy's property, interrogate his crazy daughter, kill his dog, and now you illegally run his record."

It was pointless to deny her accusations. She couldn't prove it anyway. "I'm not the bad guy here," he said. "I'm just asking you to consider the possibility the Goldbergs aren't what they appear to be."

"You think he took your boy?" she asked.

"I think he knows what happened to Matt . . . him and Cate and Jennifer. Jake knew and maybe Sister Domenic and Hellman too."

"Sister Domenic? Jesus, Angie, listen to yourself." She stopped and asked, "What's up, Max?" He turned and saw Maxwell Casey walking toward them. The homicide detective extended his hand to Angelo.

"Thanks, Angie. Got a hit on the Bennett kid. Hellman's prints were all over that dump, including the envelope with the money," Casey said without much enthusiasm. "You got anything else you can tell me about this Reverend Hellman?"

"He stinks like cat shit and he lied to me," Angelo said, pulling away from the big man's beefy grip. "It would really help if you found him." There was no way Hellman came up with his story about the homeless man with a missing finger on his own, and Angelo wanted a chance to confront him again. Charley was quiet. Her face flushed slightly and he guessed she felt guilty about letting Hellman slip away.

"Hellman knew Jake Bennett?" she asked Casey, then gave Angelo a look that said maybe you're not as crazy as Magdalene.

"Looks like it," Casey said, before returning to the homicide table.

She shook her head and asked, "Was Hellman in Jake's room at the Carlton?" Angelo nodded. "Fuck," she said.

"Can you get into Goldberg's sealed juvenile record?" he asked, emboldened by Casey's revelation.

Charley removed her glasses and ran her fingers through her unruly curls. He could practically see her thoughts as she tried to reconcile feelings for him and skepticism that someone like David Goldberg could have knowledge about a missing, possibly dead boy and not have told her. She was intelligent and confident about her detective skills, but Goldberg's criminal record and the link between Jake and Hellman might have created doubts. Angelo told her about Sister Domenic's housekeeper, hoping it would be enough to push her trust all the way over to his way of thinking.

"You need a court order. His lawyer will fight it," she said after a long pause.

"I know. But that's not what I'm asking. Can you get in?"

"Come over tonight. I've got to get back to work." She turned and walked away, disappearing behind the room divider. He saw Reggie leaning against the wall across the squad room. He was watching them.

Angelo wondered if avenging angels ever felt guilt.

THIRTEEN

Lieutenant John Delong exemplified everything Angelo hated about LAPD management. He was inept as a street cop. He hadn't learned the basics because he diligently avoided any kind of field assignment. He promoted because he knew how to study and work the system, not because he was a leader who understood his job or cared about the officers who worked for him. One of Angelo's biggest pleasures in retiring was that he never again had to work for someone like Delong.

Unfortunately Matt's disappearance had brought LAPD's Juvenile Division and Delong back into his life. There was a message on his answering machine when Angelo arrived home late that afternoon. Delong announced he would be coming to Angelo's house in about an hour to discuss the investigation. He remembered Captain Davis's warning that Delong might ask to search his house. It was an intrusion, not to mention a waste of time and effort, but Angelo already had made up his mind. He would allow the search. Although he was only a lowly detective when he retired, Angelo understood the bureaucratic mind better than most cops. It was all about process. Delong needed to go through the motions. Procedure was his bible and his crutch.

The possibility that Matt had stashed something in his bedroom had bothered Angelo since the morning he and Reggie found the bag of marijuana at Sidney's condo. He'd made a thorough search of the room and was certain it was clean. In fact, other than a few clothes, it seemed abandoned. Delong would think Angelo had something to hide and had scoured the area removing all signs of Matt. The truth was his son never treated this place as anything more than a weekend stopover. His real home, his heart, his belongings were with Sidney. Two years of trying to be a father couldn't erase more than ten years of neglect. Matt had given him that message in a hundred not-so-subtle ways.

By six P.M., Angelo had decided Delong wasn't coming. He'd waited two hours and wanted to get to Charley's place before dinner. The doorbell rang as he was turning off the kitchen lights. Delong stood on the porch carrying a computer, monitor, and a box of assorted parts. Angelo took the computer and keyboard and held open the door.

"This stuff should go to Sidney's," he said, putting the computer on the couch. "Matt didn't keep it here."

"I know, Angie. You mind getting it to his mother. I tried. I can't seem to touch bases with her."

Angelo looked at the tangle of cables and box of compact discs that covered his furniture. "You want to help me put this mess in his room and get it out of my den?" he asked, figuring it would give Delong an excuse to get into the bedroom and look around. Angelo didn't want to wait for the man to work up the courage to ask. A smarter cop would have carried it up there in the first place.

They set up the computer and monitor on Matt's empty desk. Delong walked casually across the room.

"Take a look around," Angelo said. "It's fine. Go ahead."

"He didn't spend too much time here, did he?" Delong touched the bare shelves and peeked into the nearly empty closet and dresser drawers.

"Sundays mostly. Did you find anything?" he asked, pointing to the computer.

"No. Actually that's what I wanted to talk to you about. Our investigation's pretty much at a dead end," Delong said, sitting on the bed. His contorted grin told Angelo he was struggling with a way to say something. After an uncomfortable silence, he stared at the carpet and said, "I understand you've been doing some snooping on your own."

Angelo wondered how beneficial it would be to give Delong what he had discovered. In the past, the juvenile lieutenant had proven to be an impediment rather than an asset. He doubted Delong's assistance would help but couldn't afford to overlook any avenue that might lead to Matt. He detailed the link between Hellman and Jake, described what Magdalene had said, and finally told him about the odd connection of the housekeeper Mrs. Pike to Goldberg and Sister Domenic. He didn't mention Goldberg's criminal record because he wasn't certain how involved Charley might become. He didn't want to jeopardize her career or admit that he and Reggie had broken the law. Delong listened quietly, nodding occasionally, but his expression never changed. When Angelo finished, the lieutenant stood and faced him.

"It's not much, is it?" Delong said.

"More than you have," Angelo countered without thinking. The guy annoyed him and lately he was finding it difficult to hide his feelings. "If you can locate Hellman again, it would be a big help," he added, trying gracefully to cover up his disdain.

Delong didn't respond for a few seconds and then said, "I'll find him all right, but let's get something straight. You can play Dick Tracy, but you're not a cop anymore. I understand you wanting to find your kid. I'd probably do the same, but no matter what Charley Harper says, this is my case. Anything you get comes directly to me the minute you get it or I'll personally book your ass for interfering."

The temptation to grab Delong by the back of his neck and drag him out the front door was overwhelming. But the fear of never finding out what happened to Matt was stronger, so Angelo agreed to tell him everything knowing he'd tell Delong exactly what he wanted him to know and nothing more. Besides, it was Charley's investigation.

When he was alone again, Angelo went back to Matt's bedroom. The computer was on his son's desk. He picked up the tangled cables and drew one through the other. Not intending to snoop, he couldn't deny intense curiosity about his son's life. He worked until the computer and monitor were hooked up and running.

Matt was sophisticated enough to have a password, but when Angelo opened up the desktop he had immediate access to all the files. He browsed through boring homework assignments and discovered that his son was a decent, intelligent writer. There was a folder with what appeared to be lyrics for a song titled "Holocaust" that he'd started composing. It had disturbing words and thoughts for a budding teenager. Angelo printed it and slowly read the lines out loud:

> Cry bloody man. Cry to the black, barren bottom of the earth.
> Spread your futile tears on seeds of hate scattered through the years.

The sun beats warm and friendless on forgotten signs of life,
lighting rotting corpses, burning away the last foul forms of human strife,
leaving the world dry and hard, its last, its endless sleep.
Violet-colored ocean bottoms, sealed coffin covers, close forever mysteries of the fertile deep.
Smoldering air, a cloudless, starless void fills the silent rage of sterile man,
chokes the barren women staring sightless into empty wombs of sand.
A chilling wind roars round the stony graves. No ear to hear the proud man curse,
the frightened mute who prays.
God is stumbling blind, his image faded into dust, the mirror broken and buried beside man's mind.

He closed the file and tried to remember the young man he thought he knew and loved, but had to admit this was a stranger consumed with despair. Angelo shook his head. It was his fault. He brought a son into this world and then abandoned him. If this was his kid's music, it came from some personal hell.

He hooked up the Internet. Matt had an icon for AOL and he clicked on it. Another click and he was online without using a password. His son had programmed an automatic sign-on for himself. Angelo clicked on new mail. It was empty. Reading the old mail might've been beneficial but that file was empty too. He accessed the mail sent folder . . . nothing except the message Matt had sent him the night he disappeared.

He sat back, took a deep breath. This was wrong. His son lived on the Internet. The computer and his music were all he talked about, but someone had cleaned out Matt's messages, deliberately destroyed any record of his correspondence. He thought about all the information he had naively shared with Delong and felt sick. Juvenile Division had the computer for weeks and the man had plenty of opportunity to delete everything, but why would he do it? He'd never even met Matt. Another scenario was Matt had cleaned out his own files before he sent that last message, maybe knowing he wouldn't be there to protect his privacy—scary because that meant the boy intended to leave.

The phone rang. He let the answering machine pick up while he signed off. Charley's voice came over the speaker and he ran to the kitchen, snatching the receiver before she hung up. The kitchen clock said ten thirty. He couldn't believe it was that late. He apologized and described the visit by Delong and what he had found on the computer.

"Is it too late to come over?" he asked. He wanted to know if she had looked in Goldberg's juvenile file, but hesitated to ask on the telephone.

"No, it's fine," she said and hung up.

Angelo shut down and unplugged the computer. He rolled up the cables and stacked them on the desk. He'd hoped that this intrusion into Matt's thoughts would bring them closer. Instead it made him realize if Matt walked into this house tonight, the breach between them might be insurmountable. It didn't matter. He had to find the boy . . . alive or dead.

FOURTEEN

The rancho neighborhood of Burbank looked like Hollywood's version of a Midwestern town an hour before midnight. Half a dozen residents walked their horses and dogs in the middle of Charley's tree-lined street. They lazily shifted a ton of horseflesh from one side of the centerline to the other as the occasional car passed. This was horse property, and they'd share their space but weren't willing to give an inch of it for more than a few seconds.

She was in her backyard mucking stalls and laying fresh shavings. He watched from the driveway gate for a few minutes. Charley wasn't a big woman, but she fearlessly shoved the horses out of her way. Her chatter was constant, scolding, name-calling, cajoling as if the two pea-brained animals understood every word. She finished and called her dog. Sammy darted from inside one of the stalls and jumped against her stomach, nearly knocking her down. They wrestled playfully until she glimpsed Angelo waiting quietly at the gate.

Moonlight caught the pleasant image of her full figure standing with hands on hips in tight Levi's jeans and jacket, boots, and a Shady Brady. The rottweiler leaned against her leg inspecting the intruder. Both horses stood behind her peering at him from one stall. Charley was comfortable there and seemed annoyed by the interruption. She unlocked the gate and he followed her through the back door. In the kitchen's bright lights, he saw the smudges of dirt on her face and hands. She threw her hat on the counter and splashed water on her face.

"Are you okay? You look mad," he said. She didn't answer and took a paper towel to wipe her face and hands. He wanted to touch her, but she was telling him not to without saying a word.

"I'm not. I'm tired," she said, reaching under the table to pick up the crippled little black cat, Tiny Tim. She gently stroked its head and wouldn't look at him.

"I'll go. We'll talk tomorrow."

"He molested a six-year-old girl when he was Matt's age. There was another accusation when he was closer to eighteen but the police could never prove it." She spit the words at him, didn't attempt to hide her disgust.

Without thinking, Angelo hugged her but let go when she didn't respond. He stepped back and said, "Sorry, I know getting that information wasn't easy for you, but didn't I say there was something wrong with that guy?"

"That's not it," she said, pacing in front of him before putting the cat on the floor. "I think we should do something now, but you're not going to like it." Angelo watched her and was puzzled. He expected resentment because he had persuaded her to break the law. But she wasn't angry. Her hands were trembling as if she were nervous or frightened. "We need the dive team to search Goldberg's lake," she said, but wouldn't look at him. "We'll do it on the premise that the schoolbag was found there. Can't mention the file or even hint that we suspect him. We'll say we're afraid Matt stumbled in the dark and drowned."

He didn't respond. The schoolbag was found nearby and Goldberg had a history of perversion. The kids were at the lake that night and Goldberg tried to take Jackie Dennis there when he propositioned her, but the man wasn't stupid. It didn't make sense that he'd dump a body on his own property and even Matt wasn't klutzy enough to fall and drown in that shallow lake.

"Do me a favor and talk to Jenny and Cate first," he said, thinking that searching the lake was a long shot and probably a waste of time. It should be a last resort.

She studied his face for a second or two then finally sat down, pulling him onto the chair next to hers.

"I know you don't want to hear this, but we can't find a trace of him." She said each word emphatically as if she were giving directions to a foreigner. "For a minute, think like a cop, not a father. There's no way he accidentally fell in the lake, but it's the perfect place to hide a body. I can get a search warrant. Goldberg can't stop me." She touched the heavy stubble on his face. "I'm afraid for you, Nino, for what's going on in your head."

"Look," he said, leaning back, "I can accept that my son might be dead . . . I just can't see him being in that lake."

His gut told him Goldberg was involved somehow in Matt's disappearance, but he was having a difficult time picturing the arrogant pervert as a killer and didn't think he'd be stupid enough to discard a body in the murky waters of Magdalene's lake.

"Come to bed. We'll talk more about it in the morning." She tried to help him stand, but he was dead weight.

"Will you talk to Jenny and Cate first?" he asked. His instincts told him the two young girls knew what happened. They were there and had to know. If there was a body at the bottom of the lake it wasn't going anywhere.

"Later," she said.

He stood and kissed her, held her a long time. She wasn't upset any longer, but he didn't stay. Admittedly he missed the warmth of her soft body, but the image she'd given him of Matt's flesh rotting underwater and his bones picked clean by hungry fish wouldn't allow him any pleasure tonight. She seemed to understand his reluctance and said she would pick him up in the morning. They would wait together until the search was finished.

There wasn't a star in the sky and the moon was a slim wedge of light as he drove toward home. He believed that he had survived years of police work in this dangerous city because his instincts were good, a cop's sixth sense. He could feel things and understand long before his partners got the picture, pulled their weapons, or took advantage of a situation. Maybe that's why in gun battles he was the one who always survived.

When Matt first disappeared, Angelo never doubted he would find the boy, possibly in serious trouble but alive. Lately that confidence had eroded and his sixth sense was telling him he was facing the worst possible outcome.

THE LIGHTS were on in Reggie's duplex. Angelo parked the MG at the curb and pulled up the canvas top. He wasn't certain why he'd stopped there. Was it because he didn't like to drink alone? Reggie, on the other hand, had made considerable progress by himself. He met Angelo at the door with two beers.

"Can't sleep?" Reggie asked, closing the door behind them and handing Angelo a cold beer.

"Don't know. I haven't tried." Angelo dropped onto a leather couch and glanced around the room. "Nice," he said, staring at the wide plank hardwood floors. The house was small and old, but immaculate with tan walls and elaborate crown moldings, not what Angelo had expected from a man who seemed so detached from everyday life. Charcoal sketches decorated the living room walls. "Yours?" he asked, pointing at one of the drawings. It was an old man sitting behind the window of a skid row bar—an amateur talent but well done.

"What's up?" Reggie asked.

Angelo told him what Charley had discovered and what she intended to do. He studied Reggie's expression as he repeated her conclusion that Matt might be at the bottom of the lake. The blue eyes never blinked, never looked away. When Angelo stopped talking, Reggie left the room. He came back with two more beers and tossed one to Angelo.

"What do you think?" Angelo asked.

"It's bullshit," Reggie said, sitting on an overstuffed chair and resting his feet on a polished ebony coffee table.

"You think he's still alive?" Just hearing Reggie say it would give him a reason to get up tomorrow.

"I don't think he's in the lake."

Angelo relaxed his grip on the bottle. Good enough for tonight, he thought.

FIFTEEN

Angelo stuck his badge out the passenger window of the black Mustang and a uniformed security guard waved the car through the front gate of the Goldberg estate. Reggie grinned and drove away while the guard attempted to give them directions to the lake.

"Don't bother," Reggie said, grinning at Angelo. "We definitely know the way." He parked near the footpath. Several city cars already had arrived, including the coroner's van. Angelo had slept poorly last night on Reggie's narrow couch. Half a dozen beers anesthetized his body, but nothing seemed capable of deadening his senses.

When he called Charley that morning, she sounded worried and suggested he go home. She promised to call him as soon as she knew the outcome. He didn't take her advice because like Reggie he didn't believe his boy's body would be in that lake.

They made the familiar hike. Several private security guards were stationed along the path, a silent, human barrier to anyone who might consider wandering beyond the parameters of the search warrant.

A staging area had been set up in the open space between the trees and the lake, where several men in business suits stood under a large portable canopy. The department's underwater dive unit had pulled its four-wheel drive Jeep Cherokee off-road, close to the water, and dragged out its equipment including dry suits and full-face masks. Angelo walked past the staging area and went directly to the water's edge where Charley was speaking with the uniformed lieutenant in charge of the divers. She introduced Angelo and Reggie. Lieutenant Brown, without any small talk, explained how his team would search the lake.

"The water's so dirty we'll have to do a line-tended search," Lieutenant Brown said. He looked from Angelo to Charley and added, "A line is run from that small boat to the divers. My guys keep one hand on the line and search the bottom with the other. The man holding the line directs the search."

"So what's the delay?" Reggie asked, pacing in front of the Jeep and watching the divers standing in a circle on a makeshift platform. Charley frowned at him.

"I want them to take the Sony underwater video. I think they got it ready to go now," Lieutenant Brown said as the first officer jumped into the lake.

Angelo moved closer to the edge of the water. He could see Magdalene's cottage on the other side. He guessed the lake was less than a few acres and not very deep. It should be a quick search, even though the divers seemed to be moving in slow motion. He wandered through the weeds away from the small group and followed the shore as the searchers inched toward the center. He glanced at Reggie and Charley, standing silently with Lieutenant Brown, and realized he'd gone nearly a quarter of the way around the lake. Watching from there as wind blew a stagnant odor off still water and over the grass, he felt Charley's scenario gaining momentum. It wasn't difficult to imagine this place as a graveyard.

The cottage was in full view now. He saw that storm windows had been locked in place. It was abandoned. The garden was overgrown and weeds grew in ugly clumps between the flagstones.

He turned back toward the lake and saw Reggie and Charley waving from the other side. Reggie was motioning for him to return. The divers were in the center of the water. They had stopped moving.

His legs were frozen. He wanted to go back, but couldn't move. He had experienced fear in his life and recognized the symptoms. Dry mouth and tightness in his chest stopped him for a moment, but his mind quickly recovered. He'd been a cop half his life and done things he didn't want to do. He learned how to shut down the natural instinct to flee. He always did what he had to do regardless of the cost, and even the possibility of finding his dead son couldn't make him run away.

They stared in his direction as he jogged toward them, but averted their eyes when he was close enough to see their faces.

"Listen," Lieutenant Brown said, holding a radio up where he could hear it. There was a transmission from one of the divers. It sounded as if the man was talking through a tunnel, but it was clear enough to understand they had found something. It appeared to be human remains.

Angelo looked at Reggie. This was how it would end. His boy had been thrown in this mud hole like a sack of garbage. He glared at the suits standing under the canopy. Goldberg wasn't there.

"Angie, come here," Charley shouted. She hovered over a video screen placed in the back of the Cherokee. Lieutenant Brown pushed in front of them. They crowded around the fifteen-inch screen with the fuzzy picture. "It's too small. See, the diver's hand next to it. It's a small child," she said, touching a spot on the glass.

Angelo took a deep breath. After all, it was just a reprieve. Half the lake still remained to be searched. He couldn't stop staring at the picture, focusing on the dull image of a tiny skeleton sleeping at the bottom of the lake, tangled in a bed of underwater plant life. His relief quickly turned to pity for the dead child who would never again feel the warmth from the sun or a loving mother. Reggie pulled him away from the car and the others.

"It's got to be Magdalene's," Reggie said.

Angelo remembered her crazy words that night. She might have admitted killing her child. The bones were practically on her front door.

"Do we tell them?" he asked.

"No," Reggie answered without hesitation.

Angelo didn't argue. It seemed right not to say anything. Maybe she had murdered her kid, but her punishment was already worse than prison. Magdalene no longer had any sense of herself. She lived in a fantasy world of angry memories, dreading tomorrow and frightened every moment of today. What little freedom she knew had been taken away by her father. Angelo wondered how much debt Goldberg had racked up in hell regarding his older daughter and suspected the man's soul was mortgaged to the hilt.

"How awful," Charley said and Angelo turned at the sound of her voice. She was staring at the screen and shook her head. "They think it might've been just a couple years old. Somebody's picked up another homicide."

She went back to the canopy and the suits gathered around her. She spoke for a few minutes then led a dark-skinned woman back to the Jeep. The others remained in a huddle whispering.

Charley introduced the woman, an investigator from the coroner's office. They discussed the underwater crime scene. The investigator confidently rattled off a list of procedures that had to be followed before the tiny skeleton could be removed. Lieutenant Brown told his officers to mark the location of the bones and continue the search. He left the camera in place and the hazy image watched them from the back of the Jeep.

It was nearly dinnertime when the divers stood on the opposite shore. Angelo was able to breathe normally when he saw the last man rise from the lake and undergo decontamination in a makeshift shower. Reggie stood silently beside him while Charley briefed the suits a final time. She never told him who the suits were but he guessed they included the local law enforcement and a few powerful political and legal friends of the Goldbergs'. It didn't matter.

Matt wasn't found but there were no high fives, no genuine satisfaction in being right. The hazy picture of a lost life staring at them from the back of Lieutenant Brown's Jeep wouldn't permit any sense of relief or celebration.

Charley had notified Santa Clarita and they sent their detectives to oversee removal of the skeleton, but she remained in charge. Angelo watched her coordinate the crime scene, direct the coroner, and bring the new investigators up to speed. She bossed around everyone the same way she controlled her horses—quick commands, clear instruction, and a total lack of fear. It worked. She had the crime scene wrapped up just as it started to get dark so they weren't forced to bring in heavy-duty lights or come back the next day.

Reggie and Angelo leaned quietly against the Jeep and waited. They knew if it were Magdalene's child, its DNA would link it to David or another of the Goldbergs. Angelo was certain detectives would get DNA samples from everyone who lived on the property. He felt uncomfortable not telling

Charley what Magdalene had confessed, but wouldn't change his mind. Reggie was right. What was the point? Besides, if LAPD was as diligent in helping to find this killer as it had been in finding his son, Magdalene would spend the rest of her life unmolested.

After everyone had gone, Angelo followed Reggie and Charley back to where the cars were parked. They had the benefit of flashlights this time as the security guards stood along the path and kept the trail well lighted.

David Goldberg never made an appearance at the lake, but the lights in his house were on when Angelo arrived at the gravel parking spot. He watched shadows move behind the drapes and wanted to be inside that house. He needed fifteen minutes alone with David Goldberg and the scrawny lawyer would eagerly tell him what had happened to Matt.

"Let's go," Reggie said, holding open the car door. "Don't even think about it," he added, seeming to read Angelo's mind. "Not yet."

"Why don't you come with me, Angie?" Charley asked.

"My ride's at Reggie's. I'll meet you at your place."

"Sure," she said and grabbed his arm as he turned to leave. "Angie, I'm glad I was wrong."

"Will you talk to Cate and Jenny?"

She started the engine, "I don't know." The window closed and the car slowly backed out then headed toward the front gate.

The Goldberg mansion was an elegant prison, no way in and no way out. He stared at the high windows and heavy front door. He might be able to sneak in through a basement window or some other burglary route, but he didn't want to give Goldberg an excuse to shoot him or worse, dismiss him as a nut case. There was always a way to get inside, but talking to Jenny and escaping without being arrested or killed would be the challenge.

It wouldn't be any easier to reach Cate. Sister Domenic had the key to the convent. She was a formidable obstacle that wasn't going to step aside for him.

"Want to grab something to eat?" Reggie asked, as he maneuvered the Mustang out of the driveway and into traffic. "I know a bar that serves great hamburgers and sandwiches about ten minutes from here. Okay?"

Angelo nodded. He wasn't hungry or thirsty, but a dinner break with a few beers would give him downtime to think and plan. Reggie ate more than any skinny man he had ever known and like every good cop the surveillance detective never missed a meal.

The Code-Four Bar was a cop hangout, which pleased Angelo. Policemen were pack animals that tended to eat and play together. Their disciplined veneer often deteriorated to unruly and sometimes out-of-control behavior in a friendly environment. It was a necessary pressure-relief valve.

Reggie found a table away from the crowded bar and ordered the biggest hamburger on the menu, extra onion rings and fries. Angelo did the same and watched Reggie finish two beers before their meal arrived. Angelo sipped at his drink because he had a feeling he was about to become the designated driver. After Reggie drank his second beer, he confiscated the extra one he'd ordered for Angelo.

Depression was such an overused clinical term that Angelo usually ignored anyone who claimed to have symptoms. He was certain Reggie would be the last man on this planet to admit to being depressed, but his partner's behavior was clearly telling another story.

Angelo was fearful over the fate of his son, especially after today's grim discovery, but had to admit Reggie's misery was wearing on him too. Although Reggie never talked about it, Angelo guessed his relationship with Sidney had caused considerable mental damage. The guy had learned the hard way that Sidney thrived in a world devoid of consequences. She began and ended relationships on a whim so her abrupt split from him might not have had any reasonable explanation. Unfortunately, Reggie being a hard, lean man with a mind-set to match believed that in his ordered universe every effect had to have a cause. Searching for reason in Sidney's illogical mind was not only futile but guaranteed the answers he needed to decipher her conduct would elude him. Angelo knew Reggie wouldn't find peace of mind until he got drunk enough to stop trying to understand her.

So they ate and Reggie drank. They talked about ways to interview the two girls. Neither of them could figure out a workable plan. Reggie's mind was surprisingly clear. The alcohol hadn't affected his ability to reason, but there was heaviness about him, an oppressive weight the liquor seemed to feed. When they finished, Angelo tried to take the car keys, but he refused. Reggie walked steadily to the driver's door and showed no signs of drunkenness. Angelo asked again. Reggie ignored him and started the engine.

"It's not the same thing. I can drive fine, but . . . never mind, just get in the car," he ordered, and looked embarrassed as if he had nearly revealed too much.

Angelo didn't argue and buckled himself into the passenger seat. Somehow he understood that in Reggie's world driving a car had nothing to do with drinking or being unhappy.

There was no more conversation and Angelo left him standing at his front door. He drove his MG home and was relieved to be by himself. There was nothing more to discuss. The day had tired him. This time it wasn't his boy at the bottom of the lake. But how many vacant lots and abandoned building searches would he be forced to endure before the nightmare ended? How many times would his heart stop after a hiker discovered an unidentified body or some poor soul's remains washed up on a beach? He wished for closure and then hated himself for wanting or needing the comfort of knowing, good or bad, just having an answer.

The quiet darkness of his house was soothing. He called Charley and explained that he was exhausted and didn't want to go out again. She understood but sounded tense. She volunteered to come over and be with him. He refused. He worried that his feelings for her had become a distraction. All his energy was needed to focus on finding Matt. If it were genuine, whatever was between them would survive, and they would continue, but not until he solved the mystery of his son's disappearance.

He was going upstairs to bed but went back to the kitchen for a glass of milk, or he would have missed the blinking red light on the answering machine. He played back the message and recognized her voice immediately. He'd only heard it once but she had a lyrical quality that was difficult to forget. Caitlin Bennett wanted to talk to him. Would he meet her at Our Lady of the Angels Cathedral tomorrow? Sister Domenic had business downtown and Cate said she begged the nun to allow her to visit the cathedral. Sister would leave her there for confession at four P.M. and pick her up an hour later.

He sat in the dark and listened to the recording again. "Please come," were the whispered last words of her message. Was it a cruel joke, he wondered, divine intervention, or just dumb luck? He didn't care because he was certain the young girl had answers and now he might have an opportunity to ask questions. It was enough.

SIXTEEN

Our Lady of the Angels stood like a French prison, plain cold stone devoid of the ornate trappings so essential among the older cathedrals. Dull alabaster-covered windows filling space where stained glass should have been, and modern track lighting replacing traditional chandeliers. There weren't any breathtaking Michelangelo statues. Instead, one-dimensional tapestries decorated the walls.

Angelo waited in the back of the cavernous hall and stared at the altar and the organ pipes—a cylindrical steel garden behind a barren slab of marble. His conventional Catholic upbringing should have caused him to rebel at this modernist stab at religious architecture, but to his amazement he could relate to it. The lack of flamboyant artisans or craftsmanship said a lot about today's world—something he had long suspected. The ability to evoke emotion through great art had deteriorated to cheap sentimental manipulation. He wondered what sort of sensation this architect was trying to create. The message he got was God was nowhere to be found in this cold sterile palace.

A few noisy tourists shuffled through the church. Some snapped photos of the altar or the large baptismal fountain in the back of the sanctuary. They joked and laughed, obliterating the few remnants of reverential feeling the architect hadn't managed to destroy.

It was four fifteen P.M. and he hadn't seen Cate. The confessionals had emptied and still no sign of her. He searched in each of the small chapels, but she wasn't on the main floor. He found the stairway to the catacombs and made his way into another empty chapel. The stained-glass windows removed from skid row's condemned Saint Vibiana's cathedral had found a home hidden in the basement. Alcoves reserved places for dead Los Angeles elite and chosen clergy. Beautiful glass paintings were the prizes at the end of each marble walkway. There was a respectful silence down there; he'd found a holy refuge at last.

He spotted Cate sitting under an enormous window of bold reds and blues, a picture of Christ the shepherd guiding his wayward sheep. She waved before disappearing behind a marble wall. When he got closer, she motioned for him to follow her into a secluded corner where a stone pew had been placed in front of a life-sized statue of the Virgin Mary. A tray of unlighted candles was positioned directly in front of the statue.

The young girl in her green Saint Mark's Academy uniform knelt on the pew and seemed nervous and thinner than Angelo remembered. Her long black hair was pulled back away from her face, and he could see a single diamond stud in her right ear. She directed him to stand out of sight behind a pillar ten feet from the statue.

"Sister will be angry if she finds you here," she explained. "This way you can see if she's coming."

"What did you want to tell me?" he asked, knowing he sounded a little too desperate.

"Jenny said you killed my brother, Jake. I don't believe her, but I have to ask you."

"Why would she say that?" he asked, feeling a little guilty even though he hadn't done anything wrong. He had been so obsessed with finding Matt that he'd forgotten her brother was dead, and that the boy had died in a horrible way. "I swear I didn't hurt your brother."

"I know." She wiggled uncomfortably on the narrow leather kneepad and leaned forward on her elbows. "Jenny's dad probably did it."

Angelo waited. His heart was racing and his thoughts were tripping over each other as he tried to find just the right thing to say. He didn't want to push her too hard or she might back away, but he had so many questions, and she seemed willing to talk.

"Why do you think Mr. Goldberg would harm your brother?" he asked as an older woman peeked around the wall. Angelo pushed closer to the pillar and put his finger over his lips. Cate understood and bowed her head, pretending to pray. The woman saw her and respectfully backed away. "She's gone," he whispered.

Cate looked up at him. "Mr. Goldberg's a pervert, worse than Jake . . . used to be." Her voice got louder. She stopped and seemed to compose herself. "Remember those pictures you found in his bedroom with me and my little sister?" she asked, and Angelo nodded. "My mom told me you saw them, but Jake took lots more." She hesitated and her eyes narrowed. "He sold them to Jenny's father."

"How do you know that?"

"Jake told me. He swore there was a bunch of these rich old guys that bought them and passed them around like Pokémon Cards or something."

"Did he tell you who the men were?"

"No, but he said one of them was a cop and that's why they could never get caught . . ." She stopped and quickly added, "I don't know who else."

Angelo shook his head. "You're a smart girl. Why would you let him do that to you and your sister?"

"He gave me money. Who cares about some stupid pictures anyway."

"So then why tell me now?"

"Jenny's father killed Jake and . . ." She stopped and moved closer to him until she was leaning against the pillar and whispered, "I think he did something to Matt."

A rush of blood hit his brain. It wasn't nerves. It was excitement, the expectation that finally he might know. "What did he do?" Angelo asked calmly.

"Matt was going to Jenny's house when he left the lake that night. He was really mad at Mr. Goldberg . . . already beat up Jake when my brother showed him some of my pictures . . . said he was gonna get Jenny's dad next." The words rushed from her like a story she had to tell before she lost her nerve.

"Matt beat him up?" Angelo asked, having a difficult time picturing his son fighting with anyone, but felt pride for a boy he had obviously misjudged. He reached into his pocket, removed the earring he had found in the clearing, and handed it to Cate. She smiled, a rare but beautiful smile.

"Where did you find it?" she asked, putting it in her left earlobe.

"Near the lake."

"I lost it that night." She looked sad again. "Matthew was such a child," she said in a world-weary way that made him think about her reassuring kiss on Jenny's head. "That wasn't his first time at the lake, but he never understood. The pictures were no big deal. I warned him to stay away from Jenny's father."

"Why were you kids there?"

"We always went to the lake. We snuck out all the time, smoked grass and stuff. Jake would wait until mom passed out and take her car. It was fun until Jenny's crazy sister found out and wouldn't leave us alone."

He was afraid to pursue what "stuff" was and instead asked, "Did he go?"

"What?"

"Did Matt go to Goldberg's house?"

"I guess. We all left, except crazy Maggie. Next day he was missing, then Jake ran away too."

"Maybe Matt never got there." He looked up at the sound of hollow footsteps, a woman's heavy heels on the marble floor, and he gently shoved Cate back toward her pew. The steps retreated and she leaned forward.

"Jenny said he was there," she whispered without turning toward him.

Sister Domenic walked around the wall and Angelo quickly ducked behind the pillar. Cate bowed her head and acted surprised when the nun tapped her on the shoulder.

"Are we ready, Caitlin?" Sister Domenic asked, glancing suspiciously around the empty room. "What do you think of Our Lord's splendid home?"

"It's nice," Cate said. She picked up her schoolbag and hurried away with Sister Domenic a step behind.

Angelo waited a few minutes to give them time to reach the parking garage and hoped Sister Domenic hadn't parked anywhere near the MG. His next thought was Charley. He wanted to share Cate's story with her. Certainly she would want to interrogate Goldberg and at least try to talk to Magdalene. Angelo knew how pedophiles worked. Some of the weirdos just looked at pictures, but there were others who would pay a lot of money for the real thing and if they were prominent enough, they'd kill to keep their secret. The fact that one of them might be a cop complicated matters. Who could he trust now? The answer was actually easy—no one. That way he wouldn't make a mistake. He, Reggie, and Charley would have to do everything themselves.

As he drove home, he left a message on Charley's cell phone asking her to meet him at his house. When he arrived half an hour later, he saw her Crown Victoria parked on the street. His determination to keep their relationship strictly business deteriorated as soon as she smiled at him. She waited on the front porch, leaning lazily against the wall in her work jeans and a flattering pink sweater. He kissed her, thinking abstinence was a stupid idea anyway.

As soon as they got inside he repeated what Cate had told him. It didn't seem to surprise Charley as much as he thought it would. She was a clever woman and had some growing suspicions about David Goldberg.

"Knowing it and proving it are two very different things," she said.

He handed her a glass of chardonnay and dropped beside her on the couch. They sat silently for several minutes. He sipped on his beer, hoping her quick mind would find a way.

"Cop could be anyone," he said, thinking out loud.

"Or Jake lied and there isn't any cop."

"How about Delong? He had the computer and an opportunity to clean it."

"How do you know Matt didn't erase everything?"

"We need to talk to Jenny," he said and she sighed. "Don't close your mind to the idea. I know he's her father but she's not a happy little girl, and I'm guessing she's seen stuff she might want to tell someone."

"These kids hardly ever give up their parents, even the real monsters. Besides, Goldberg would never allow it. If you try to talk to her without his permission, he really will sue all of us."

"I don't care."

"Well, I do," she said, sitting up. "I won't put the department and the city in jeopardy if there's another way."

"And if there isn't?" He spotted a tiny crack in the armor and grinned at her.

"Fuck you, Angelo. I'm not going there. We'll watch him. We've got enough for surveillance."

He knew he and Reggie would have to do the surveillance themselves until they figured out whether or not Jake was telling the truth about a dirty cop. Before he could say anything, she rolled over on top of him, kissing his neck, nibbling playfully on his ear, and was seriously working toward his eager mouth when the doorbell rang. It startled her and in an attempt to sit up she nearly slid off the couch. Her face flushed and she straightened her sweater as Angelo steadied himself and opened the door.

"Bad timing?" Tony asked, standing under the porch light with Lucy a step behind him. Angelo wasn't good at hiding his feelings and at this moment his feelings were throbbing throughout his body. Lucy squeezed by her hesitant husband and was stationed in front of Charley, introducing herself before Angelo had closed the door.

Tony asked how the investigation was going and what the dive team had found, but before Charley could answer, Lucy interrupted with a list of questions.

Charley glanced at Angelo and tried to answer but Lucy interrupted again. "I'll make us some coffee," Lucy said. "Come with me, Detective Charley. You can help."

"Want a beer?" Angelo asked, ignoring his sister, and Tony nodded. He went into the poolroom, took a cold beer from the refrigerator under the bar, and waited until Tony took a long swallow before asking, "So why did my sister drag you here tonight?"

"She's worried about you."

"What else? If Lucy came to my house every time she was worried about me, she'd be living in my spare room."

"She thinks Sidney did something to Matt and that's why he ran away."

"Did what?" Angelo prepared himself for another one of his sister's convoluted, farfetched theories on what had happened to his son. Since Matt's disappearance, she had come up with a new one every week.

"Who knows? She got this harebrained notion last night and that's all she's talked about all day."

"She hasn't said anything to Sid, has she?" Angelo asked.

"She means well," Tony said, but didn't look at him. He coughed and rubbed his left eye nervously. He looked tired and uncomfortable.

"You have to talk to her," Angelo said, trying to stay calm.

When the two women returned, Charley carried a tray with a pot of coffee and cups. Lucy had a small plain yellow cake that she placed on the coffee table. The plate landed a little too hard and Angelo looked up at Charley, who focused on the coffee pot, trying not to smile.

Angelo recognized the signs that Lucy had been put in her place. She was subdued and sat quietly beside Tony.

"To answer your question, Tony, the investigation is picking up a little," Charley said, taking a sip and peering over the porcelain rim at Angelo.

"Good," Tony said. "That's good. Isn't it, honey?" he asked. Lucy didn't respond, but shrugged with a noncommittal grunt.

After an hour, Angelo faked a yawn and Tony announced that it was late. Lucy barely mumbled a good night and sat in the car while Tony hugged Angelo and thanked him for his hospitality. The big man politely offered to shake hands with Charley but changed his mind and put his arm around her shoulder, gently pulling her toward him for a hug. Laughing, he whispered something in her ear. She snorted and kissed him on the cheek.

Angelo watched the car drive away from the house before turning off the porch light and going inside. He wondered why Charley kept smiling but couldn't decide whether or not to pry into what had happened in the kitchen.

"What did Tony say?" he asked, hoping it would encourage her to start talking.

"He had a good time," she said, giggling again.

"What's the joke?"

"Do you know what your sister thinks?"

"Practically never."

"She thinks your ex-wife sold your son to those Mexican dayworkers that stand in front of Home Depot."

He laughed. That was absurd, even for Lucy. "Is that what you argued about in the kitchen?"

"We didn't argue. I told her she was wicked to accuse a boy's mother. She actually said those terrible things to Sidney. I told her she should be ashamed and God would send her to hell if she didn't stop."

They finished washing the dishes and turned off all the lights downstairs. Angelo brought two glasses of chardonnay back to the bedroom and left them on the dresser while they took a shower together and played on the bed long enough for her to come. He followed within seconds. Her full body aroused him so quickly and completely that he had little control when she touched him. Pleasure compensated for longevity.

"I like Tony," Charley said, as she lay naked and sweaty on top of the bed.

He put his glass on the nightstand and cuddled close to her. "What did he really say to you?"

She grinned. "I think you should talk to Sidney tomorrow. I'm afraid your sister might have distressed her." She lifted her head and kissed him before he could respond. He tasted her sweet saliva and felt her warm, damp breath on his face. Every painful, anxious thought paled as her gentle hands slowly rubbed his back and thighs. He felt himself harden again. She crawled on top of him and this time he came inside her. With a soft, satisfied moan, she rolled over and they both fell asleep.

The sound of the shower woke him. He was on the bedspread and didn't remember falling asleep but had slept comfortably with Charley tucked in his arms. The alarm clock said four A.M. She was out of bed and suddenly it was chilly. He crawled between the sheets. As he drifted back to sleep, his thoughts were mixed with memories of Sid when Matt was a baby, her frustration and clumsy attempts to be the perfect mom. Crying one minute, laughing and confident the next, she knew immediately motherhood was a mistake. Babies were for other people. But he loved her because she tried.

A kiss on his forehead woke him. Charley was leaning over him.

"Sorry, I couldn't help it. You were smiling in your sleep."

He pulled her toward him and kissed her. "Why are you leaving?"

"I've got to get home, feed the horses, change, and try to be at Hollywood early. There's a ton of work. You and Reggie may have to watch Goldberg without me today."

"No problem."

"Promise me you won't try to talk to Jenny."

He didn't hesitate. "I promise."

She seemed satisfied and kissed him again before leaving. Angelo lay in bed feeling guilty. If the opportunity were there, he knew he would talk to Jenny. It was an empty promise, but she should have known better than to ask.

After she left, he found sleep impossible. He thought about his sister confronting Sidney with her ridiculous accusation. Sidney felt enough remorse without having to contend with Lucy's bizarre imagination. Matt would have found a way to get out of the condo that night even if Sidney had been home. If Cate was telling the truth, Matt had escaped from his bedroom on prior occasions.

He put on his robe and wandered into his son's room, took a copy of the lyrics to Matt's song that he'd printed from the computer file. Downstairs, he poured a glass of VSOP brandy and carried it to the cellar. He sat in the lounger across from his wall of photographs and read Matt's words again. This time, to his surprise, he enjoyed the verse and the picture the boy had created. The scene was desolate but not necessarily the state of its author's soul. He hoped imaginative minds might recognize and understand despair without having to experience it. It would be unbearable to think his son felt such hopelessness. Tommy Lamada smiled at him from the cluttered wall. He could almost hear his partner warning him, "Relax *paesano,* you make everything into a bad opera." Easygoing Tommy died thinking the world was good.

"There's evil in this world, Tommy," he said, raising his snifter to the picture. "God swept them out of heaven, but not all the bad angels landed in that first hell or even purgatory. There's a third hell here, partner. It's worse because Satan has learned to look and act just like you and me." He gulped the remainder of his brandy and leaned the recliner back as far as it would go. "Sometimes he is you or me." His eyes closed, but he couldn't sleep. The paper with Matt's words slid off his lap onto the floor, and he tucked the empty glass beside him on the chair. "The hardest part is finding the devil, Tommy. After that, we both know what to do," he whispered.

SEVENTEEN

"Your sister is a moron," Sidney said matter-of-factly. "Why would I listen to anything she says?"

Angelo nodded. This morning was a wasted trip. Of course Lucy wasn't a moron, but he couldn't argue that she sometimes didn't do and say incredibly stupid things. Sidney looked tired but very attractive in an expensive business suit. She impatiently tapped her fingers on the kitchen table as he apologized for his sister's behavior. She kept checking her wristwatch and offered him a second cup of coffee before he had finished the first.

"Anyway I'm sorry she said those things. Do you need to get going?" he asked, but it was obvious she couldn't wait to get away from him.

"I said don't worry about it, Angie." She stood and took his half-empty cup. "I've got a meeting later. Business has picked up. I've got four, practically incompetent women working with me. We'll probably have to hire two more just to keep up." She finally had a few words for him. Even if the conversation was one-sided, at least she was talking. Sidney was always interested in matters that concerned her.

It was irritating to him that she hadn't mentioned Matt or the investigation. Her life was continuing its hectic pace as if their son had never existed.

"I'm glad you're coping so well," he said. He'd meant to sound nasty and succeeded.

"Fuck you, Angie. It's been a long time. I won't hide for the rest of my life. My doctor told me to stay busy, so I'm busy. Besides, your concern hasn't kept you from screwing your little detective friend, has it?" Tears filled her eyes and she turned away. He felt miserable. He had come to support her, fix any hurt Lucy had caused, but he'd made it worse. She faced him again. Her mascara had smeared a little and she wiped her nose with the back of her hand. "I think you should stay away from here. You make me feel bad about myself. Matt's gone. There's no reason for this anymore," she said, and added, "for you and me."

There were a million things he wanted to say—first, we don't know what's happened to Matt, and second, you were an insecure mess when I met you; you're a self-centered greedy woman—but he didn't, because he knew he'd already hurt her. That wasn't why he'd come, but he couldn't deny his anger. He never actually said anything, but he still blamed her, and she knew it. It wasn't rational. It wasn't fair. Something evil might've taken their son and she most likely wasn't responsible, but he'd never forgiven her for allowing it to happen, so she was right; he needed to stay away.

Sidney had money and beauty. Matt was a bonus, and she had adjusted to life without him. Angelo left without trying to mend the ugly rift that had grown between them. He sat in the MG and dialed Reggie's cell phone number. As he backed out of the driveway, he caught a glimpse of her standing inside the balcony door, nearly hidden behind the drapes. She was peeking out at him like a frightened child, waiting for the monster from her worst nightmare to jump out of the shadows and do what she couldn't bring herself to do.

He left a message on Reggie's answering machine. The man never picked up his phone or returned messages, so Angelo decided to go to his house. He knew Reggie was on his long vacation without plans to go anywhere. Angelo expected to find him sitting alone in his tiny bungalow scribbling in the little notebook that he carried everywhere these days. It hadn't been that long since his split with Sidney, but he hadn't coped any better than Angelo had. Reggie's drinking tapered off; nevertheless, he preferred seclusion to anyone's company. When Angelo asked about the notebook, Reggie let it slip that he'd been seeing the department shrink. "Things were piling up," is the way he put it.

The psychiatrist had suggested that Reggie jot down his thoughts and at the end of the day go back and read them. Reviewing the entire day was supposed to put things in perspective. It had become an obsession, but Reggie actually seemed better, and he said he liked to write. He had stacks of notebooks filled with his thoughts and observations sitting on his kitchen table and the pile got bigger every time Angelo saw it.

When Reggie opened the door, he was dressed in baggy shorts and a tank top with a fading picture of Diamond Head on the front. The house was well lighted and clean and smelled of french fries.

He invited Angelo inside and closed a notebook that was lying on the couch.

"Still at it," Angelo said, pointing at the notebooks.

"Want coffee?" Reggie asked, walking into the kitchen without waiting for an answer and returning with two mugs. "What's up?" he asked, giving one to Angelo.

"I need your help, again."

"Okay."

"You might want to hear what I'm asking before you agree."

"It's about Matt. Otherwise you wouldn't ask." Reggie didn't like to complicate matters and he knew that he and Angelo had no other business together except finding his son. Angelo figured Reggie's life with the enigmatic Sidney must have driven the man crazy.

"I want to follow Goldberg," he said, and told Reggie everything he had learned from Cate Bennett.

"I got a week and a half vacation left. We can use my city car." There wasn't the least bit of concern in his voice.

"No way—they'd seriously burn you if they found out you were using that car for something like this," Angelo warned.

Reggie laughed and shook his head as if Angelo were a child afraid of the dark. "You want to start now?" he asked, and added for Angelo's benefit, "Why would I worry about driving the city car off-duty when we both know I've done far worse shit?"

"This afternoon we'll pick him up from his house," Angelo said. He needed Reggie, but the man always made him nervous. Experience had taught Angelo it took a hellhound to catch the devil but he understood you never really had control of the beast.

"Anybody else know?"

"Just Charley," Angelo said. "She's okay with it."

Reggie frowned but didn't say anything. They agreed that Reggie would pick him up at his house in East Los Angeles in about two hours. Angelo had no idea what Goldberg's schedule was and didn't know if he worked at home or from an office, but they had to start somewhere and the estate was the only address he had.

He drove home and packed a small utility bag with his binoculars, a flashlight, a camera, and extra ammo. He started to slip his holster over his belt but changed his mind and decided the Berretta would go in the bag for now. A small water bottle and protein bars got stuffed in the side pockets as well as some light reading material. Reggie wasn't someone who enjoyed conversation so Angelo feared the hours would go by very slowly unless he had something to read.

When Reggie arrived, Angelo was waiting on the porch. Reggie had cleaned out the Mustang and there was plenty of room for Angelo and his gear as well as blankets and map books on the backseat and a small cooler with soft drinks. Angelo sat in the passenger seat and Reggie handed him a radio that fit in his pocket with an earpiece and microphone, then showed him how to use it. The earpiece and the tiny microphone pinned under his shirt's lapel were barely visible, and another wire hidden inside his right sleeve had a small plunger that allowed Angelo to key the microphone and speak. He could stand on the street and broadcast without any sign of a police radio.

"Put this rig on every morning," Reggie said. "And don't take it off until we're done."

Angelo nodded. He wasn't about to argue with a guy who did this for a living. He was willing to defer to Reggie's surveillance expertise, but couldn't help remembering the dead dog in Goldberg's backyard. Before the day was over he'd have to be more assertive, set some boundaries for his peace of mind and his desire to stay out of court or jail.

They explored the terrain outside the Goldberg estate and eventually found high ground across the road that afforded them a surprisingly good view of the house and surrounding buildings.

Reggie searched in the trunk of his car and replaced Angelo's binoculars with state-of-the-art digital electronic viewers. He also dragged out two folding chairs that they hid behind overgrown scrubs and wild grass and settled in for long, boring hours of waiting and watching.

By six that evening, they had seen a parade of gardeners, housekeepers, David Goldberg, and a woman they surmised from her behavior was his wife. Unlike her husband, Susan Goldberg was a robust figure; she dressed well but not as meticulously as her spouse. Her round face was a blank page with features seemingly lost in excess pounds and bottled-up emotions. Angelo guessed she was a woman who had never experienced a good belly laugh, someone who plodded along and made things work without humor or passion. Husband and wife were together several times during the day, so he was able to see some interaction. They never appeared to make eye contact or touch but she did most of the talking, and he listened.

David Goldberg's step quickened and his posture improved noticeably when he walked toward his Mercedes to leave shortly before seven P.M. He was smiling as he drove out the gate. Angelo gathered the chairs and water bottles as Reggie opened the trunk and started the car. Thanks to Reggie's skilled driving, they were on a side street waiting when the Mercedes slowly passed them heading toward the freeway. Reggie was a master at sliding into traffic and keeping half a dozen car lengths or more between them and their target, but David Goldberg helped by driving like an old lady and signaling miles ahead of his intended turns and stops.

His destination was Saint Mark's Academy where he parked the Mercedes in one of the empty spaces in front of the rectory. Reggie continued driving past the school and stopped on the street a block away. Angelo got out quickly and ran back to the gate where he hid in a secluded corner but had an unobstructed view of all the school buildings. He felt his gut muscles tighten when he caught a glimpse of Sister Domenic standing in front of the convent. She was clearly visible to Goldberg too, but he failed to acknowledge her and instead went directly inside the rectory, appearing to be a man on a mission.

The nun stared at the door to the priest's house long after it closed. She crossed her arms under the mantle of her habit, and Angelo thought he saw anger in her expression. She wasn't a woman who had on prior occasions shown much emotion, so he was surprised. A few minutes later, Jennifer walked slowly down the steps of the academy and waved at Sister Domenic, who nodded but didn't move. Goldberg's daughter climbed into the backseat of the Mercedes, glancing over her shoulder at the convent where Sister Domenic shook her head before going inside. The girl had added a few pounds since Angelo talked to her in the classroom, but she managed to curl up on the backseat, apparently tired but not expecting her father to return anytime soon.

It was nearly forty-five minutes before David Goldberg left the rectory. An older, frail-looking man stood in the doorway and waited until the Mercedes backed out and drove toward the gate before he retreated inside again. Angelo slid around the corner and jumped onto church grounds seconds before the gate closed. He stood in the driveway trying to understand why he was on this side of the fence, because he hadn't given any thought to his actions. Reggie looked annoyed as he backed up the car and stared at Angelo locked behind the wrought iron gate.

"Do I follow the asshole or what?" Reggie's irritated voice was in his earpiece.

Angelo pushed in the plunger. "Go. Come back and get me when he sets down," he said, trying to convince both of them that he had actually planned this . . . whatever this was.

It wouldn't be difficult for Reggie to catch up to Goldberg, but Angelo felt stupid anyway. He had changed the game plan without telling Reggie and without clearly thinking it through. Instinct had taken over and that sixth sense he relied on when he was a working cop had resurfaced. If only he had a clue why or what had triggered it. It could have had something to do with that old man who lingered on the step like a worried parent before going back inside or maybe it was Goldberg's deliberation in getting to the rectory.

It was dark now, but he realized he was standing in the open; a few steps to the right put him in the shadows. The school buildings appeared locked up and deserted, and the convent had light only in the upper windows. He moved behind the security floodlights staying in the shadows until he reached the rectory. A series of clever lies ran through his head, but by the time he knocked on the door he still hadn't decided what he would say.

It took what seemed like a long time for a man's voice to ask, "Who's there?" and then, "Is that you, David?"

Angelo identified himself and waited, another lengthy delay, but finally the door opened a crack and the man peeked out. He pushed it open another few inches and looked around as if expecting someone to be with Angelo. The illumination from inside was a spotlight and Angelo was nervous that Sister Domenic would look out her window and see him.

"Can I come in for a minute and speak with you?" Angelo said, pushing past the surprised man and not waiting for a response. "I promise I won't take long. Father . . . ?" he asked, guessing this had to be the priest that lived there.

"Daly. Who are you and how did you get on school grounds?" Father Daly asked. He was standing in his stocking feet and had on a pair of baggy gray pants and an old sweatshirt. Up close he looked pale and sickly. He turned off the light in an adjoining room and closed the door. His house was plain, but clean and comfortable, with small rooms and bright lights, but it was sparsely furnished and had little character. There were indications that several men with varying tastes had occupied the place at different times, but no one who had the inclination or had stayed long enough to give it some personality.

"What do you want?" Father Daly asked.

Angelo explained who he was and reminded the priest about Matt's disappearance. Father Daly looked confused but led Angelo to his office and offered him a glass of brandy, which Angelo accepted. The priest sat behind his desk and finished his drink in one gulp.

"I'm not sure why I'm here," Angelo admitted. "I guess I was hoping you could tell me something."

"About what?" Father Daly asked, scratching the top of his head and leaving his few strands of gray hair standing straight up. He removed his reading glasses and put them on the desk. "I'm very tired, not well. Is there something you want?" He did appear weary with dark circles under his bloodshot eyes, but there was coldness, indifference in his voice. Angelo had been around priests all his life and even the worst ones pretended to care, to offer comfort, but this guy was about as compassionate as a cranky old waitress at closing time.

"I want to know if David Goldberg harmed my son or had anything to do with his disappearance." The words came out before he could organize his thoughts, but they expressed exactly what he had wanted to say. Father Daly didn't blink, didn't act surprised or angry or outraged or anything he should have been.

Angelo instinctively keyed the microphone and left it open, hoping Reggie was within range to hear the conversation. He wanted a witness.

"I can't imagine why you would believe that," Father Daly said. He was composed and far more alert than he'd been a few seconds ago.

"I think you do know."

"David Goldberg and his wife are exemplary people. They have been remarkably generous to this school. You should be careful who you malign, Mr. Angelo. David is a fine attorney, and he won't hesitate to protect his family name." Father Daly was standing by the time he had finished his sharp if polite reprimand.

"Would you protect him?" Angelo ignored the hint and remained seated while Father Daly edged toward the door. He wasn't surprised by the priest's staunch defense of his benefactor Goldberg, but thought it strange that Daly didn't deny any personal knowledge.

"You'd better go," Father Daly said, abandoning subtlety and holding open the front door. Angelo noticed that the hand resting on the knob had a nervous tremor. "Press the button to the left of the side gate to open it," the priest said, avoiding Angelo's stare. "Do it quickly or I'll be forced to call the police."

The porch light at the convent came on before Angelo reached the end of the driveway, and the light was on in Sister Domenic's sitting room now, the curtain pulled back, and someone was watching him. He got outside the gate and walked half a block to the corner trying to reach Reggie on the radio. Finally Reggie answered and told him he was on his way back because Goldberg had gone directly home.

"Did you hear any of that?" Angelo asked.

"Some of it," Reggie said after a few seconds.

"What do you think?"

"Hold on, I'm almost there."

Angelo sat on the curb and tried to fit together pieces of the puzzle. Cate's photos connected Goldberg, Jake, and some unknown cop. Sister Domenic, Father Daly, and Mrs. Pike were tied to Goldberg, and they had demonstrated complete loyalty to the wealthy man. Susan Goldberg knew about her husband's earlier indiscretions but was still living with him. The wild cards were the Reverend Hellman and Magdalene. How did Hellman know Jake, and what was he doing in Jake's room when the boy was killed? He rested his forehead on his knees and thought about Charley. If she found out he had crashed Father Daly's rectory, she would be livid, and he figured Reggie wasn't going to be too happy with him either.

None of it would matter if he'd gotten any closer to finding out what happened to his son, but he hadn't. He heard the Mustang coming down the street and looked up. Reggie stopped at the corner and the passenger door flung open as Angelo approached.

"Sorry," was all he said.

"I'm going back to Goldberg's house. He's there and the lights are still on."

"What about the priest?" Angelo asked.

"My guess is he knows what Goldberg's doing."

"He's a priest." Angelo felt stupid as soon as he said the words. His Catholic upbringing had stymied his reasoning for a moment. "Okay, so it's possible."

"We still can't prove anything."

Reggie was a man of few words, but he had a way of concisely saying what needed to be said. They had a lot of suspicions, uncorroborated hearsay from a young girl, who posed naked for her brother, and the ramblings of a crazy woman who might have thrown her child into a watery grave. Hope of finding out what had happened to Matt was sinking in a quagmire of unconnected, unsubstantiated clues.

They returned silently to the observation point on the hill and watched the Goldberg mansion until the lights went out. Angelo was packing up the equipment and chairs when Reggie called him back to the bushes. A light over the side entrance had been turned on. The door opened several minutes later, and the figure that emerged was unmistakably Mrs. Pike's. The bulky frame stepped off the stairs onto the driveway. She was carrying two large bags and had a ring of keys in her right hand. She walked to a dark-colored Volvo parked near the stables and placed the bags on the passenger seat. She drove to the main gate. It opened, and she disappeared into the night. He looked up at Reggie who didn't say anything and was quietly snapping the cover on his viewer. There was no point in following her. They both knew she would be returning to the convent.

Without the benefit of either moonlight or flashlight, he took a few cautious steps several yards behind Reggie as they worked their way down the hill in the dark toward the car. His attention was focused on the ground where a misstep or gopher hole might cause him to trip and fall.

He had lost sight of Reggie when a sudden movement exploded from the bushes and he felt a blow to his chest. Air burst from his lungs as he fell forward onto the ground. The weight of several bodies pressed against his, and he couldn't move his arms or legs. He tried to call out to Reggie, but a hand covered his mouth, and then duct tape quickly replaced the hand. Someone pushed his face into the ground. He couldn't get enough air through his nose and thought he would pass out.

"This is private property," a man's voice said. "Whatever you think you're doing, don't." The man's breath was close to his ear, and he felt the cold metal of a gun barrel touching, rubbing against the back of his neck. "Be careful. Jake wasn't careful," the man whispered. Someone stepped on his back, and unable to cry out he grunted into the duct tape. Angelo felt the pressure ease as the man moved away.

Hands gripped his arms and legs, and tape was wrapped around them. Someone grabbed his hair and lifted his head. Strips of tape were placed over his eyes and covered his ears. His head snapped forward again and pounded into the ground. The smell of dirt and crushed grass filled his nostrils. He rolled over onto his back expecting another blow, but didn't have any choice; he was suffocating. In his taped cocoon, he lay there on the ground waiting, but nothing happened for several minutes. He couldn't see or hear but guessed they had gone.

He turned onto his side and managed to slide his right hand into his pants pocket. The pocketknife was still there. It took him several minutes to work the knife out of the Levi's, and then open it. Once the blade was extended, he easily cut the tape from his hands and legs. He ripped the tape off his mouth and took a deep breath before attempting to remove it from his eyes and ears. It was wrapped around his head and he felt clumps of hair pulled out with each strip. He called Reggie's name over and over . . . no answer.

It was too dark to see more than a few feet in any direction, and when he stood, his chest hurt and his body ached as if he'd been trampled by a herd of cattle. When his head cleared, he found the car and a flashlight. He didn't care if anyone saw the light. He had to find Reggie.

A soft moaning came from behind him, and he shined the light in front of the car. Reggie was crawling to his knees, coughing and spitting. Angelo ran to him. He held Reggie's shoulders until the convulsive hacking stopped.

"Are you okay?" Reggie asked, when he was able to speak and stand. He took the flashlight and turned it on Angelo as he explained how he'd been grabbed as he reached the car. A smelly rag was forced over his face and he was dragged to the ground, and then remembered nothing until he woke up feeling sick to his stomach and dizzy. Angelo could smell a faint chemical odor on Reggie's clothes.

"They were stalking us while we were watching Goldberg," Angelo said. He leaned against the car, trying to take some pressure off his lungs, a little worried the blow might've dislodged the spent slug the surgeons had left in his chest. The doctors had assured him it would never move, but he wasn't convinced they'd anticipated baseball bats.

After brushing the dirt from his pants and shirt, Reggie used the flashlight to search the area around the car and found his .45 semiauto where it had been tossed in the brush. He took an old towel from the trunk and wiped the gun clean before turning his attention to Angelo.

"That looks bad," he said, shining light on the patches of raw skin on Angelo's face. "I'm taking you to the emergency room."

"He had to hire somebody to do this. That might help us," Angelo said.

"Sure, we got him right where we want him."

"A guy like that can't contact goons without leaving a trail."

Reggie slowly shined the light on Angelo's body, starting with his face, around the back of his head, down his torso to his feet.

"What'd they hit you with?"

"The first blow was a baseball bat. I grabbed it when I brought my arms up to protect my face; after that fists, feet, who knows. It all hurt."

Angelo didn't feel as if he was injured that badly. He was sore and would be miserable tomorrow, but nothing felt broken. The tape had actually done more damage than the hits and kicks. Angelo guessed the lawyer was trying to let them know, in the most painful way, that he was aware of the surveillance and didn't like it, but he was badly mistaken if he thought this would change anything.

Angelo convinced Reggie to take him home by reminding him that hospitals get very nosy when battered bodies show up in their emergency room. The doctor's first call is usually to the local police station. Neither of them wanted to explain what they were doing up on that vacant property in the middle of the night. A hot bath and a handful of codeine would have to do.

They were silent on the ride home. The air was uncomfortably cold, but the windows were down to keep Reggie from dozing off or getting dizzy. Before they reached the downtown area, Reggie drove the Mustang onto the emergency lane and stopped.

"You okay?" Angelo asked when Reggie closed his eyes and lightly tapped his head with his closed fist.

"He didn't hire thugs. It was the cop. I saw, but I couldn't remember—a tattoo. The guy had a tattoo on his arm."

"You know him?"

"So do you . . . that morning, the command post, Sergeant Hill . . . same picture, Chinese winged dragon."

Angelo tried to remember the man he talked to, the busy, arrogant, not very helpful sergeant. He could clearly recall his face and hear his words promising that the canyon search behind Sidney's condo was just a formality. Sergeant Hill ran the command post, made the decision to stop the search. He declared Matt a runaway and brought the investigation to a disappointing halt. Angelo could feel his breathing accelerate. His mind was flipping through the events since Matt's disappearance, the frustration of realizing all that could or should have been done maybe hadn't been.

He bombarded Reggie with questions. How could he be certain? Where was the tattoo located on the arm? How did he see it if he went out so quickly?

"The guy just doesn't look like one of them," Angelo finally said in the face of Reggie's unwavering certainty.

"I saw it the first time when he took off his long-sleeved uniform shirt to help set up the canopy for the command post. The dragon on his forearm isn't big but real ugly. Nobody cares about tattoos anymore, but his guys said Hill hid it because it was such a crappy job . . . it looks like a deranged gecko." Reggie eased the Mustang back onto the nearly empty freeway. "Hill's arm was around my chest tonight and I saw that stupid-assed dragon before I passed out."

As Angelo considered the number of ways Hill could have hampered efforts to find his son, his anger grew and the stinging on his face and hands fueled his agitation. He closed his eyes to calm the turmoil. Seemingly respectable men connected by an evil addiction. Pornographers, pedophiles, maybe kidnappers or murderers, it sickened him to think of the harm they had done, might still do. If his son had somehow stumbled into their world, Angelo couldn't imagine a good end to this nightmare.

EIGHTEEN

Angelo thought they were driving to his house in East Los Angeles, but there was a change of plans, at least on Reggie's part. The car pulled up into a driveway, and Angelo opened his eyes expecting to see his magnificent oak trees standing sentry over his tiny domain. Instead the headlights rested on the imposing figure of a rottweiler sitting behind Charley's gate in Burbank. The dog didn't bark or growl. It didn't need to.

Charley led them into the spare room and told Angelo to lie on the sofa bed while she searched for disinfectant. He detailed the day's events, as much as he could remember, intentionally providing sketchy facts related to his encounter with Father Daly. Reggie filled in the rest. She didn't say a lot but listened intently while she scrubbed his face and arms and dabbed cream on his raw skin. The yellow stuff in the tube smelled bad, but he didn't care. As soon as it touched his bruises, the burning stopped, and he felt better.

"What is this?" he asked, dabbing a little more on his face.

"Don't know but it works on my horses," she said, shrugging.

"Can we get the department to put Reggie's team on Hill?" he asked.

Reggie shook his head. "Not us. Internal Affairs surveillance maybe."

"We don't know if Sergeant Hill is the only one," Charley said. "Do we?" The apprehension in her voice was understandable. It was getting difficult to identify the good guys.

"He wasn't alone tonight," Angelo said, thinking about the strangers who crushed him into the ground.

"How many do you think?"

He tried to remember—the talking man, one to hold his arms, and one on his legs. "At least three."

"I'm talking to Captain Davis tomorrow. I trust him. He can go to IA to set up the surveillance," Charley said. She was pacing in front of the sofa, making decisions again. "No point staying on Goldberg," she said, and added, "Obviously, he knows we're there."

"Bring in Mrs. Pike," Angelo said. He had been thinking about her since they saw her leave the Goldberg house. She was the link between Saint Mark's and Goldberg.

"For what?" Charley asked and seemed frustrated with the suggestion.

"Scare her," Angelo insisted.

"Scare Attila the Hun?" Reggie asked, shaking his head.

"Maybe," Angelo said. He tried to sit back and get comfortable, but his face itched like the worst rug burn he'd ever had. "But my guess is she's never been arrested. It's easy to be tough when you're in your own environment. Get her in a holding cell at Hollywood station, then see."

"I'll ask this again. What reason do I have to detain her?" Charley asked.

They both looked at him, waiting for an answer. He didn't have one. It was simple finding a bogus excuse to take a drug dealer or petty criminal to the station. They went because they hoped cooperating would keep them out of jail. Mrs. Pike, on the other hand, was a middle-aged housekeeper who probably got a few dollars to keep her mouth shut and do what she was told. The real question was how much loyalty did that money buy. Angelo was guessing it would be minimal. Especially if the Goldbergs treated her with the same condescending, dismissive attitude they used with everyone else.

"Tell her you know Goldberg was responsible for the dead kid in his lake. Tell her you know she was staying at the cottage with Magdalene at the time the kid died. Tell her anything to scare her. It looks suspicious. She won't know you're lying," Angelo said. He was frustrated. Act like a detective was what he wanted to say, but didn't.

"That's not my case and nobody knows yet how or when that child died." Charley shook her head and walked toward the kitchen.

"Mrs. Pike doesn't know that," Angelo said before she was out of sight. He couldn't understand why it was so difficult for Charley to do what was needed to get the job done. He wasn't suggesting anything immoral or illegal. Catching criminals was a game without rules. You adjusted, used tricks, and lied if you had to. How did she ever solve any crime, he wondered?

"But I'll know," Charley shouted from another room.

"What happened tonight gives you a legitimate reason to talk to the woman," he said loud enough for her to hear anywhere in the small house.

Charley appeared again, carrying three glasses of wine. She put one on the table in front of him and gave one to Reggie, who sat quietly on a rocking chair in a corner of the room.

"No," she said. "Think of something else."

Before Angelo could argue, Reggie stood, emptied his glass, and put it on the table.

"I'm tired. Let me know what you two decide," he said.

"What do you think about bringing her in?" Angelo asked.

"I think it's a lot of work for nothing. You won't scare her. Let me think about it some more when this stuff wears off and my head doesn't hurt so bad."

Charley walked Reggie out to his car. Angelo leaned back and stretched out on the sofa. He could hear their voices coming from the porch. It sounded like an intense conversation. Reggie said one or two words then Charley raised her voice and talked for several minutes. She wasn't a woman to let anyone have the last word if it wasn't the same as hers. Stubbornness was one of the qualities he admired in her even when he knew she was wrong. She had strong convictions. Unfortunately many of them weren't consistent with his idea of good police work.

If he got up and moved closer to the door, he could probably hear what they were discussing, but he'd found a comfortable position and knew he wouldn't like what she was saying anyway. Love was a strange condition. He couldn't explain his feelings for Charley, but he knew she had become an essential part of his life. She annoyed him and yet he respected and worried about her and felt that making her happy was something he wanted only a little less than finding out what happened to his son.

The voices stopped and the Mustang's engine roared. He waited several minutes, expecting to hear the front door open, but it didn't. He pushed himself off the couch and looked out the front window. She wasn't on the porch. The dog was barking behind the house, so he opened the back door and saw her standing near the stall of the big red gelding.

They weren't touching, but stood side by side, staring into the night.

"You two want to be alone?" he asked, but didn't wait for an answer as he sat on the rail beside her.

"I've had this horse nearly thirteen years," she said, rubbing the animal's nose. "He has bad legs. The vet says if it gets much worse I might have to put him down. I can't imagine doing that."

"You love him. When the time comes, you'll do it because it's the right thing."

She turned and studied his eyes as if looking at him for the first time. "How have you endured all these weeks of not knowing?" she asked, and quickly added, "I'm sorry if I disappoint you. I know I'm not always as strong as you'd like me to be."

"Charlene," he said and she smiled at his use of her full name. She told him no one except her parents ever called her Charlene. "I love you. You are an intelligent, beautiful woman. I don't expect us to always agree." He surprised himself because he meant every word. He wasn't trying to manipulate her to do something or change her mind.

She kissed him on the cheek. "I love you too. Go to bed and let me think." He slid off the fence with a painful groan and she snatched his shirtsleeve for a second. "Sleep on the couch. Dad's coming for breakfast."

He rubbed more of her smelly horse cream on his face and arms then threw towels on the sofa to keep it from staining. When he woke in the morning, scabs had formed in a few places, but most of the bruises were a pinkish hue and didn't hurt. He looked in the mirror and was surprised how little damage was visible. Maybe they hadn't meant to seriously harm him and it was a warning to back off. But they had invoked Jake's name. Bringing that dead boy into it definitely made the incident more than a warning. He didn't want to believe a cop could be capable of killing anyone as young and pathetic as Jake Bennett, but he knew better.

He dressed, poured himself a cup of coffee, and drank it standing by the back door where he could see Charley and her father sitting under an umbrella at a table near the pool. The morning sun was steaming off the damp deck. She was in a swimsuit, wrapped in a towel, and had her elbows on the glass tabletop leaning toward Rizzo. Her father was saying something, gesturing with his open hands as she listened intently. Angelo stepped outside, and they both looked up. Charley sat back and waved at him.

"Come sit with us, Angie," she said, holding her hand out for him. He leaned over and kissed her and was amazed how little any of his body parts hurt. "Dad's got a couple of old swimsuits inside if you want to do a few laps before breakfast."

He laughed and shook hands with Rizzo. "Thanks, I never swim before meals."

They made some small talk but almost immediately lapsed into yesterday's events. It was clear Rizzo had been well briefed prior to Angelo's arrival. The older man exchanged glances with his daughter, and she nodded.

"Tell him," she said to Rizzo. "Dad knows Hill."

Rizzo shifted uncomfortably in the patio chair. "I know of him. Ray Hill was Chief Denby's adjutant when he was at Parker Center. He went to Hollywood just before I retired. I heard he got accused of fondling some clerk typist and Denby had to send him away."

"Was he charged with it . . . a personnel complaint?" Angelo asked, but had a good idea what the answer would be. LAPD's management protects its lackeys because they see and hear too much incriminating stuff.

"Nope."

"Then how do you know about it?"

"Staff and command officers in PAB need their shoes polished, and they ain't gonna do it themselves. They sat in my chair and talked about stuff like I wasn't there or was too stupid to understand and remember."

"What did Denby say about this guy?" Angelo asked. It didn't surprise him that the deputy chief would have someone like Hill working for him.

Rizzo glanced at Charley. Her expression didn't change. "The chief says to another deputy chief that this Ray Hill is a player. He can't keep his hands to his self, but he's a good writer, and the chief depends on him to do stuff. Hill went too far with this pretty, little clerk typist, so the chief says he had to move him. He gives Hill his choice of divisions, and Sarge picks Hollywood."

"Did you ever see Hill?"

"Sure, he'd come down every morning for a shine. Good-looking, gray-haired guy. Had a Macy balloon impression of hisself, bigger-than-life ego. Always talking private details of what woman he had, and how he did it. I just shut him out, stop listening."

"So Denby allowed a sex addict to work in sin city?" Angelo asked. He couldn't believe any deputy chief would be that stupid. Hollywood was a cesspool of temptations. It was the last place to put a guy like Hill.

Rizzo laughed. "Yeah, the chief even had a chuckle betting Hill wouldn't survive a week without getting caught up with some drag queen on Santa Monica Boulevard. But he said he didn't give a shit 'cause Hill was Captain Davis's problem now."

"Denby's a sleazebag," Angelo said. "Were there any rumors among the troops about Hill when he got to Hollywood?" he asked Charley.

She shook her head. "Not a word. He's well liked, works hard. Captain Davis uses him as an adjutant whenever he can. He is a good writer and knows what the bureau wants in completed staff work."

"Reggie's so positive it was him last night I gotta believe it. I wonder how much Davis knows," Angelo said. He guessed Captain Davis probably knew everything. A captain would never win an argument with a deputy chief, but it's a safe bet he fought to keep Ray Hill out of his division. Guys like Hill are time bombs that sooner or later go off and inevitably take a lieutenant or captain down with them.

"I still trust Captain Davis," Charley said. "He's not a genius, but he's a good man. He'll do the right thing."

Angelo didn't approve of her sanitized approach to police work, but her instincts about people were usually good, and he was willing to rely on her judgment regarding Captain Davis. She volunteered to phone Davis and tell him everything, convince him to bring in the internal surveillance unit to watch Sergeant Hill.

"It won't take long. Guys like Hill can't help themselves. It's an addiction. If he's into kids, surveillance should catch him right away. Then we make a deal with him to give up the others and find out what happened to Matt," Angelo said. It sounded so simple, but he knew it wouldn't be. They had to keep the investigation away from Chief Denby since he had a vested interest in protecting Hill. If it were ever proven that a deputy chief buried an allegation of sexual misconduct, his career would be toast. "What happened to that clerk typist Hill molested?" Angelo asked, figuring she might be someone they could use to tell the truth.

Rizzo snorted. "She's Denby's third wife and the mother of his new baby boy."

"Fuck," Charley said. "The guy leads a fucking charmed life." She kicked off her sandals and jumped into the pool. Angelo watched her long, graceful strokes cut through the water and was sorry Rizzo was there. Her glistening body and those sexy wet ringlets had stirred up an urge to make love with her on the closest floating raft.

ALTHOUGH IT was the weekend, Charley reached Captain Davis at Hollywood station and made an appointment to meet with him that afternoon. She would attempt to start the surveillance as soon as possible, maybe today if Captain Davis agreed, and they could get the Internal Affairs surveillance squad working on their regular days off.

As soon as Charley left for Hollywood station, Rizzo opened a bottle of pinot noir that he had purchased for Charley on his last trip to a cousin's winery in Northern California. He left it on the counter in the kitchen and sat with Angelo at the dining room table where Angelo was looking through a picture album he'd found stacked with magazines on a table in the den. He was a born snooper and enjoyed rummaging in other people's cupboards. There was no shame in admitting the compulsion. All the best cops had it.

The album was stuffed with pictures of Charley growing up, surrounded by a hoard of relatives at family gatherings, her first communion and confirmation, graduation from college. Rizzo appeared several times as a handsome, young man with his pretty wife.

Rizzo pointed at the picture of his wife. "Maria ain't so thin anymore, but she's still a beauty. Just like her baby."

"Charley's your only child?"

"She had two brothers. Mike, he died in Afghanistan, and that's Pete." Rizzo pointed to a black-and-white photo of a handsome, dark-haired man who stood next to a much younger Charley. "He was our baby. Got cancer and died the day before he turned twenty-one. So much wasted talent; he played the violin like a master." Rizzo stopped. Years later it was difficult for him to talk about his dead sons.

"I'm sorry," was all Angelo could say.

"Me and Maria, we always wanted lots of kids and grandkids. It ain't gonna happen. Charley's all we got left. Nothing's gonna hurt her," Rizzo said, and Angelo didn't need to look up to know the old man was warning him. It wasn't necessary, but now wasn't the best time to discuss his future with Charley. Angelo would gladly agree to spend the rest of his life loving and protecting her from harm, but what she wanted, aside from their intense and pleasurable lovemaking, was still a little fuzzy in his mind.

NINETEEN

Rizzo drove Angelo home after lunch. He decided to leave after Charley called from the station and told them the surveillance squad had agreed to meet her and Captain Davis at a secluded parking lot near the Griffith Park observatory. She expected the briefing to take most of the afternoon. Her father was good company, but Angelo wanted to be in his own house. A strange restlessness was growing inside him. Not being involved in executing the plan was difficult for him. As a working cop, he was always the one calling the shots, making the decisions, and the role of a worried father standing on the sidelines didn't suit him.

There was only one thing he knew that kept his mind off police work. He disconnected the kitchen phone and carried it out to the workshop where he looked around at the tarp-covered machines connected to the walls and ceiling now by threads of delicate spider webs. A ten-minute sweep with his shop vac had the garage clean again, and he folded the covers determined to spend a few minutes every day working out there again. It was good for his mental health. He needed to see the beginning and the end of something even if it was only a cabinet.

The plans for Matt's display case were covered with dust, but it didn't matter. The design was in his head. He started ripping wood and estimating the size and number of pieces he would need. It was strange. Before his son disappeared, Angelo had difficulty imagining something that would please him. Weeks of searching for the boy, discovering who he was, his strengths and weaknesses, peeking into his intimate thoughts had given Angelo a clearer picture of the young man. He wanted so badly to be with Matt now. All those wasted Sunday afternoons were a painful memory. It was a cruel joke to give sight to a blind man and then abandon him at the bottom of a dark well.

As the display case began to take shape, his mind focused completely on the task at hand. It was what he had hoped would happen. Creating didn't allow room to think about other painful things. It was as if a switch turned off, and his work was all he could see, all he could remember, and everything of consequence in the future.

The sharp ringing of the phone broke his concentration. If it hadn't disturbed him, he might have worked through until the first light. It was two A.M., and the project stood in the center of the workshop ready for sanding. Hours of steady labor had produced a sturdy, but handsome display table, one he was certain would have pleased his son. The creative spell had been broken, and he was disappointed, but he answered the phone because no one should call him at this hour unless it was important.

"It's me," Charley said.

His immediate thought was to tell her about the table, and then he remembered the surveillance and Sergeant Hill.

"Did they get something already?" he asked.

"Where are you? What's that noise?"

He looked around the shop and realized his compressor had turned on. He hadn't thought about the noise he was making and realized his neighbors would hound him in the morning.

"I'm in the garage working. I'm making Matt's display table for the knives. I want you to see it."

"Angie," she said, interrupting him. "I saw something tonight. A couple of blue suits picked up Reverend Hellman. I think he's talking."

Angelo waited for more, but finally asked, "What is it?"

"I'll be there in fifteen. We'll come back here. I don't know anything yet."

He hung up and leaned against the workbench. She was a terrible liar. He could hear the concern in her voice. He needed to run the shop vac but glanced at his watch and thought better of it. Everything would stay the way it was until he got back. He found a plastic paint cover to drape over the display cabinet but before covering it, stared at the little piece of furniture and was amazed, as always, that he actually had created it. Before turning out the lights, he checked each machine to be certain it was switched off and felt a peculiar sadness as he locked the doors and returned to the house.

Less than fifteen minutes later, Charley's red Honda pulled into his driveway. After he gave her a quick kiss, they drove without any conversation until she parked in the back lot of the Hollywood station. Several morning-watch officers were sleeping in their black-and-whites. Angelo smiled. He understood. Morning watch was torture for any normal human being.

He walked toward the front of the station, but Charley called him back and insisted they use the back door. His retired ID card wouldn't open the door so he never attempted to use the employee entrance. A lot of retired guys did by getting someone to open the door for them, but he had no illusions about his status. Charley walked quickly, twisting at every sound as if a ghost might jump at her from the shadows. She was acting as if they shouldn't be there which told him they probably shouldn't, but he wasn't asking any questions. The woman was on an undertaking that he sensed would benefit him. They went directly to the detectives' squad room where two uniformed officers sat alone at the homicide table.

Angelo attached his ID card to his shirt, but the two young officers stared hard at him as he followed Charley into the room. She was wearing her gun and badge on her belt and he was obviously with her, but like all good cops they were suspicious of someone they didn't know.

"Casey here yet?" she asked as if she had a reason to know. The younger men continued to stare at Angelo. She glanced casually over her shoulder and said, "This is Detective Nino Angelo. He's working Hellman as a suspect in another case."

Angelo reached around her and shook hands with both men. He was surprised how convincingly Charley could lie when it suited her. The P-III training officer had a cocky smirk, but from the condition of his uniform, Angelo guessed he had two or three years at most on the job. The blue hadn't begun to fade yet from the dry cleaning needed every few days.

"Where's Hellman?" Angelo asked, surprised neither of the officers noticed his retired ID.

The patrol officers looked at one another.

"He's in the interview room," the training officer said, nodding at the closed door across the squad room. "But Detective Casey said not to talk to him till he got here."

"That's okay. He knows I've got a few questions to ask Hellman," Angelo said. "It won't interfere with his homicide investigation."

"It don't bother me. You guys are the detectives. You work it out." The mind-set among some uniformed officers—that once they made an arrest the case didn't concern them anymore—was working in Angelo's favor this time. Usually it irritated him.

"Thanks, guys, you did a great job," Angelo said. He and Charley walked toward the closed door, but catching a whiff of an unpleasant odor, Angelo stopped and asked, "Has he been dipped?"

The probationer laughed. "Yes, sir. He's got on jail clothes. Still stinks a little, but the shower and lice soap helped." The boyish-looking officer glanced at his partner for approval or the scowl that said he should have kept his mouth shut, but the training officer ignored him.

Angelo stepped into the interview room, and a sour smell engulfed him. The Reverend Hellman, with one hand cuffed to a chair, was dressed in a faded green jumpsuit that revealed the sickly white of his arms above the weathered hands. Hellman turned to see who had entered and when he recognized Angelo and Charley nearly fell over the table trying to move away from the door.

"Sit down, Hellman. You aren't running away, not with that thing attached to your arm," Angelo said, and helped him put the chair upright behind the table.

"Satan's henchman captures me again," the reverend said, looking up at the ceiling. "Save me, Jesus."

"You keep acting stupid and I'll let them hang a murder charge on you," Angelo said.

"I didn't kill nobody."

Angelo sat across the table from Hellman and Charley stood behind him. She leaned over and whispered in his ear that she was going to see if Max Casey had arrived yet and would try to stall him as long as she could.

"Why did you kill Jake Bennett?" Angelo asked when Charley was gone. He didn't have time to make this the perfect interrogation.

"You crazy? I never killed nobody. I told you."

"Your prints were all over his room."

"That pimply faced boy was dead when I got there. I seen his ratty ass and I run like the devil was in my legs."

"Why were you there?" Angelo asked and Hellman turned away from him. "Come on, Reverend; once Casey walks through that door, I can't do anything for you."

"What can you do for me now?" Hellman asked, looking over his shoulder. He knew the game.

"First, why were you there?"

Reverend Hellman looked around the room and wiggled uncomfortably. "You recording me?"

"No."

"I brung him his money." He hesitated, scanning the walls again. "I seen him dead so I stuff it in his shirt. If I didn't leave it, I knowed what they think . . . that I killed him for it and now they gonna think that anyhow."

"Why were you giving him money?" Angelo asked. Hellman looked down at the table. He tugged at his wet, frizzy hair with his loose hand. "They're going to fry you for this. Somebody set you up to take the fall."

"He kill me anyway if I tell. Either way, I'm a dead man, Jesus," Hellman said, staring at the ceiling.

"Who?"

"The man."

The door opened and Charley gestured to him to cut off the interview. She pointed behind her and closed the door quickly. Angelo knew he was out of time. Casey was in the station, so he took a chance.

"Sergeant Hill's the man," he said and Hellman's bloodshot eyes grew wide with terror.

"You crazy? I didn't speak nothing 'bout him."

Angelo stood and moved away from the table. "Fine, but here's my story. I'll tell him you couldn't wait to give up his name."

The reverend took hold of Angelo's arm before he reached the door. "No, wait. Give me time to think some."

"There is no time. Tell me now or I walk."

Hellman cleared his throat and sat back. "The sarge he arrests me, says he won't put me in jail if I do him a favor. Tells me to say I seen your boy and what all to lie about. He says if I lie good, you probably give me some money. But I get scared and run when we was at the river."

"What else did he say about my boy?" It was becoming difficult to control the anger.

"Nothing, nothing else, that was it. I didn't even know the child's name."

"What about Jake Bennett?"

"Sergeant says bring the money to that room and give it to the boy. I says, like joking, the boy he must of got something on him for that kinda money, and he smacks me aside the head for saying it. I suppose to pick up a package from the boy, but there ain't nothing there 'cept his cold dead ass."

"What was the package?"

"Don't know. Don't tell him I talked. He kill me."

"Are you certain he didn't say anything else about my son?"

"God strike me dead, nothing." The reverend hurriedly made the sign of the cross and tried to clasp his cuffed hand.

Angelo needed to know more, but before he could ask another question, the door to the interview room opened slowly. This time it was Maxwell Casey. His ruddy, Irish complexion was a shade brighter than usual as he stood framed by the doorway with his arms crossed and his short red hair not quite combed. Angelo had worked with the man long enough to know his former partner was severely pissed and he was looking at the redheaded lid on a boiling cauldron.

"Can I see you a minute, Detective Angelo?" Casey asked with a crooked, painful smile. His knuckles were white as he clutched the doorknob and waited for Angelo to pass in front of him. When they were outside the interview room, Casey carefully closed the door behind them. "Captain's office," Casey said without turning around and led the way.

Captain Davis was pacing in front of his desk, speaking to Charley when they entered the room. Charley sat with her arms crossed. She peered over the rims of her glasses, following the movements of the agitated captain.

"The coconspirator," Captain Davis said to Angelo and pointed at the chair beside Charley's. "Sit," he ordered.

"I'm retired, remember. I don't work for you anymore."

"Fucking right you don't work for me. So what the fuck are you doing in my station impersonating a working detective and messing up my homicide investigation?"

"If you give me five minutes without yelling, I'll explain," Angelo said, but Captain Davis interrupted him and moved to within inches of his face.

"Fuck no. I won't give you five seconds. I should throw your retired butt in one of those cells right now. Then you'll have lots of time to talk to that smelly bum." Captain Davis was as angry as Angelo had ever seen him. Tiny drops of spit sprayed Angelo's nose and cheeks, but he didn't move to wipe them. He stood still hoping that when the tirade was over he would have an opportunity to give an explanation.

Help came from an unexpected source.

"What did Hellman tell you?" Maxwell Casey asked, interrupting his boss.

"What the fuck do you care?" Captain Davis said, turning his anger on the homicide detective. "Go fucking talk to him yourself."

"Look, boss, Angelo might be an asshole, but he's also a good detective and if he's found something I want to know what it is."

That seemed to calm Captain Davis a little. He stared at Casey for a second and then turned to Charley, who hadn't moved. He raised his hands in frustration, took a deep breath, walked behind his desk, and dropped onto his leather chair.

"Okay," he said to Angelo. "Tell him."

Angelo did. He recounted all of Hellman's statements and watched Davis sit up and move forward, leaning over his desk.

"Did you tape it?" Casey asked.

"No, but he'll say it again. He's scared shitless."

"Detective Harper, get the surveillance squad to bring Hill in here and call IA to send a team of investigators," Captain Davis ordered. Charley jumped up quickly as if she'd been waiting for an excuse to escape, but then lingered by the door not wanting to miss anything. "Casey, you get that jackass reverend on tape before he has a memory lapse," Captain Davis added.

"What surveillance team?" Casey asked. "Have you been watching him?"

"Don't worry about it. Just do what I say." Captain Davis's temper was flaring again. He was irritated with everyone now. Angelo was glad. At least it took some of the attention and heat off him. Davis put his elbows on the desk and rested his head in his hands.

"Captain," Angelo started to explain, but Captain Davis interrupted him again.

"No, I don't want to hear it," Captain Davis said without lifting his head. "Your boy is gone and you got an excuse for acting like a dumbass. I'll deal with Detective Harper's part in all this at a later date."

Charley smirked at Angelo. Little Miss By-the-Book was treading some deep water, but she didn't seem all that concerned about it. He wanted to hug her but thought that might send Captain Davis over the edge.

"Thanks, Bill," was all he managed to say.

"Get out of here and stay out of this investigation," Captain Davis said, looking up at Angelo. "Let us handle this, Angie, before you do something really stupid. In case you haven't noticed, you're not helping."

"Maybe I'd best make those calls in here, boss," Charley said and picked up Davis's phone before he could object.

Angelo nodded and left the room. He waited outside and after a few minutes Charley came out. She raised her eyebrows and pulled him into the supervisors' office off the watch commander's area. It was nearly change of watch and the sergeants and officers from the day shift were mulling around outside the room waiting to go upstairs to roll call.

"Might be too soon to bring Hill in," Charley whispered.

He shook his head and said, "I don't think so. They have enough for a search warrant. He doesn't know we're looking at him. I know we'll find the pornography and he'll talk to stay out of jail."

"Unless he killed Jake," she said. "Then why say anything?"

Before he could consider the possibility, Angelo saw the good-looking man with the thick gray hair walk past the jail toward the back of the station. Sergeant Hill was smiling and still unaware that if what Hellman said was true, he was probably spending his last few hours dressed in that tightly tailored LAPD uniform. Two men in casual clothes walked several yards behind him. In a few seconds, in a more secluded part of the station, they would stop him and advise him that he should come with them. Angelo was certain they would escort him out of the station and take him to the West Bureau Internal Affairs office just down the street.

"I need to be at his interview," Angelo said.

"Right." Charley breathed hard and shook her head. "And how do you think that's going to happen. They won't let either one of us within a mile of him."

"Not you, just me. You've done enough."

"Damn right, I have," she said, still feeling smug about her minor transgression.

"Come with me, Angelo," Captain Davis shouted from the hallway where he was impatiently shaking his car keys. He had his jacket on and was carrying a police radio. Angelo shrugged at Charley and followed the commanding officer into the lobby and out the front door. He didn't know what Davis had in mind for him, but he guessed it wasn't something he was going to like. He had broken a lot of rules to get to Hellman.

Captain Davis unlocked the passenger door of his shiny blue Crown Victoria and motioned for Angelo to get in, and then he walked around the car and sat in the driver's seat.

"Look," Angelo started to say. He wasn't about to be hauled off if he didn't know where he was going.

"Shut up, Angie. I'm taking you with me because you'd figure out a way to get there on your own and screw things up. So sit back and keep your mouth shut because I'm not done being mad."

Angelo didn't talk, mostly because he was too surprised to say anything. Captain Davis drove to the West Bureau Internal Affairs building on Sunset and led him to the fifth-floor lobby where Detective Casey met them. He had notes on the recent admissions made by Reverend Hellman, this time on tape. Angelo looked at the pages and added anything Hellman had left out the second time. They waited an hour for the employee representative that Sergeant Hill had chosen. He was a lieutenant who was working a Vice unit in Hollenbeck. An attorney from the officers' union arrived a few minutes after him.

Captain Davis told Angelo to sit in one of the empty rooms until everyone was inside the interview location. A few minutes later, he returned and directed Angelo to a large, dark closet with a one-way mirror. On the other side of the glass, Sergeant Hill sat at a table with his lieutenant, a bald rumpled-looking man, and next to him sat an older, confident guy in a gray silk suit that Angelo guessed was the union lawyer. They were facing the mirror. The two IA investigators and Detective Casey sat across the table with their backs to Angelo. There were places to sit in the dark room but Angelo and Captain Davis stood close to the mirror. He didn't move, fearing any noise might be heard through the flimsy wall.

Hill and his representative were talking and laughing quietly. The lawyer seemed bored and played with his cell phone, scrolling through text messages and pecking out responses. Finally one of the IA investigators raised his voice and got their attention. Captain Davis played with the volume control on a panel under the mirror until they could almost hear everyone's voices.

The investigator clarified the procedure for the interview. Everyone except the lawyer acknowledged the rules and agreed to abide by them. The attorney continued to stare at his phone and seemed unconcerned with the entire process. After the formalities, administrative and criminal rights were given to Hill; the lead investigator asked if Sergeant Hill understood and if he knew why he was being interviewed. The soft-spoken sergeant said he understood his rights but not why he had been detained. Angelo listened for a few seconds and then closed his eyes. He couldn't be certain. The voice was nicer but similar to the one he'd heard as he lay struggling on the ground, gasping for air. Casey asked Hill about his relationship with Hellman and he denied telling the homeless man to lie about Angelo's son.

The Internal Affairs questions were polite, hedging and weaving, avoiding nastiness. Detective Casey was squirming and made no attempt to hide his disdain of IA's interrogation techniques. Hill's representative objected to everything, albeit in a nonconfrontational manner keeping with the tone of the interrogation. After hours of softball questions, Sergeant Hill didn't appear the least stressed by Hellman's allegations. He calmly and sincerely denied everything. The union lawyer yawned and stretched several times. His body language very clearly said: Why are you people wasting my valuable time with this nonsense?

When Angelo had lost all hope of getting any admission of guilt from the cocky sergeant, the interview room door opened, and the investigator said they would take a ten-minute break. Angelo saw this delay as his opportunity to deal with the two investigators, berate their wimpy asses, and try to motivate them to demonstrate a little aggression. He reached for the lock, but Captain Davis cupped his hand over it.

"Don't even think about it, Angelo. This is their show."

"They're treating him like he lost his damn ticket book. What's the matter with them," he whispered impatiently. What good was it being there if they weren't going to even try to accomplish anything?

After a few minutes, Hill returned to the interview room with his representative and the lawyer. They didn't talk. He stood staring out the window. The bald lieutenant scribbled notes and chatted on his cell phone.

Almost twenty minutes later, one of the original IA investigators returned with another man in Levi's and a T-shirt. Angelo knew him: Tom Weaver was the officer in charge of the surveillance squad. Weaver sat at the table beside Detective Casey, who was grinning.

Sergeant Hill came back to the table and sat between his lawyer and representative who began by objecting to the length of time Hill had been detained.

The lead IA investigator apologized but said they'd better get comfortable because the process had just begun. He placed a document on the table in front of Hill. The sergeant picked it up, and the color visibly drained from his face.

"You can't do this," Sergeant Hill said as Angelo strained to see the piece of paper through the glass.

"Search warrant," Captain Davis whispered in his ear.

"We can, and we will," Sergeant Weaver said. "Your home, computer, cell phone, car, and your locker at the station. I'm here to take you back to your house to stand by while we search."

"No, my wife and daughter are there," Hill pleaded and turned to the lawyer who had snatched the warrant and was carefully examining it. "I need to piss," Hill said and stood to leave.

"Okay," the IA investigator said. "But Sergeant Weaver will go with you."

Hill left, followed closely by Weaver and the representative. When they returned a few minutes later, Sergeant Weaver stood and waited until the IA investigator started his video recorder.

"For the record," Weaver said matter-of-factly. "Sergeant Hill just vomited all over the men's room."

"Oh, come on," the lawyer said. His phone was out of sight now, and he waved the search warrant at Casey. "I'm not certain this is even legal."

"See that judge's signature at the bottom. She thinks it's legal," Casey said.

Angelo watched Sergeant Hill's face. His expression was frozen somewhere between fear and arrogance. It was priceless—the clever criminal who thought everyone else was too stupid to catch him—the moment after he's caught. His eyes seemed to be searching the room for an escape route. Should he jump through the window, fall five stories, and spare himself the indignity of capture and incarceration or succumb to the disgrace that was about to follow. Angelo could almost hear the man's frantic thoughts.

The lawyer argued for a delay to construct a legal challenge to the warrant, but the IA investigator dismissed his concerns and advised him to do what he needed to do on his own time. The court had given them permission to search, and they weren't required to wait for appeals.

Arrangements were made to assign teams of supervisors to search Hill's residence and car, but first they would return to the Hollywood station and go through his work locker.

Captain Davis drove Angelo back to the station. It would take several hours to rummage through the house and garage. Casey would let him know when the locker search at work was finished. Angelo hoped when investigators returned from the residence, the real bargaining would begin. Depending on what they found, it might be time to play "let's make a deal." Angelo hoped the arrogant man would give up anything he could to save his worthless skin, and he didn't care what kind of agreement was made as long as he found out what had happened to his son.

As soon as he got back to the squad room, Angelo found Charley sitting at her desk working on a stack of overdue follow-ups. She stopped writing and listened intently while he described Hill's interview.

"As soon as they're done, if they find anything, I'll go back to Internal Affairs with Davis," Angelo said.

"I gotta feed my horses. You want to come? The search won't be finished for hours. I'll bring you back in plenty of time." She was cleaning off the top of her desk as she spoke and finally had to move in front of him to get his attention.

"This scumbag Hill says he has a daughter. How much you want to bet she goes to Saint Mark's Academy?" Angelo asked, looking up at her. He knew she was talking about something else but he couldn't keep his mind off the possibility of another easy victim.

She shook her head. "There's got to be a special place in hell for these guys."

"Look around you. We're there," he said, feeling as if he'd been living in agony for what seemed like an eternity.

As Charley locked the last file cabinet, Maxwell Casey stomped into the squad room followed by an entourage of IA investigators and Captain Davis. They were all talking at the same time except Casey who marched straight to the homicide area and tossed a bulging manila envelope on one of the squad tables. Another detective set a box of magazines and computer discs beside the envelope.

"Book him," Casey said, loud enough for Angelo to hear across the room.

Captain Davis looked up and saw Angelo and Charley standing by the juvenile table.

"Detective Harper, get over here," Davis shouted.

Angelo followed her and stood quietly as Captain Davis explained what they had found in Sergeant Hill's locker. Charley was the juvenile expert. He wanted her to look at the photos and confirm that they qualified as child pornography.

"Isn't anybody up in Vice?" Charley asked. "They're the real experts. I hate looking at that sick crap."

"I called their supervisor. He's on his way, but I want as many opinions as I can get before I start incarcerating one of my supervisors," Captain Davis said, looking directly at Casey as he finished speaking.

Angelo was listening to Davis, but he couldn't stop staring at the envelope. Without giving it much thought, he reached across the table and picked it up. Casey saw him and started to say something but they made eye contact, and the big detective didn't stop him.

The rest of the group had their backs to them and were discussing the legal requirements for child pornography. Angelo carefully emptied the contents of the envelope onto the table. Hundreds of black-and-white or digital photos, all sizes, covered the center of the table. Streaks of chemicals and poorly contrasted prints indicated an amateur had developed them. Young girls and boys in various stages of undress, to total nudity, posed seductively. They looked up at him with an innocence that denied the outrageous things their bodies were suggesting. He searched so many different faces trying to find the one he hoped would not be there.

"Hey, what the fuck," Captain Davis said, glancing over his shoulder at the table. Everyone turned now to see what Angelo was doing. They looked at him and then down at the pictures. It was eerily quiet as they stared at the shameful mosaic. There were several photos of Caitlin, her sister, and younger brother—Jake's legacy. The rest of the children were strangers. Angelo was sickened, but should have been relieved. Matt wasn't among them. He felt an odd sensation of fear, gratitude, and then disappointment.

"This is more than enough," Charley said softly, breaking the silence. She gathered the pictures one at a time, replaced them in the envelope, and handed it to the closest IA investigator. "I'm going to feed my horses," she said without looking at anyone.

"Bring Hill back. We need to talk to him again," Angelo said. He had heard Charley but let her leave without him. He couldn't go now.

"Hold on, partner. There's no 'we' here." Casey was firm but the anger was gone and he was treating Angelo like a member of the family again. "I'll handle it. Don't worry." The huge redheaded leprechaun grinned at him.

He would still worry but felt a shift in momentum and wanted to believe the many possibilities were about to give way to an ending; good or bad was the only remaining question. Matt had been gone so long that he knew the odds of finding his son alive weren't good, but hope was a powerful ally.

TWENTY

The break room was empty as he and Casey sat with their feet on the table drinking stale coffee and waiting for word to come that Sergeant Hill was back at Internal Affairs. They had already heard from Captain Davis that more digital photos were found inside the house and on the computer. To no one's surprise, except his wife's, Hill's ten-year-old daughter was among the victims. When Mrs. Hill found out her predator mate had pissed in his own backyard, she packed two bags, one for her, one for the little girl, and moved out before the search had been completed.

Shortly before midnight, Angelo was back in the cramped, dark room at Internal Affairs. He watched through the mirror as Hill's attorney and representative huddled with him in a corner of the interview room. The casual indifference of the earlier interrogation had been replaced with some sense of urgency in finding a way to keep their client out of jail, but they had no delusion about the man retaining his job. This was the critical moment Angelo had anticipated. Sergeant Hill had to offer these investigators something because he'd been a cop long enough to know if he didn't, one of his cohorts certainly would and only the first sleazy rat to jump ship would have any chance to save his skin.

In a surprisingly firm voice, Sergeant Hill described how the pedophile network operated, and if he felt any shame, the man hid it well. Jake took pictures, and the priest developed them at first. Then when everyone started using digital cameras they were able to swap pictures on the computer. The discs were copies he had made for himself. The magazines were his private collection. All of them were obtained through subscriptions directed to a post office box and, while loathsome, apparently some were legal. Casey placed a list of names in front of him.

"Is this everyone?" Casey asked and glanced up at the mirror. Hill's attorney, in the spirit of cooperation, had given Casey a list of associates his client had hastily compiled before they went back on tape and Casey had shown it to Angelo prior to the interview. Father Daly sat prominently at the top, but David Goldberg's name wasn't there. Angelo refused to believe Goldberg wasn't involved and made Casey promise he would at least mention his name.

"Everybody I know," Hill said.

"What about David Goldberg?"

"No."

"Are you certain?" Casey asked.

"I told you, no."

"Why did you kill Jake Bennett?"

"What?" Sergeant Hill wasn't expecting the question and seemed genuinely surprised. "I didn't kill anyone," he said, looking from his representative to his attorney. The lawyer tried to calm him, but Hill pushed him away. "No, damn it, I didn't kill that dirtbag."

"Hellman says you gave him money to pay off Jake because the kid was blackmailing you. You killed him to shut him up." Casey was on a roll. He had been a homicide detective most of his career, and this was the part of every tough case he liked best, making guys tell you things they could hardly admit to themselves.

"No way," Hill said and paused a minute to compose himself. "I wouldn't kill anybody, especially that termite, for a few lousy pictures. Jake pressured Daly for cash. Daly gives me the money. Says he's too scared and too sick to meet with Jake. I give it to Hellman. I was never even there. Hellman comes back the next day and says Jake's dead and the pictures are gone. Besides, if you check, I was in court most of that day."

Even listening from the closet, Angelo could tell Sergeant Hill was lying. He had worked with Casey enough to see that the homicide detective didn't believe him either, but Hellman and Sergeant Hill weren't the only suspects. Casey would have to go through the list, and he might find someone else with a strong enough motive to kill the teenager.

"Why did Father Daly pay to get the pictures back?" Casey asked. Angelo thought it was scary how similar he and Casey thought. That was his next question.

"I don't know," Hill said too quickly. "He didn't tell me, but I figured there must have been kids from his school in the pictures, and Jake threatened to expose him."

"What happened to Matt Angelo?" Casey asked. Angelo held his breath and turned up the volume.

Sergeant Hill shook his head. "Ask the priest," he said.

"I'm asking you," Casey said, raising his voice for the first time and leaning forward on the table.

"The priest told me the kid ran away. I'm supposed to leave a trail so nobody starts looking too close at the school and accidentally finds out what we were doing. So I get Hellman to convince the kid's father he ran away. Naturally Hellman screws it up."

"Why would the boy run away?"

"Don't know. Like I said, ask the priest."

"Maybe you tried to recruit him."

The sergeant laughed, "That kid? Jake told me he almost ripped his head off after he found pictures of Jake's little sister. Jake convinced him to keep quiet, so the girl wouldn't get in trouble."

In spite of his concern, Angelo felt a twinge of pride. His son had stood up for someone else. Surely the boy wouldn't do that and then run away. It didn't make any sense.

The interview continued for another hour. Sergeant Hill had talked himself out of a night in jail. He would be booked for felony possession of child pornography and be allowed to post bail. He had skillfully constructed a story that left him as nothing more than a participant. According to his version of events, he accessed the computer and received the pictures but never admitted soliciting material or sending anything to anyone. He had painted himself as a low level conspirator and gave up Father Daly as the primary suspect, a man with a purported affection for children and the natural ability to manipulate them. Hill described how over the years, the priest moved from one parish school to another compiling an extensive collection of pornography; in every parish, he managed to connect with a community of like minds and tastes. The computer had allowed him to build a huge network.

By the time Casey turned off the recording machines and the IA investigators were ready to process Sergeant Hill, Angelo had stopped watching the mirror and sat slumped on boxes of old files stacked along the walls of the room. He was exhausted, drained by the knowledge of how many young lives had been damaged by these men and the fear that his son was no match for this kind of evil. He hadn't learned as much as he had hoped but knew Father Daly was the next step. Casey opened the door and turned on the light.

"You still awake?" Casey asked, handing him a cup of black coffee. "More good news. Detectives served a search warrant on Father Daly. He was gone, along with his computer discs and any pictures he might've had. The other players were all squeaky clean too. Apparently Hill or his attorney dropped a dime before he spilled his guts."

"Was there a photo lab at the priest's house?"

"An ancient Canon printer, cartridges, paper, but no pictures."

"Where is he?" Angelo asked.

"Sister Domenic swears she doesn't know. She thought he was still in the rectory."

"Bullshit," Angelo said. "She's protecting him."

"That was my gut feeling too," Casey said. "Come on, I'll take you home. Don't sweat it, Angie. I'll find the priest." He held out his hand and helped Angelo stand. "Sorry I couldn't get more on your kid."

Angelo shrugged. He had learned something in Hill's admissions that Casey apparently hadn't. If a guy like Hill balked at revealing more information about Matt, then either something really terrible had happened, or his son's disappearance had nothing to do with this case. Either way it wasn't good news.

He wanted to call Charley, talk with her, and make certain she was okay, but it was too late. On the way home, he thought it was peculiar that nothing seemed real lately unless he shared it with her, but things were moving too fast. No time to think or plan. He didn't want to sleep or wait for Casey to find the priest. He was certain Sister Domenic knew everything, including where Father Daly had gone.

Angelo asked Casey to drop him off at Reggie's bungalow. The Mustang was parked in the driveway, and a light was on in a back room. If he hadn't been so tired, maybe Casey might've been curious about who lived there, but he didn't ask. He said very little during the trip and only a quick goodbye before driving away. That suited Angelo. He didn't want to answer any questions. All he could think about was finding the priest.

Reggie was awake and fully dressed when he answered the door. If he was surprised to see Angelo standing on his porch at this hour, he didn't show it. His expression as always revealed nothing. Without waiting for an invitation, Angelo went inside and stood in the middle of the living room.

"What do you need?" Reggie asked, and continued walking past him into the kitchen. He came back with a fresh cup of coffee, gave it to Angelo, and sat on the couch with his feet resting on the coffee table. "I'm supposed to meet my squad in an hour, new surveillance. Is this about talking to Mrs. Pike?"

"No," Angelo said. He looked at the cup in his hands for a second. His abdomen tightened at the thought of pouring more of the black acid into his empty stomach. He put it on the table and paced in front of Reggie while he told him what had occurred with Reverend Hellman and Sergeant Hill, most of it anyway. He made the story sound as if it was coming to an end and the priest was the final chapter.

"Goldberg's part of it," Reggie said, when Angelo had finished. "Is Casey going to let him slide?"

"Will you help me find the priest?"

"Casey will find him."

"Casey needs to solve a murder. I want to know what happened to my son."

Reggie sat up and took a sip of Angelo's coffee. His blue eyes seemed to see through Angelo, making him wonder what sort of thoughts bounced around in the man's brain. There was a disconnect somewhere between Reggie's emotions and his intellect. He would decide to help or not, but his reasons would most likely remain elusive. He lived by some code of honor and decency, but Angelo hadn't been able to decipher it. Right or wrong, good or evil, everything and everybody got sorted into one of Reggie's mental buckets, but how they got there wasn't clear to Angelo. He looked at the growing stack of therapy notebooks on Reggie's breakfast table and wished when all this was over he could spend a day or two reading them.

After a few seconds without any explanation, Reggie picked up the phone, punched in a number, and told whoever answered that he wasn't coming to work. He hung up without further conversation and sat back.

"Thanks," Angelo said.

"We'll talk to Sister Domenic."

"Thanks," Angelo repeated.

"I'm not doing it for you."

TWENTY-ONE

The doors to Saint Mark's chapel were open. A note taped to the wall announced that all morning masses had been canceled, but Angelo heard voices inside the church and opened the inner doors. The mission-style adobe building accommodated fewer than one hundred worshippers. Blue-tinted stained-glass windows kept it dark and depressing. He instinctively reached for the holy water and crossed himself. Rows of pews on either side of the small sanctuary were empty. A dozen nuns in identical brown habits knelt at the altar and prayed together chanting familiar Hail Marys and Our Fathers. A lingering odor of incense triggered his memories of the corduroy pants and stiff white shirt he had been forced to wear in parochial school.

Sister Domenic's commanding voice led the prayers. Eventually Angelo recognized her compact body kneeling near the center of the railing.

He genuflected beside the last pew and sat on the hard wooden bench. Reggie did the same and slid in beside him.

"You Catholic?" he asked and Reggie nodded. Angelo had difficulty associating any religion with this man but especially Catholicism. It was a humbling faith with mysterious beliefs that had to challenge Reggie's unyielding and complicated mind.

Reggie seemed to know what Angelo was thinking and without looking up whispered, "Not practicing."

The rustling of beads, starched collars, and leather shoes shuffling on the tile caused him to look up at the altar. The nuns dusted off their habits where they had knelt, then marched in a line toward the rear of the church. As they passed, Angelo examined each face searching for Sister Domenic. She was the last one to leave and paused in front of their pew as soon as she recognized them. Her hands were hidden inside the mantle of her habit, and she seemed to bite the inside of her lip. Angelo couldn't decide if her expression was anger or nervousness, but either way Sister wasn't happy to see them and sighed as she stopped and bent forward.

"Come with me," she whispered and walked away.

They followed her to her office near the school. This time she made no excuses for the clutter and didn't offer them a place to sit.

"I want Father Daly," Angelo said as soon as they were inside the room and before she could speak.

"He's gone."

"Where?"

"I don't know."

"Bullshit," Reggie said. He was picking at the paperwork on her desk.

"Watch your language and get away from my things," Sister Domenic ordered.

Reggie stepped away from the desk. "You're right. I should wait until I have the warrant. Have you ever seen a place after a search warrant's been served, Sister? It takes weeks, months sometimes, to get things back in order. That's if I don't confiscate all this junk."

"What are you talking about? I haven't done anything wrong."

"You had to know what he was doing," Angelo said. He followed Reggie's lead. There wasn't any warrant, but his partner could tell a convincing lie.

"I want both of you out of here and off church property."

"Afraid not," Reggie said, sitting on the leather chair behind her desk. "We stay until the warrant's delivered and then we search. Can't imagine you'll have much of a school anyway when parents find out the extent of this pedophile ring."

For all her toughness, Sister Domenic was not a woman of the world. She could be stubborn and arrogant, but chances were she had never dealt with anyone quite like Reggie Madison. He bullied and dared her to challenge his authority. Angelo watched as she scrutinized Reggie's face waiting for the telltale blink, a drop of perspiration, or any other sign of nervous bluffing, but there wasn't anything. Her shoulders sagged just slightly, but enough for Angelo to know Reggie had succeeded.

"Where is he?" Angelo asked.

She hesitated, looking at a stack of papers on her desk. "The archdiocese sent him away," she said.

"Where?" he asked again.

"I don't know. I wish I did. He's a sick, evil man."

"Then why protect him?"

"You're wrong. I didn't know until the detectives told me. I thought he and Mr. Goldberg were doing what was best for the school. They said you blamed us when Matt ran away, that you were trying to harm Saint Mark's." She covered her face with both hands. "Those terrible pictures . . . poor Caitlin."

"You saw the photos?" Reggie asked.

"The detectives thought I might recognize some of the children." She looked up and removed her glasses. Her eyes were red and watery. She wiped the back of her hand across them and replaced the glasses. "Of course, I did."

"Do you think Goldberg knew?" Angelo asked.

"Jenny wasn't one of them."

"I know, but do you think he was aware of what Father Daly was doing."

She didn't answer immediately which told Angelo a lot. Priests were the closest beings to heaven she would encounter on earth. They were anointed by God and did his work, but Father Daly had done terrible, evil things. The idea that Goldberg, who gave great sums of money to do good deeds, might be evil as well only compounded her confusion and literally left her without words. She shook her head and drew her arms in like a frightened, little turtle. No one spoke for several seconds.

"Can I take my manuscript before you search?" she asked, glancing at the stack of papers on her desk. "I swear to the Holy Mother I don't know any more about all this." She looked up at the ceiling as if to say, see, it's not falling on me.

"Not necessary," Reggie said. "If you've told us everything, then we'll forget about the search warrant for now." Angelo nodded. He was agreeing not to do something they couldn't do anyway.

Sister Domenic seemed grateful and promised she would do the best she could for Caitlin and the other children. Angelo felt sorry for her. She appeared tired and frail, and for the first time, her religious garb looked uncomfortable. He thought this betrayal must have been unbearable for someone like her, devoted to an idea and dedicated to a life that certainly had less value this morning since her God had been foolish enough to trust and empower a man like Father Daly.

They left her alone in the office. As they walked back to Reggie's car, the empty campus and church grounds reminded Angelo of a Mojave ghost town. The heat increased; an odor of jasmine carried on the warm breeze made him think of Charley. He had his cell phone and dialed her number at home. Rizzo answered and said she'd gone riding for the day.

He'd forgotten it was Sunday. Riding on the hilly trails around the equestrian center and hearing nothing but the sound of horse hoofs on the baked ground, was her religious experience. He was disappointed that she went without him. They had been riding together every Sunday for the last few weeks. She rode her big red gelding, and he would gingerly mount her other horse, an old chestnut mare named Ramona, a plodding, dim-witted, overweight nag, but enough of a ride for him or any man who didn't know or care much about horses. He had begun to look forward to that time alone with Charley.

Once the disappointment passed, he was glad she had gone. It gave him pleasure to think about her solitude. He wondered if the answers he'd sought for so long would finally bring him the peace of mind to be alone with his thoughts and memories again.

Reggie had just reached the driver's door when the large, slightly stooped figure of Mrs. Pike stepped from behind the convent and gestured at them to follow her. Angelo looked around, remembering the pain of being taken by surprise on that dark, deserted hill, and he was determined not to let it happen again. Reggie didn't hesitate, so any misgivings Angelo might have had were quickly put aside in the interest of not abandoning his partner.

They followed her to a garden shed behind the back wall of the convent. The big woman was dressed in a clean but faded white uniform and an apron. Her sleeves were rolled up as if she had been washing dishes or doing some other housework. She wouldn't look directly at either of them but kept wiping her hands on the apron.

"You want the priest," she said. The words seemed to stick in her throat. She didn't enjoy doing this. Angelo glanced around the yard to see if anyone was watching, coaxing her to speak, waiting in the bushes to attack them again.

"Yes," Angelo said. "Do you know where they've sent him?"

She laughed, but it was an angry, hollow sound. "No one sent him. He's hiding."

"How do you know that?" Reggie asked, and added what they were both thinking: "Why tell us?"

"He's a bad man."

"What do you care?" Angelo asked.

"He's nothing to me. I seen those dirty pictures when I cleaned for him. They made my stomach sick," she said, her face twisted with disgust.

"Where is he?"

"Skid row downtown . . . Saint Paul's Place . . . nobody's gonna find him there."

"How do you know he went there?"

"They forget I'm around when I clean. I hear stuff."

"What about Goldberg? You hear stuff when you clean for him?" Angelo asked.

"No," she said and this time looked directly at him. "He's got nothing to do with this. I wouldn't a said nothing if I thought you'd drag him in."

"Have you told the detectives?" Angelo asked.

Shaking her head, she said, "Nobody asked." She wiped her sweaty face with a corner of the apron. She was a burly woman, but her skin was delicate and thin as parchment. Spider veins lay just below the chalky surface. Even the heat couldn't bring color to those cheeks, but perspiration covered her forehead and stained the collar of her uniform. "Gotta go," she said abruptly. "Can't be gone so long." Mrs. Pike was done and it wasn't in her nature to linger. She was nearly around the convent wall but stopped when Angelo called her name.

"Does Sister Domenic know where the priest is?" he asked.

Mrs. Pike stared at him for a second, swallowed a laugh, and then continued around the wall without answering.

TWENTY-TWO

Angelo remembered Saint Paul's from his time on the department. It was a halfway house run by the Catholic Church and a convenient drop-off spot for patrol officers to unload drunks and bums. Father Daly could easily disappear among them. Angelo worried that Casey might question Mrs. Pike again or Internal Affairs might be clever enough to figure out Daly's destination, but Reggie reminded him investigating wasn't IA's strong suit and Casey's people had no reason to talk to the woman again. They should have plenty of time to question the old man.

Reggie drove from Saint Mark's to the halfway house and even in downtown traffic they arrived in thirty minutes. The place hadn't changed much over the years. It was covered with graffiti, surrounded by a chain-link fence with an open gate and street people sitting on steps or on the dirt-filled planters. A row of folded tents in shopping carts was pushed against the fence reserving space on the sidewalk for later that night when the LAPD would allow them to be set up and occupied.

The front door was open and the young man behind the lobby desk reluctantly admitted Father Daly was staying there, but he insisted on escorting them to the priest's room. It was a private room on the first floor and when they arrived, Angelo gently nudged the man out of the way and knocked.

"What do you want?" a woman's voice asked.

"We've come to see Father Daly," Angelo said, opening the unlocked door and pushing past her. Reggie followed, and they found themselves standing in a cramped bedroom with the priest lying in bed, his naked arms and chest barely covered by a gray sheet. Except for a dresser by the bed, the room was empty. The woman moved closer to the priest, standing between him and the two men.

"My name is Sister Julia. This man is very sick and you need to leave." She spoke deliberately, but without anger. She was barely five feet tall but stood with her arms crossed ready to stop them.

"Sorry, can't do that," Reggie said. "We need to talk to Father Daly."

She sighed, motioned them away from the bed, and whispered, "He's dying. You can't disturb him."

"Either we talk to him here, or I drag him in handcuffs to Central police station. He can die in the street for all I care," Reggie said matter-of-factly.

Sister Julia glared at him. Her jaw dropped, parting her lips slightly and her expression was unmistakable. She was horrified, but his cold blue eyes didn't blink. Reggie had an advantage. Angelo knew he wasn't bluffing. She looked at Angelo, but he felt little pity for Father Daly and offered her nothing.

"Why are you here?" Angelo finally asked.

"I promised not to leave him alone. What has he done?" she asked and glanced back at the bed, but the priest hadn't moved. She turned to Reggie. "He's a good man."

"What's wrong with him?" Angelo asked.

"He has a bad heart, terminal cancer. I don't understand why, but he refuses to go to the hospital."

Father Daly groaned, and Angelo and Reggie stepped around her and stood near the bed. The priest's skin was sweaty and a pale yellow. His thinning hair was damp and stuck against his forehead. He was awake and seemed frightened. He called for Sister Julia, but Reggie kept her away. The smell of perspiration grew stronger, and Angelo backed away as the priest's pungent breath polluted the air around the bed. Angelo remembered a similar stench when he stood over his dying father, the inevitable rotting odor of death.

"Mr. Angelo," Father Daly said with a clear strong voice. His eyes were open now, and he seemed coherent.

"The police know what you've done," Angelo said. "Ray Hill told them everything."

"Everything?" Father Daly laughed and then grimaced in pain, closing his eyes before speaking again. "Pictures gone . . . burned them. Too bad."

"What happened to my son? Where's Matt?"

Father Daly looked confused. He shook his head. "Not me," he said.

"What do you mean? What have you done?" Angelo tried to control his anger. He couldn't force the dying man to talk, but didn't understand why he wouldn't admit the truth now. What difference could it possibly make?

"Jake Bennett told your boy things he shouldn't have," the priest whispered as tears streamed down the sides of his face onto the pillow. His eyes narrowed and he stared intently at the ceiling as if he recognized something or someone. "Can you forgive me?" he asked the emptiness above him.

Sister Julia tried to move closer to the bed, but Reggie held her back again. "For God's sake, let me comfort the man." She was crying.

"What happened to my son?" Angelo asked, louder this time, closer to the priest's face. He was nauseated by the dying man's breath but wouldn't allow himself to back away. He refused to go another day, another second without knowing.

"Goldberg," Father Daly whispered.

"Goldberg took Matt?" Angelo asked.

"That night." Father Daly took a deep breath, grimaced, and then continued. "David said the boy was there and knew . . . all of it . . . not to worry . . . he'll fix it."

"Goldberg, but Hill said . . ." Angelo mumbled.

"Fix it," the priest whispered and closed his eyes. Reggie leaned over him and shook his head.

"Still breathing," Reggie said.

"What did Goldberg do?" Angelo shouted in the man's ear, but Father Daly didn't move. Without thinking, he grabbed the priest's arms and forced him to sit up. Father Daly's head dropped forward, his chin touching his chest, and Angelo heard a squeaky, distressed cry from Sister Julia. He looked at the clammy flesh he held in his hands, wondering how it got there, as he pushed the man's dead weight back on the pillow.

The nun was frantic. She touched Father Daly's neck and tried to find a pulse. Taking a corner of the bedspread she wiped the saliva that ran off the side of his gaping mouth, and finally saying a prayer, she covered his face with the sheet.

"He's died without Last Rites," she whispered as if the corpse might be roused by this information. She hurried to the front desk to have someone find another priest for the dead man. Angelo shouted after her to call the police.

While they waited for the Central division cops, Angelo searched the contents of a small suitcase that had been shoved under the bed. The priest had told the truth. There weren't any pictures or other evidence of pedophilia, just an old man's clothes and a prayer book. Reggie was anxious to leave, but

Angelo insisted they tell their version of the story to balance the account of the distraught nun's.

When the uniformed officers arrived, Reggie talked with them while Angelo located a telephone in the lobby and contacted Maxwell Casey. Predictably the Hollywood detective was upset that they hadn't given him Mrs. Pike's information. But then he was relieved the priest had been found, dead or alive . . . actually, dead was preferable—less complicated. The pedophile/pornography angle just confused the fact that someone had killed Jake Bennett. Casey didn't care about prosecuting perverts. He wanted a killer. Father Daly couldn't help solve his homicide. He was a loose end, and might be just a convenient scapegoat for Sergeant Hill who, according to Casey, deal or no deal, was looking more and more like his prime murder suspect.

Angelo insisted Casey hear every bit of what Father Daly had said about Goldberg and Matt, and he carefully repeated the priest's words.

"David Goldberg is dirty," Angelo said. "You can't deny he's mixed up in this. Goldberg told Daly he had Matt at his house the night he disappeared."

"That's not much by itself, Angie, the ramblings of a delirious old guy who's now dead and can't repeat them to anyone."

"He had no reason to lie, Max."

"What do you want me to do? Search the Goldberg mansion, see if he's got Matt buried in the cellar."

"Yes."

There was silence on the other end of the line until Casey cleared his throat. "Come back to Hollywood. We'll talk."

"No, we'll talk now. I'll drag Sister Julia back with me if I have to. She heard; Reggie heard. They can corroborate what that depraved son of a bitch said."

"I believe you already. I just don't know what to do with it. Get a statement from the nun and tell them to send me a copy of the death certificate." Angelo was about to hang up when Casey asked, "Remember that skeleton the divers found in Goldberg's lake?"

"What do you think? Of course I remember."

"DNA came back. Sheriff's lab people say it doesn't match anyone in the Goldberg family."

"Magdalene?" he asked.

"Nope. They think it's been in the water for years, long before she was old enough to conceive. Besides, according to her doctor, the oldest daughter's never been pregnant."

Reggie expedited the interview with the uniformed police, and by the time Angelo finished his conversation with Casey, the cops were satisfied the priest had died of natural causes. Sister Julia refused to concede Father Daly's demise wasn't affected by the cruel questioning of the two "Gestapo bullies." She begrudgingly gave Angelo a statement, but wouldn't admit hearing most of what the priest had said.

"You didn't let me near the poor man to hear his last confession. Thank the Lord, he's in a place where his soul at least will find peace and comfort," she said, crossing herself.

"I wouldn't take the odds on that one, Sister," Reggie said under his breath as they left the room.

TWENTY-THREE

There were two messages from Charley and one from Lucy on the answering machine when Angelo returned home. He was physically exhausted and emotionally drained by his encounter with the priest. The prospect of finding out what happened to his son had been so promising a few hours ago, and now it seemed murkier than ever. He was convinced the priest had been telling the truth. Matt was with Goldberg that night, but what had happened?

Lucy's message said she was worried because she hadn't talked to him for several days. He telephoned his sister and she invited him to dinner that night. Lucy hesitated only a second or two when Angelo asked if Charley could come along. He needed to be with Charley tonight because he felt his will waning and she had become his source of strength.

Lucy loved her brother and in her own way relented and invited Charley. "*Capisco*," she said sadly. "Love me, love my dog."

He let it go because it was Lucy. Charley was doing paperwork at the Hollywood station and wanted to hear every detail of what had happened that day at the school and the halfway house.

"Goldberg's too smart," she said when he had finished.

"They all think they're too smart."

"Angie, I doubt you'll find anything in his house or on his property now that Sergeant Hill's been arrested, and, if Jennifer knows anything, she won't rat on her father. Believe me I've seen parents do terrible things to kids who still refuse to get them in trouble."

"I don't understand why Ray Hill won't implicate him," Angelo said, thinking the LAPD sergeant had to understand that he could help himself by giving investigators a fish as big as Goldberg. "Why would he protect him?"

"My snitch in the DA's office says someone's paying all Hill's legal expenses and keeping his wife and little girl comfortable in a suite at the Beverly Hills Hotel. It's being handled through an attorney, so there's no way to know for sure, but my guess is Goldberg's money."

"Maybe Casey can figure out something. I'm just too tired to think straight anymore."

"Come to my place tonight. I'll cook, and I guarantee you'll sleep like a baby."

"Can't—promised Lucy I'd go there for dinner. She said you could come too."

Charley laughed. "Do I get a food taster?"

"She swore she'd be good."

"Love to," she said too sweetly. "As long as Tony's there. I'm crazy about your brother-in-law. He reminds me of dad."

"Of course, bring Rizzo."

"Did she invite him?" Charley asked.

"Doesn't matter. She expects two and cooks for a dozen. He'll save me from having to eat for three people."

Before hanging up, Charley offered to pick him up about seven P.M., and Angelo knew she intended for him to spend the night at her place. He was pleased. She was the only good thing that had happened to him in a very long time. Life before Charley and life without her were unimaginable now. He wished Matt could've known her and her father, ridden her horses, and hung around that bunkhouse. She was the essential ingredient missing from their relationship, the glue that would've put him and his son together.

The doorbell woke him. He had fallen asleep on top of his bed. As soon as his head cleared enough to remember where he was and what he was supposed to be doing, he scrambled downstairs to open the door. It wasn't a restful sleep, but revived him enough that he was hungry. Charley and Rizzo played pool while he went back upstairs to take a shower. When he finally stood in the game room awake and clean, she welcomed him home with a long, intense kiss. If her father hadn't been standing there with a pool stick in his hand, Angelo might have been tempted to lead Charley back upstairs and after some passionate lovemaking fall asleep in her arms. But he had promised Lucy and disappointment was not something his sister forgave. Besides, Rizzo still looked at him like he couldn't decide whether Angelo was a potential son-in-law or another jerk his misguided daughter had chosen to mess up her life.

Lucy's home wasn't far from his in East Los Angeles. The neighborhood was still mostly Italian families. Tony's garage was attached to the house and his business had expanded until he owned most of the block. Their one extravagance, a blue Cadillac, was in the driveway beside his Buick Regal.

He and Charley sat at the wood-block table in a corner of the kitchen while Lucy finished preparing the meal. The room had all modern appliances and a large center island with a sink. Lucy used every inch of space for cooking.

They drank glasses of the heavy red wine Rizzo had brought and watched Tony and Rizzo hover over the wine rack trying to pick another bottle for dinner. The two older men who hadn't met before tonight had emigrated from different parts of Sicily and argued in a friendly way about the best places on the tiny island with shouts in Italian from one man or the other when either of them recognized a location or person. Angelo had heard similar expressions from his father and knew they were swearing, but wasn't certain what they meant. Charley smiled at their banter. The wine and the warm kitchen brought a blush to her cheeks, and Angelo thought she looked prettier than he had ever seen her.

Lucy brought a tray layered with slices of tomato covered with pieces of mozzarella cheese and basil leaves and put it on the table in front of them.

They drank more wine and sat at the kitchen table until all the dishes were empty. Angelo was comfortable and to his surprise was enjoying the evening. Lucy was preoccupied cooking, but Angelo knew she was eyeing him and Charley, a furtive glance as she carried a pan from the stove to the sink or took a tub of butter from the refrigerator. Charley didn't seem to notice or care. She was laughing and joking with her father and Tony. Rizzo made a toast and said how much he loved his daughter, and she kissed his hands. Angelo saw Lucy smile when it happened. He understood his sister well enough to know she had softened toward Charley. Love me; love my dog.

Dinner was almost too much after the appetizers, but they ate everything—pasta with sausage and chicken, salad, garlic bread—and drank more wine. They ate and talked. No one mentioned Matt or the investigation. Angelo could think of nothing else. He tried to put it out of his mind just for tonight, but it wasn't happening. Goldberg was a bad taste in his mouth that wouldn't go away regardless of how much wine he drank.

Angelo sat in the living room with Tony and Rizzo sipping serrano limoncello with an espresso chaser while the ladies cleared the table and washed dirty pots and stacks of Lucy's best dishes. He was tired and probably very drunk. His eyes refused to stay open and conversation became background noise to his alcoholic nightmares. The most vivid dream was about Father Daly and the child's corpse in Goldberg's lake descending hand in hand through the bowels of Dante's inferno. Angelo watched them on a blurry monitor, a perverse revision of "Divine Comedy" for the small screen. In Angelo's nightmare, the monitor was sitting on top of his pool table at home.

His sister's cackling laugh woke him, and he opened his eyes in time to see the two women enter the room together. The bitterness of their last kitchen encounter had diminished. He was happy they were getting along, but female bonding always disturbed him. One woman was more than he could handle; two of them working together were formidable.

With a couple of double espressos, Angelo's caffeine level topped out, and he felt his energy returning. It was an addict's false sense of enhanced ability, but he didn't care. He was invigorated in an edgy sort of way, although he knew the eventual crash when it arrived would be ugly.

The call came as they stood on the porch saying good night. Angelo held Charley's hand and was thinking how nice it would be to be snuggled with her in her cozy double bed. Tony had run back inside to answer the phone, but after a few seconds of listening to whoever was on the other end and shaking his head, Tony walked over and handed the phone to Angelo.

"It's your ex. She's crying. I can't hardly understand nothing she's sayin'," Tony said, as Angelo took the mobile phone and moved toward the living room. For a few moments, he couldn't speak. He wanted to but the sound wasn't there.

He coughed and cleared his throat. "What are you saying, Sid?" he asked.

She wanted him to come to the condo. A teenager hiking in the canyon near her building had found something. The police had shown her pieces of cloth. She was confused. They asked her to call the father. Could he come? Sidney was quiet. He could hear a man speaking in the background. A hand covered the receiver for a second or two.

"Angie?"

"Yeah," Angelo said, trying to place the familiar voice.

"This is Joe, Joe Denby. You'd better come."

"What's going on? She's not making any sense."

"No, not on the phone. Come to her condo, please."

Angelo hung up, and the dreaded downer hit him like a medicine ball thrown by a gorilla. Everyone had wandered back inside his sister's house, surrounding him as he talked. Now they waited silently for an explanation.

"I have to go. Can I borrow your car, Tony?"

Tony took a ring of keys out of his pants pocket and gave it to Angelo. "You want me to go along?" he asked. "Maybe I can help."

"No. I'll call you." Angelo looked at the keys in his hand. He didn't want to do this, not tonight, not ever. Charley didn't say anything and wouldn't look at him. She leaned against Rizzo. Her father had his arm around her shoulder. She was a smart lady. She understood.

"What is it?" Lucy asked. "What does that woman want?"

Angelo kissed his sister on her cheek. "I'll call you," he said. Poor Lucy, he thought . . . poor Sid . . . poor me.

It was another dog skeleton, a smuggled monkey, or pot-bellied pig, a buried pet that no one was supposed to find, perhaps someone else's child but not his son.

Stubborn denial gave him the strength to get in Tony's Buick and drive to Sidney's place. He tried to miss traffic lights, refused to pass even the slowest cars on nearly empty streets, but nevertheless he arrived at the Hollywood condo in less than half an hour.

Police cars cluttered the end of the cul-de-sac. Portable lights made the street look as if it were the middle of the afternoon. Yellow crime-scene tape had been stretched across the intersection, preventing additional cars from entering. He got one of the young officers to lift the tape, and he parked the Buick in Sidney's driveway behind a new, silver, four-door Ford with too many radio antennas and a showy red light in the rear window. It had to be Joe Denby's ride. He guessed that Denby, because he was an ex-husband, had been called by someone at Hollywood station, but Angelo knew that wasn't the case when Denby opened the condo door. The deputy chief was comfortable, the way a man is in his own surroundings. His shoes were under the coffee table, and he retrieved matches and a pack of Camels, his favorite brand, from a kitchen drawer.

With a quick scan of the condo, Angelo saw Sidney in the den. Reggie was sitting on the sofa beside her.

"She couldn't find you so she panicked and called him," Denby said, indicating Reggie. "Does it bother you, him being here?"

Angelo shook his head. Reggie's self-control was a calming influence, and seeing him made his heart stop hammering against his chest. Reggie noticed him, whispered something to Sidney, and got up. She slumped back against the couch and stared at the wall.

"Sorry," Reggie said, reaching to shake Angelo's hand.

"Did she take the Valium?" Denby asked.

Reggie nodded, and the three men—two ex-husbands and her ex-lover—watched the woman none of them could satisfy for very long curl into a ball, tucking her body as close as she could to the overstuffed arm of the sofa.

"I want to see what they found," Angelo said. He had been conditioned by a frustrating search of dead ends and false leads. Why would tonight be any different? Let me see the pile of decaying coyote bones, he thought, so I can go home and get what passes for sleep these days.

"No, you don't," Denby said quickly.

"They're human remains, Angie. The coroner says a young male." Reggie spoke softly and was herding him away from the front door.

"They searched the canyon right after Matt disappeared. You know that . . ." Angelo's voice trailed off because he knew it was Sergeant Hill who had organized the investigation in the canyon and had told the explorers where to look. He could still remember his surprise and confusion when he returned that night and found the command post gone. It was Hill who convinced Captain Davis that Matt had run away.

"The coroner's taken the body. They'll do DNA," Denby whispered. He twisted his torso to see into the den to make certain Sidney wasn't close enough to hear.

"Then why call me? This is no different than the others," Angelo said, knowing in his heart this was completely different from the myriad of bogus discoveries and sightings he had endured the past several weeks.

"There's pieces of cloth," Reggie said and waited. There was more, but his mouth tightened. "Looks like animals got at the body . . . material's torn and faded, but she thinks it could be his pajamas. He was wearing them under Levi's."

Angelo glanced at the couch in the den. Her head was resting awkwardly on the arm of the sofa, buried in a stack of pillows. She might be sleeping. He moved closer and saw the barely discernible spasms in her shoulders. She was crying, muffling the sound with the pillows. How slender and pale she had become in the last few weeks. He didn't think it was possible for her to get any thinner.

He hadn't intended to think about Charley but the image of her plump womanly body and healthy blush flashed in his mind for just a second. Annoyed and feeling guilty about the mental distraction, he knelt beside Sidney and rubbed her back. She jumped, frightened by the sudden touch, but relaxed when she realized it was him.

"Do you hate me?" she asked, scarcely able to mouth the words.

Angelo sat on the couch beside her and drew her closer to him. He held her for several minutes without speaking while her tears soaked through the shoulder of his shirt. This was a woman he had loved and when he was honest with himself, in spite of himself, still loved. There were too many times he was disappointed, even blamed her, but he could never hate her. He always knew she was a terrible mother, but then he was no prize as a father.

"We don't know it's him, Sid," he whispered in her ear and gently pushed the damp hair away from her eyes.

She buried her face on his shoulder again, and he held her for a very long time until he felt her body go limp. Exhausted, she had fallen into a deep sleep. There was nothing more to do. He carefully laid her on the sofa and covered her legs with an afghan.

Reggie and Denby were in the kitchen. The sun had risen and flooded the room with the brightness and warmth of morning, but the promise and hope of a new day remained tangled in the grief that had fallen over his life. The combination of too much alcohol and sleep deprivation had left him drained and ill-prepared to face the aftermath of grim, if not unexpected, news. He had thought too little of his former wife, doubted her grief and love of their son. He had allowed their differences and his anger to distort how he had perceived Matt's disappearance would impact her life. Sidney's devastation was genuine. Of that he was certain.

Denby poured a cup of black coffee and offered to make breakfast, but Angelo wasn't hungry. DNA analysis could take weeks. He felt impatient and nervous but would have to wait for answers from the coroner. His hatred of Hill and the others had been diminished by the possibility that his search would end badly. Until the identity question was answered, his desire for vengeance had nothing left to fuel it.

"She was with me," Denby said, after several minutes of silence. Angelo and Reggie stared at him. "That's why she didn't know the boy was gone." The deputy chief stood and walked away from the table. "I'm so sorry. We locked the condo and went to the Bonaventure, never imagining he'd go anyplace during the night."

Denby folded his arms and leaned against the counter. He took a deep breath as if a terrible burden had been lifted from his conscience, but avoided eye contact with Angelo, mumbling again how sorry he was.

Angelo stared at the tall man with the flecks of gray in his expensive haircut and the beginnings of a middle-aged paunch. Denby had put Hill in Hollywood, let him slide on charges that would have led to discipline and a ban from such high-risk divisions.

"You're a piece of shit," Angelo said without emotion. Denby looked up. His mouth tightened and anger replaced the tears.

"He was told not to leave his room," Denby said.

"You knew Hill was a pervert when you transferred him to Hollywood."

Denby seemed to panic. "Who told you that?" he asked in a shaky voice. "Personnel transfers are confidential," he added, trying to sound in charge again.

"What else have you done to protect him?" Angelo asked. "How many other little records clerks or explorer scouts were there, Joe? You couldn't marry all of them."

"You're crazy. I didn't know what he was doing. Why would I do that?" Denby turned to Reggie for support.

Reggie stood and faced him. "Easy answer," he said. "You wanted to protect your worthless skin from all the insider dirt Hill had collected working for you."

"You're both crazy," Denby said. "And Davis or anybody else that says I knew about him is crazy. Nobody can prove anything." He pushed past Reggie and left the kitchen.

"What do you need?" Reggie asked Angelo when they were alone.

"I wanna see where they found him," Angelo said.

Reggie cleared the table, and told Denby they were leaving. Denby was sitting across from Sidney watching her restless sleep and ignored Reggie. Angelo had mixed feelings seeing Sidney and Denby together. After his divorce, Angelo had gone back, tried to live in her world again. Memory has a way of blocking the disagreeable stuff and enhancing those ordinary pleasant moments until he believed life could be better with her, even in a bad marriage. It wasn't. It caused him no anxiety when he finally walked away. Angelo always suspected Denby was her perfect match, the man Sidney really wanted. He hoped so because she would need someone. Angelo loved her, but not enough to live with her again.

The yellow crime-scene tape had been removed from the street. The sun was up and the cul-de-sac open again. Detectives threw the orange cones, shovels, and plastic bags into the trunk of their car, preparing to leave. Three uniformed officers huddled near the edge of the canyon, laughing and catching up with the latest department gossip. They stopped talking when they noticed Reggie approaching with Angelo. There was a quick nod and curious stares from each of the officers before they returned to their black-and-whites. Angelo caught a glimpse of them watching as he climbed down the side of the canyon toward the gravesite. Loose rocks and weeds covered the dirt trail worn into the canyon. Fresh bicycle tire marks and several piles of animal feces were indications that this was the primary entry route for man and beast. Kids and coyotes played there and died there.

A carpet of dead leaves and plants sheltered the floor of the canyon providing ground cover for an assortment of ugly, scrawny trees and brush. Angelo's boots slipped on a sludgy pool of mud and decaying weeds. He fell forward but managed to grab a tree limb and stay off the ground. The season cycles of vegetation and animal droppings were mixed in an odd brew of life and death. The smell got stronger as they closed in on the isolated spot. He took a deep breath in this suburban jungle and thought there were worse places.

The area around the small mound of dirt had been trampled and dissected by investigators searching for any piece of evidence that might yield a clue to identity, the victim's or the last person to see him alive. Angelo was startled by the size and depth of the hole. It was only a few feet long and wide, not big enough or deep enough to hold a twelve-year-old chubby boy. He looked up at the sky and imagined how lonely and frightening it would be there at night, gazing at the heavens from the bottom of that shallow grave.

Reggie tapped his arm, "You ready?"

"What did they find with the body?" Angelo asked.

"Just the cloth and pieces of Levi's," Reggie said and took a few steps away from the mound. "You know what happens when animals dig up a grave. Let's get out of here."

"I want to see him."

"What?" Reggie asked.

"The body," Angelo said.

Reggie sighed and squatted a few feet from the hole. He rubbed the back of his neck for a moment while he intently observed an endless trail of ants marching into a grassy thicket where they disappeared. Angelo didn't persist. Somehow he knew what the answer would be.

"Whatever," Reggie said, finally standing and stepping over the relentless little army.

Without speaking again, the two men walked side by side, climbed the dirt wall up the canyon until they stood looking out across the cul-de-sac at Sidney's building. Joe Denby, wearing a white bathrobe, was standing on her balcony, watching. He returned to the condo as soon as they reached the asphalt. Apparently there was no need for discretion any longer. He had a young wife and a baby at home, but Sidney had lured her last ex-husband back into the web of her life.

"I've got to get my brother-in-law's car back. You mind following me?" Angelo asked, glancing up at the balcony. He didn't know why, but he expected her to come out, say something to him, and try to take control the way she always did. That Sidney might be gone forever.

He left the Buick in the street in front of his sister's house. Tony came out the door as Angelo dropped the keys through the mail slot.

"You okay?" Tony asked, holding the screen open with his foot and retrieving the keys from the tile entryway.

"Does Lucy know?" Angelo was worried. His sister would normally hover behind Tony when he answered the door. She never wanted to miss anything.

Tony nodded. The sagging skin around his eyes pulled his features into a tired, wrinkled mask. He hadn't slept much and said Lucy had cried most of the night. Charley had tried to calm her, explaining that no one knew anything for certain. Eventually Rizzo convinced his daughter to take him home, and they left at dawn.

"Your lady and her papa have good hearts. Come in, your friend too," Tony said, and moved aside so Angelo and Reggie could pass. "I got lots a room. You can sleep."

"No, we're okay. I've got to go. I just wanted to bring your car back and see how Lucy was."

"She feels bad about all the terrible things she said to the boy's mother. I'm sorry, Nino," Tony said, pulling Angelo toward him and hugging him with surprising strength. In Italian, the old man whispered he loved him like a son and kissed him on the cheek. He stepped back and Angelo saw tears fill the craggy lines of his face. "*Benedice, figlio,*" Tony said and closed the door.

"Maybe you should stay with them," Reggie said. He waited on the porch as Angelo walked toward the Mustang.

"Are you driving or do I get Tony's car?" he asked, standing by the passenger door.

Reggie didn't respond, but unlocked the car doors. He drove to the coroner's office without speaking. When they arrived, Angelo thought about apologizing for snapping at him, but before he could say anything Reggie turned to him.

"You want me inside?" he asked.

"Yes," Angelo said, but he really didn't care.

With Reggie trailing a good distance, he led the way into the freshly painted county building. He asked for the coroner and was surprised when Gabriel Martinez, the man himself, agreed to meet with them. Martinez shook hands with Reggie and patted him on the back. He was a short, heavyset, Latino man who looked more like an investment banker than a morgue dweller.

"Are you on vacation, Detective Madison? I haven't had a corpse on my table with your slugs in him for at least a month," Martinez said wryly.

Ignoring the comment, Reggie said, "This is Nino Angelo. He wants to see the body from the Hollywood Hills this morning."

Martinez shook hands with Angelo and studied his face. "You're the father?" he asked.

Angelo wanted to deny the possibility, but didn't. Instead he said, "I don't know. That's what you're supposed to tell me."

"Hmm. Don't usually do this," Martinez said mostly to himself. "But . . . you're a cop."

"Retired," Angelo said.

Martinez shifted his weight from his right to left leg and folded his arms. It was obvious he didn't like what he felt he had to do.

"It's not a good idea for a parent to see this extensive decomposition . . . partial remains."

"Gabe, he knows what he's doing," Reggie said with a tone that suggested he believed something quite the contrary.

"Normally I wouldn't permit it, but I have a lot of respect for you guys, so I guess I'll let you do something really stupid."

Angelo didn't say anything. He stared at the well-dressed little man and waited, knowing eventually he'd allow them to see the body—professional courtesy prevailed even in the game of life and death.

"Where?" Reggie asked, moving in the direction of the freezers.

"No," Martinez said. "In the decomp room for DNA sampling," he added, getting in front of Angelo who was headed for the autopsy room. "Wait, Mr. Angelo; let me go back there first, clear everyone out, and turn on the fans." He held up his hands as Angelo started to protest that it wasn't necessary. "We do it my way or not at all."

Angelo stepped aside and noticed Reggie's worried expression.

"You don't have to come in. I can handle this alone."

"Maybe, but he won't let you in there by yourself."

Over the years, Angelo had seen strong men faint in that room. Some guys couldn't take the smell. Others got queasy watching human flesh treated like a slab of beef. He wondered how Reggie would react. He figured the stoic cop didn't mind putting the bodies there, but that didn't mean he was anxious to gawk at the results of his handiwork. Angelo was always able to separate the living from the dead. The latter didn't need his pity or emotional attachment. Until now.

After a long ten minutes, Martinez returned and led them back to one of the autopsy rooms. The combination of odors from decaying flesh and chemicals was powerful even with the air-conditioning and heavy-duty fans. Polished metal tables were freshly washed and empty except one. It was cold, undertaker cold, a meat locker for human carcasses. Angelo folded his arms to keep warm. A white plastic cloth covered what looked like the figure of a small body, much smaller than Matt's should be, he thought. He remembered the overweight young man struggling to get out of his MG that morning and tried to imagine what was waiting for him under the sheet.

His chosen profession had exposed him to an assortment of life's horrors, but suddenly he feared his imagination and memory less than what lay on that table. He knew as soon as he saw the remains, this would be the final nightmare.

He thought maybe the life force, the intuitive connection between father and son would reveal the truth as soon as he got close to the body. He felt nothing and yet he knew.

"Are you ready?" Martinez asked, clutching the top of the cloth as if he were prepared to unveil a new piece of art.

Angelo turned and walked quickly out of the room.

TWENTY-FOUR

During the weeks that followed, Angelo concluded there weren't any real revelations in life, just realities that people were unwilling to acknowledge, and others that they preferred to lie to themselves about until the truth was unavoidable. He denied the certainty of Matt's death until that moment he stood in front of the autopsy table and had to admit his son was gone. The circumstances of the boy's disappearance and the lack of clues or credible leads should have warned an experienced detective like himself that foul play was the most likely culprit. Denial had only delayed the inevitable and didn't make it any easier to accept the truth as it lay under a plain white cloth in front of his eyes. Uncovering the horror wasn't necessary, so he didn't. His heart finally told him everything his intellect had rejected.

The call came in days, not weeks, but it wasn't necessary. The coroner confirmed what he had felt since that day in the morgue. The preliminary tests were positive, confirming that the boy he loved would never grow old or have a son of his own or learn to love and forgive his father.

The *LA Times* ran a single paragraph on the last page of the California section that stated the remains found in the

Hollywood Hills had been identified as the missing son of a retired Los Angeles police detective. Sidney must have given the reporter Matt's last school photo. It showed a serious, handsome boy in his Saint Mark's Academy uniform, a child who wasn't remotely similar to the moody boy Angelo thought he knew or the young man he had discovered.

After a statement to the media claiming the cause of death was most likely blunt force trauma to the back of the head, Martinez released the remains to Sidney. Angelo wasn't certain how many weeks had passed since his trip to the coroner's office. Like today, he got up early every morning, made coffee, ate a slice of toast, and went out to his workshop. The phone would ring. He didn't care who was calling. There were messages on the answering machine, but he never bothered listening to them. The noise of the table saw, the air filled with the cleansing smell of sawdust, commanded his attention and total concentration. The result was creation: small pieces of woodwork slowly renewed his faith in the possibilities of life. He'd made a jewelry box for Charley from scraps of mahogany, but what form the project took didn't matter. The process was healing.

Matt's display cabinet now occupied the center of the room. Angelo had sanded it and put a thin layer of stain on the dark walnut. The piece would go in Matt's room for now, but he knew at some point he would probably sell it. He never really liked the idea of putting his expensive knives in a glass case. It was a burglar's dream come true.

When he stopped the saw, he heard rummaging noises coming from the house. He knew it had to be Tony and Lucy. They came every day about this time and stayed a couple of hours, so he had developed the habit of leaving the front door unlocked. This routine had become comfortable for all of them. Lucy made lunch, while he and Tony sat in the backyard and usually talked about anything but Matt. There had been a funeral and he went but couldn't remember any of it, or who was there. Reggie drove him to the church, the cemetery, and back home.

Sidney had buried their son beside Angelo's parents. He was grateful to his ex-wife for her thoughtful gesture, but it was another grave he would never visit. A headstone was a poor substitute for the flesh-and-blood, bad attitude, and smart mouth of an irritating teenage boy. Tony seemed to sense his reluctance to reminisce or ease the pain by talking about the boy, so he avoided the subject.

"You still see the pretty detective?" Tony asked and nervously picked at a gardenia bush growing near the patio. He covered his eyes with his hand, pretending to shade them from the sun. Angelo guessed Lucy had put him up to asking.

"Sure," he said and moved the table umbrella to put Tony in the shade.

"You think maybe it's serious?"

Angelo laughed. "I think maybe it's serious. You want me to tell Lucy."

"Your nosy sister, she can't sleep at night worrying about you. He needs a wife, she says. He can't stay in that big house alone. Let's make him live with us," Tony said, mimicking his bossy wife. "She's making me crazy."

"Better you than me."

"She loves you, Nino." Tony was serious again.

"I know, *cognato.* I need some time. You tell Lucy I'm fine. Charley knows I'm crazy about her. It'll be okay," Angelo said, not certain which of them needed the reassurance.

He worked in his shop for a couple of hours after lunch, mostly cleaning and organizing, killing minutes until he thought Charley might be home from work. At four P.M., he locked up the house and garage and drove to Burbank.

Angelo sat by the pool with Rizzo and Sammy and waited. Detectives had better hours than most cops, but occasionally she had paperwork or an interview that kept her late. The rottweiler had become his constant companion, curling up to sleep at his feet. Charley complained that the dog wouldn't play with her any longer and moped around the yard until Angelo made an appearance.

After an hour or so, the back gate opened, and Sammy lifted his head but didn't move. Charley, wearing a black pantsuit, waved and smiled at them. Angelo thought she looked pale and tired lately. He had lied to Tony. They hadn't been intimate since the funeral. She didn't push him, but he knew heavy hugging wouldn't satisfy either of them much longer. She leaned over his chair and kissed him on the cheek, then did the same with her father. She gossiped for a few minutes about department events. Angelo watched her nervously pull on the buttons of her jacket as she talked. She seemed distracted and hardly glanced at him. Sammy stretched and rolled over, scratching his back on the deck. She rubbed the dog's belly and excused herself to change clothes. The wind shifted and the odor of alfalfa and fresh horseshit blew from the corral across the deck. Angelo put his head back and breathed deeply. He liked the smell. It reminded him of television cowboys and wasted Saturday mornings as a child watching Gene Autry and Roy Rogers westerns. It wasn't until years later he discovered that horses were stupid and fragile and shooting bad guys didn't always make you a hero.

Half an hour later, Charley was in the corral behind the pool saddling up Sarge and Ramona. He took Ramona's reins, and they led the horses down several blocks, across Riverside Drive to the equestrian trails. Charley didn't want to ride tonight, so they walked the horses around the equestrian center, circling the huge barns and turnouts. Ramona was fat and lazy and didn't object to the easy stroll, but Sarge rebelled at the lack of genuine exercise, forcing Charley to turn him loose in one of the empty corrals.

Except for the horses, he and Charley were alone there leaning against the corral gate; the sun was setting in a rusty autumn sky, and it was the perfect moment to tell her how much he cared for her. He wanted to apologize for pulling back from her affection and assure her his misery did not change his love for her.

All of that was unspoken. Instead he asked, "What's wrong?" They'd been together long enough for him to know she was troubled too. Suddenly he was terrified his behavior had destroyed their relationship and damaged any feelings she had for him. How little he'd learned from Matt.

"I've got to tell you something," she said. He held his breath and waited for the knockout punch. The blow could come from any direction—I've found somebody else. You're too distant. You have too many problems. The list was endless. "Casey wants you to go with him to David Goldberg's tomorrow," she said after a brief hesitation.

He exhaled. "Christ."

"What?"

"I thought . . . never mind," he said, then realized she had mentioned David Goldberg's name. "To arrest him?"

"No, he wants to question him about his relationship with Father Daly. Casey's whiz kid partner found there was a lot of Goldberg money going into Saint Mark's."

Mourning the loss of his son hadn't allowed Angelo much time to think about the circumstances of Matt's death. The weeks of solitude had left him at peace but empty and just the thought of renewing his search was as satisfying as a full meal after fasting. He could taste the sweet anticipation of the hunt, and it revived him, gave purpose to his life.

"Why include me?" he asked, remembering how irritable Casey had been about allowing him in the investigation.

"You talked to the priest. The priest implicated him. Hill, Daley, Goldberg, they're deep in the mix. Casey thinks you may have had the best read on this all along."

"On what?"

"He believes Jake's death was linked to them. And now," she said, looking at him, "maybe Matt's too."

"He thinks they killed a couple of kids over dirty pictures?" Angelo asked, knowing the three of them might kill for much less if it meant their reputations and livelihoods.

"I know you won't listen, but I think this is a bad idea."

"Does Casey want me to call him?" He heard what she said, but her objections weren't relevant now.

"He's been trying to call you. You never answer your phone, so I agreed to pass on his message, but you're crazy if you go," she said.

"They killed my son."

"Fine, let Casey do his job. He shouldn't be dragging you in to do his dirty work."

Sarge charged the fence, stopping a few feet from the post where Ramona was tied. The big horse showered them with dirt and saliva, shaking his head before he moved cautiously toward Charley, nudging her hand with his nose. She reached into the pocket of her jeans and put several pieces of peppermint candy in her palm. The horse gently removed the treat, leaving a trail of sticky drool. Ramona protested with a snort, so Angelo gave her a couple.

"That's enough for you, lady," Angelo said, rubbing the animal's nose. "Or pretty soon, we'll need a wheelbarrow to move your ass out of the barn."

Charley smiled. "I thought you liked chubby."

"My women, not my horse," he said, leaning over to kiss her and adding, "I've gone way beyond liking you. You know that." She nodded. For the first time in his life, he didn't think about what he was going to say to a woman but just said it. "I'm sorry for shutting you out the last few weeks. It's an inherited character flaw. My dad did it to me most of his life. I did it with Matt. You'd think I would have learned. I love you, Charley, and want to marry you. I wouldn't blame you if you turned me down, but Lucy will be really disappointed."

Charley laughed when he mentioned his sister's name and kissed him again. "Yes," she said and jumped off the railing. "I was worried. I thought you were tired of me and couldn't think of a way to say good-bye. Dad insisted you loved me, but you got so distant."

"I'm stupid. I could've lost you too."

"Not likely," Charley said, pulling him off the fence. He held her, and they kissed until Sarge stuck his head over the railing and nudged him, nearly knocking them down. The horses were ready to return to their stalls. Angelo mounted Ramona and let her have her head. She couldn't get him back to Charley's house fast enough, which suited him fine.

They quickly mucked stalls and groomed the horses and threw their clothes in the laundry room before taking a long shower together. They made love as if the past couple of weeks had never happened. Charley had a way of making the bad things disappear for a while. She snuggled close to him, and within minutes he heard her quietly snoring. He couldn't sleep. In the morning, he would call Casey. If he couldn't have his son, he would at least have the satisfaction of seeing Goldberg and Sergeant Hill in prison for the rest of their lives.

How strange life was, he thought, his body still tingling from the effects of lovemaking while his mind plotted revenge.

TWENTY-FIVE

The ground rules were simple. Let Casey ask the questions. Don't accuse Goldberg of anything, especially homicide, and definitely resist making the arrogant little lawyer "do the chicken" on his marble floors. Angelo hadn't put a chokehold on anyone for years, so it was easy to agree to Casey's last condition.

"Your instincts have been good, Angie. Don't screw it up by thinking too much. Tell me how you read him; play off me," Casey said as they walked over the gravel driveway to the front door of Goldberg's mansion. "You should know what you're doing. We've done this a million times."

Angelo nodded. He knew what to do and had tuned out Casey's admonitions five minutes after they sat in the car.

Goldberg was rich, but Angelo figured he couldn't be too smart if he surrounded himself with losers like Ray Hill and Father Daly. Angelo would follow Casey's lead, but he had already decided, when the time came he would ask the questions that needed to be answered.

The front door was opened before they reached the porch. David Goldberg stood there, all five feet, four inches of him, in a three-piece Armani suit, looking elegant and stunted. The jacket was buttoned, and his shoes were shined. It was the kind of outfit someone would wear to a board meeting, not attire to knock around in at home.

Goldberg didn't offer to shake hands. Angelo was relieved because he would have refused the gesture and probably touched off the first crisis of their interview. The little man led them through long, empty hallways to a den in the back of the house.

Goldberg invited them to sit on meticulously placed leather chairs as he poured drinks. Angelo watched as Goldberg almost disappeared behind a full bar near the bay window. The view from this room was spectacular. The backyard was an English garden complete with a white gazebo, lavender, roses, and manicured lawns surrounded by a maze of neatly trimmed hedges. The woods and lake were barely visible from there. A white marble fountain depicting three naked children pouring a pitcher of water onto the head of another child was the centerpiece of this garden. Angelo had never seen anything so beautiful and peaceful, but knowing Goldberg's past, he cringed at the figures in the fountain.

"That fountain is nearly a hundred years old," a woman's voice said. He turned to see Susan Goldberg standing behind him. She looked matronly in a full-length cotton dress and less imposing in person. When he and Reggie had spied on her that day, the lens and distance had added pounds and harshness to her features.

"It's magnificent," Angelo said, feeling a little guilty about having watched her from the hill.

"My father bought it for me in Italy as a wedding gift."

"You're very fortunate," he said.

"Am I?" she asked and didn't smile.

"My wife, Susan," Goldberg said, making an offhand introduction while giving Angelo a glass of beer, barely glancing at the woman who stood a few feet from him. She, in turn, ignored him.

Goldberg gave another glass to Casey and sat behind a carved mahogany desk. "Sorry, Susan, did you want something?" he asked, but made no attempt to get up again. She didn't answer and sat on the couch beside Angelo.

"My husband told me you've lost your son. I'm so very sorry. I promise to make a special novena to the Blessed Virgin for his innocent soul."

Despite his hatred of her husband, Angelo found it difficult not to like the woman. She was plain and soft-spoken without pretense, almost childlike. She was a heavier, older version of Magdalene, and her big puppy dog eyes and expressionless face made him want to protect her. Her coldness toward David Goldberg only enhanced Angelo's impression of her.

"Susan, these detectives want to talk to me. It would be best if you left us alone," Goldberg said in his deep baritone voice.

She didn't look at him. "Actually, I'd rather stay," she said calmly.

Casey interrupted, "It's fine with me if she wants to be here. I don't have any objection."

"I do." Goldberg's voice cracked slightly. "I'd prefer to speak to you privately."

There was an uncomfortable silence during which Susan Goldberg didn't move. Casey and Angelo exchanged looks.

"You two work it out," Casey said, opening his notebook. "As long as my questions get answered, I don't give a fuck who's in the room. Sorry, excuse my language."

"No need to apologize, Detective. My husband misspoke. He has no problem with me being here. Do you, David?" The gentle tone was gone from her voice; control had shifted.

Angelo saw the little man seem to shrink several inches before his eyes. Apparently the rumors were true. Susan Goldberg had the money and, therefore, the real power. Angelo wondered why she tolerated the little weasel. She wasn't pretty, but she wasn't ugly either, and enough money tends to make most men overlook a multitude of beauty flaws.

"What was your relationship with Father Daly?" Casey asked Goldberg, not waiting for him to respond to his wife.

Goldberg glanced at her before answering. She didn't look up.

"We donate money to Saint Mark's Academy," he said, clearing his throat, and then more confidently added, "My daughter Jennifer, as you know, attends the school. Father Daly is . . . was the principal and pastor."

"Did you at any time exchange photographs or e-mail pictures with Father Daly or Sergeant Ray Hill of the Los Angeles Police Department in exchange for that money?" Casey asked. He didn't look up from his notebook.

"No."

"Aren't you going to ask what kind of pictures?" Angelo added.

"I really don't care," Goldberg said.

"What kind of pictures?" Susan Goldberg asked.

"Really, Susan, do we need to hear all the sordid details," Goldberg said, pushing away from the desk. He returned to the bar and poured himself another martini.

"How do we know they're sordid, dear?" she asked. Her face was a mask, but Angelo could smell a hint of perfume or bath oil now. She was close enough for him to see a thin layer of perspiration building along the side of her neck. She was nervous or angry or both.

"I read the newspapers. I know the story of Father Daly and Sergeant Hill. I assumed he was talking about their pornography," Goldberg said, sitting behind the desk again. He sipped daintily around the olive and leaned back, holding the glass and staring out the window. "I'm insulted you'd imagine I'd have anything to do with such filth."

"Would you mind if we took a look around your house to reassure ourselves you don't currently have any such filth in your possession?" Casey asked.

Goldberg began to say no, but Susan spoke over him and said, "Yes, we mind."

"I could get a search warrant," Casey said, looking up with a raised eyebrow.

"I suggest you do that," she said.

"Why are you paying Ray Hill's attorney's fees?" Casey asked. Now he was looking at Susan, but she didn't answer.

"How I spend my money is none of your business," Goldberg said. "I haven't done anything illegal."

"Why did my son come here the night before he disappeared?" Angelo asked. He knew Casey was getting nowhere. These weren't people he could threaten. He wanted to ask about Matt before the Goldbergs regrouped and threw them out.

"He didn't," Goldberg said.

"Father Daly said he did," Angelo insisted.

"Father Daly's dead," Susan said, turning to him and almost smiling. "And he's hardly a man anyone would find credible."

"Would they believe Magdalene?" Angelo asked and she blinked.

"My daughter is seriously disturbed," Goldberg said. "You will not bring her into this." For the first time, he seemed angry. His face blushed, and he twisted around, searching for assistance from the woman who seemed his least likely ally.

"She's coherent enough to remember that night," Angelo said.

Susan Goldberg turned toward Angelo until their knees nearly touched, and said, "You haven't seen Magdalene for a while. My daughter doesn't communicate any longer."

"I think your husband killed my son and maybe had Jake Bennett murdered. He's an evil man. Why would you want to protect him?" Angelo said, staring at her but catching a glimpse of Casey grimacing and closing his notebook. David Goldberg's face turned bright red. He jumped up and started to say something, but his wife spoke first and glared at him until he slid back behind his desk.

"And you say that based on what?" she asked coldly. "A dead pervert priest and a disturbed childlike woman. Or is there more, Mr. Angelo?" She was calm and didn't seem as incensed by the accusations as her husband.

"You can't live with a man and not know what he's done, what he's really like," Angelo said, before deciding to play his trump card. "You have another daughter, Mrs. Goldberg. Do you really want this guy around her?"

"Just a goddamn minute," Goldberg said and stood again, so quickly he bumped his knee against the desk.

"The priest had no reason to lie." Angelo ignored Goldberg and was talking directly to his wife now. "Why is your husband paying Sergeant Hill's legal costs? You're a smart woman. These things should bother you."

"I want you to leave, both of you," David Goldberg said in his booming voice. He was standing in the doorway and pointing down the hall. Casey got up, but Angelo stayed on the couch facing Susan Goldberg, who ignored her husband and continued staring at him.

"As you've probably guessed, my family is very wealthy and influential," she said softly and directly to him. This was between them. "They have enormous investments throughout the Midwest and own a substantial chunk of California," she said, not trying to impress him but merely stating facts. Angelo started to speak, to tell her he didn't give a fuck about her money or influence, but she raised her hand, and he waited. "I know my husband's . . . weaknesses."

"Susan," Goldberg pleaded from the doorway.

"My family can never be involved in a scandal. That's not wishful thinking. It's a fact. David is Jennifer and Magdalene's father. I won't allow my daughters to be tainted by his failings. I'm a religious woman and detest violence. I'll pray every day for you and the soul of your son, but be mindful that any attempt to drag my husband or my family into this sordid business will ruin you and everyone close to you."

She never raised her voice and didn't appear irritated or angry. She spoke in the same tone she had used to describe her fountain, a docent conducting a tour through her protected, influential life. The corner of her mouth twisted slightly when she finished, and she turned to Casey and spoke in a louder, friendlier tone. "Of course I'm speaking strictly in a legal sense," she said, and stood. "Please, let me show you out."

David Goldberg moved awkwardly aside and seemed to fade into the wallpaper as they followed his wife from the den. She was a stocky woman who walked deliberately and didn't bother to confirm they were following. Her confident stride said she knew they wouldn't dare disobey her wishes. When they were a few yards from the entry hall, she slipped away without another word. A female servant appeared and led them to the front door, holding it open until they were barely outside. Angelo heard it close quietly behind him.

"We're fucked," Casey said.

"Get a search warrant." Angelo knew this kind of pedophile predator never destroyed his trophies. Those pictures were too important to him. Angelo was certain they would be there.

"No judge in his right mind is going to sign a warrant for that house, Angie. Besides, she's right. We don't have enough unless Hill sprouts a conscience overnight and gives him up. If we tried to get a warrant, her lawyers would eat us for breakfast and shit us out before lunch."

"She practically admitted his guilt. He can't walk," Angelo said, knowing that's exactly what was about to happen. He got in the car, slammed the door shut, and sat there alone fuming. After a few seconds, Casey opened the driver's door and leaned in.

"What are you, some kind of alien? Of course he can. It happens all the time," Casey said.

"So you're just gonna let a murderer walk?"

"That slimy piece of shit is no killer. He might of ordered and paid for it, but my guess is Ray Hill did the actual killing, at least in Jake's case."

"David Goldberg killed Matt and threw him in that hole like garbage. He can't look me in the eye. You heard her. She knows it, that priest knew it, and you know it."

Annoyed, Casey sat behind the wheel and backed the car down the driveway in a shower of gravel and dirt. He turned the wheel sharply inches before the gate, nearly colliding with the guard shack. The wannabe cop in the dirty gray and yellow security uniform stepped outside his glass cage and blocked the driveway. He was angry and marched to Casey's side of the car, swearing at no one in particular.

"You got a problem?" Casey yelled at him and stuck his badge outside the window. The man stopped and retreated reluctantly to his perch in the guard shack.

Angelo watched him in the side view mirror until they drove away from the estate. The old man's lips never stopped moving, and he could only guess at the variety of nasty names he was directing at Casey.

"Must have added the guard shack after somebody shot their dog," Angelo said. He was thinking about Reggie and wondering how he would have handled Susan Goldberg.

"Fuck you, Angie. Is that what you want? We go in there and blow everybody away because we can't prove anything?"

That wasn't what he wanted. He needed somebody to pay for what happened to his son. They might never be able to prove how Matt died or who put him in the ground, but everything pointed to the hand of David Goldberg. If Ray Hill killed his son, he did it at Goldberg's bidding. Every instinct, every ounce of his investigative experience, told him Caitlin and Father Daly had spoken the truth, and he believed in his heart that Matt would be alive today if David Goldberg hadn't wanted him dead.

Casey was angry and didn't speak to him until they were in the Hollywood station parking lot. That was fine with Angelo. He wasn't in the mood to hear any more about how powerful and clever the Goldbergs were.

"Look, I'm pissed because I know I let you down," Casey said, gathering his notebook and briefcase from the backseat. "I'll do everything I can to lean on Hill. I've got a good circumstantial case against him on the Bennett boy. I'll get him charged with Matt too. I don't give a shit if it gets filed or not. Maybe that will shake his loyalty to Goldberg."

"You got him charged on Jake Bennett?"

"You bet. My tight-ass partner got a trace on that money Reverend Hellman left in Jake's pocket. It was Hill's, not Daly's. Hill took it out of the credit union that morning. And I got an almost sober resident that saw Hill inside the hotel in uniform before the dead body call came out, and we can prove he wasn't in court all day. He probably thought Hellman would bring his money back and never figured he'd be stupid enough to leave all that cash on a dead body. DA thinks it's plenty with the admissions Hill made and the other stuff we found in his locker."

"I'm not like that," Angelo said.

"Like what?"

"What you said before. I'm no vigilante. I want justice for my son. That's all."

"I know. Forget what I said. That cold Goldberg bitch pissed me off. I say stupid stuff when I'm mad. She ought to know better than to threaten an Irishman with three ex-wives. I got nothing left to lose."

"What's next?" Angelo asked. He was energized now, knowing about the charges on Hill. Maybe this wasn't over yet.

"For you? Nothing. Let me do my thing. Stay away from the Goldbergs. She thinks we're screwed. Let her believe she's won."

He agreed not to interfere but couldn't deny he wanted to do something. Casey was a good cop. If there were any way to make Hill talk, the homicide detective would find it. So Angelo would stay out of his case for now, but knew he couldn't enjoy his new life with Charley until Goldberg sat in a jail cell surrounded by hundreds of soulless men who hated nothing more than baby killers and pedophiles.

TWENTY-SIX

Charley told him she wanted a winter church wedding but Angelo preferred a quick, uncomplicated ceremony in the courtroom of his favorite judge. Sylvia White had signed nearly every warrant he had written during his police career, and she remained a good friend. She was willing to perform the marriage rite but Rizzo said Charley's mother wouldn't attend unless a priest did it. With Lucy's prodding, Angelo relented. The only hitch was a formality—both their former marriages had to be annulled. In the church's eyes, he had never married Sidney. Technically, his life with her and Matt had never happened. He wished it were that simple.

The date was set and preparations began in earnest. Lucy and Charley huddled daily to make lists, place orders, and share endless shopping sprees. He didn't participate because the two women preferred it that way. It bothered him that the anticipation of a new life with a woman he truly loved wasn't enough to fill the void created by his loss; nevertheless, he tried to make her believe he was ready to start again. He wanted a chance with Charley. He told himself the sadness and lethargy would pass.

Mrs. Pollard had the day off, and he was looking forward to spending the afternoon alone in his backyard, drinking beer and napping. Lately he wasn't doing much anyway except the occasional ride on Ramona, but he always felt tired. For weeks he had waited every day for Casey to call and report on his progress. The calls had tapered off to once a week or less. The news was always the same—nothing. David Goldberg was a nagging pain, an itch Angelo couldn't scratch. Charley mostly ignored his moods, but kept telling him if he changed his mind about the wedding, she would understand but couldn't speak for Rizzo and Lucy. They laughed because they both knew he wouldn't change his mind. The one thing in this world he was certain of was his love for her.

After lunch, he settled in the lounger ready to let the autumn smells and light breeze carry him into a deep sleep. He had barely closed his eyes when Rizzo arrived, then Reggie, and finally Tony. They gathered in the backyard under the sprawling oak tree where Angelo had a small concrete patio slab.

"I know the three of you didn't accidentally come here at the same time. So what's up?" Angelo asked when everyone had found the beer and a comfortable chair.

"I'm your best man, right?" Tony asked and got nods from everyone.

"I told you that weeks ago, *cognato.* You think I changed my mind?"

"No, but me and Rizzo figured I should do something, like a get-together for you before the big day."

"Not necessary. Are they trying to drag you into this, Reggie?" Angelo asked. Reggie was sitting with his feet stretched out on top of the geranium-filled planter sipping his beer. The dark sunglasses made it difficult to see who or what he was looking at.

"I told them to take you to my shrink. Any guy that wants to get married more than once has got to be crazy,"

Reggie said and turned toward Rizzo, adding, "Even if she's a beautiful woman like Charley."

"Thanks. What's the matter with you?" Angelo asked, but didn't get a response. He watched Reggie take another beer from the ice chest under the table and drink half of it in one gulp. Angelo shrugged and said to Tony, "Don't do anything. I don't need any of that."

Tony seemed to relax. Angelo was certain Lucy had convinced him he was obligated to throw some kind of bachelor party. Angelo wanted Charley to be his wife. The rest of it didn't interest him.

They drank and talked for most of the afternoon. When the temperature started to cool, Angelo threw scraps of unusable wood from his shop in the fire pit he'd built in the middle of the patio. The chill and the smell of burning wood reminded him of the camping trips and long hikes he'd taken with Sidney when Matt was still a toddler. Angelo would carry his backpack with Matt strapped across his chest. He could walk and climb all day like that, never feeling fatigued. The sweet sticky baby smell from his son's hair would fill his nostrils and give him more pleasure than Sidney's most seductive perfume. Everything fascinated the boy—moss growing on the side of a rock, a trickle of water down a dead tree trunk; even the bugs he found under a rotting leaf were treasures that made the world such an awesome place for him and forced Angelo to look at life again through new eyes.

It wasn't until it grew dark that Angelo talked about Matt. Maybe it was easier when they couldn't see his face. Stories of Matt's childhood, words of regret for all the years he missed as his son grew older and more independent. Among these friends, he felt comfortable explaining how hard he had tried after the separation to be a father again. Tony remembered some of the funny, little-boy stories that Angelo had forgotten, those times when the stubborn, individual personality of his son was fighting to exist. The two men laughed and recalled a lifetime of events. It was easy; the boy's allotted time had been so short.

Angelo knew Rizzo and Reggie were listening. They didn't speak, but he needed them to understand his son had been more than the surly adolescent Reggie saw, more than a discarded pile of rotting flesh and bones.

When they finished, the fire was smoldering coal. The only light was reflected off the red tint of intense heat and a nearly full moon. Angelo wiped the tears from his face. He had never cried, but in the silence and emptiness of the night, he realized how impossible it would be to forget.

"You still believe in God, Nino?" Tony asked through the stillness.

"I don't know," Angelo said. He thought evil seemed the stronger force in this world. If all God could do was collect souls after their demise at the hands of wicked men, how relevant was he anyway? "Maybe Reggie's right. There doesn't seem to be anyone out there keeping things in balance. The good guys can't seem to win anymore."

"It's not that they can't win. They won't do what's necessary," Reggie said. He had been so quiet Angelo thought he was asleep. He had consumed at least a six-pack of sixteen-ounce Budweisers but didn't slur a word.

"If they did, then they probably wouldn't be such good men anymore," Rizzo said.

"By whose definition," Reggie countered, moving closer to the fire.

Rizzo wasn't one to back down from a good philosophical argument, even with someone as intense as Reggie.

"Other good men who make the rules," Rizzo said.

"When bad people use the rules to get away with murder then it's time to fuck the rules and do what you got to do—what you know you should do."

"What are you talking about here, Reg?" Angelo asked, but knew what was gnawing at his friend. Reggie had been angry since Angelo told him about his and Casey's interview with the Goldbergs. Several times Reggie had mentioned that Casey would never be able to prove Goldberg was involved in Matt's killing. Goldberg would get away with murder unless someone stepped in and did the right thing. The beer and the darkness made Reggie's argument sound less extreme.

Rizzo stood and patted Tony on the back. "*Paesano,* I got to go. You ready?" He offered his arm as support, helping Tony to his feet. The two older men hugged Angelo and shook hands with Reggie before shuffling toward the driveway. Rizzo stopped and came back a few steps, pointing at Reggie. "You know, my friend, if you got no rules, you got anarchy. I been there in the old country. Believe me, you don't want to live like that."

When Rizzo and Tony were out of sight, Reggie picked up the ice chest and dumped the water on the lawn. He helped Angelo toss the empty cans in the recycle and poured sand on the dying embers before they went inside the house.

Under the bright kitchen lights, Angelo saw the dark shadows under Reggie's eyes. He recognized the symptoms of someone who wasn't sleeping or eating. He had seen the same symptoms in the mirror for weeks after Matt was found.

"You look like hammered shit, Reg."

"Got things on my mind."

"You're not thinking of doing something stupid, are you? Because if you are, don't," Angelo said, but he knew if Reggie was planning something he was wasting oxygen trying to change his mind.

"How can you sleep knowing that garbage is living like a king while . . . ?" Reggie asked, and added quickly, "Never mind, I drink too much."

"I don't sleep very well because I want to kill the bastard, but I can't," Angelo said. He had thought about this so many times. It always came down to who he was. In his imagination, Angelo had executed Goldberg a hundred different, painful ways, but he couldn't throw away a lifetime of principles because the law wasn't smart enough to catch a monster. He had to trust that the system would eventually work or everything he was and believed in was a lie.

"I don't sleep very well because I want to kill the bastard and probably will," Reggie said dispassionately.

"So you kill him and go to prison or worse. Scumbag wins again." Angelo tried to sound calm and reasonable, but his heart was pounding. In spite of his lofty principles or maybe cowardice, he wanted Goldberg dead, and Reggie was offering to do it.

"I don't think he'd be around to celebrate much," Reggie said, grinning.

"No, this isn't something you need to do."

"How the fuck do you know what I need." Reggie didn't seem angry but wouldn't look at Angelo. "Maybe I need to drag his fucking ass out of bed tonight and blow his arrogant brains all over his rich, snotty wife."

"Okay, then it's something I don't want you to do."

"I've got a lot of respect for you, Angie, but I'm not you. I can't find a way to live with this. All this justice crap is out of balance. The bad guys aren't supposed to win. Besides, don't worry about it. You aren't responsible for what I do. I'm not telling you anything. Read about it in the papers tomorrow." He stepped around the table and walked out the back door.

Angelo didn't try to stop him. Why should he? It was what he wanted, an avenging angel who had the guts to do what he couldn't.

TWENTY-SEVEN

The satisfaction didn't last. Angelo paced through the house for less than ten minutes before backing the MG out of the driveway. It's probably easier to kill someone than it is to think about someone dying when you know you can stop it. That last morning in the desert, Matt wanting to shoot the rabbit, it kept replaying in his mind. Reggie was his friend. The cost was too great.

Angelo had thought about calling the police to intercept him before he got to the Goldberg estate, but couldn't think of a way to do it without jeopardizing Reggie's career and future with the department. Attempted murder isn't something the LAPD generally condones even when it involves a lowlife like Goldberg.

What if Reggie was bluffing and didn't go to Goldberg's home, and Angelo called out the cavalry. He'd look like an idiot. There was no one he could call for help. His only recourse was to race up the freeway and hope the Highway Patrol was distracted with something else. Fortunately there wasn't any traffic, and his little sports car got him to Canyon Country in less than an hour. He drove through the quiet rural area and was relieved he'd been there before and didn't need to read street signs in a place where there weren't any lights.

He felt nauseous as he pulled up to the front gate of the estate. He had passed the black Mustang parked a hundred yards down the street. It was empty, and so was the guard shack. He backed up and parked in front of Reggie's car. Getting over the wall wasn't something he had considered, but it was the only way inside the grounds. The gate might be easier to climb, but floodlights exposed every inch of it. He could probably be seen from the house, but there wasn't much choice. It might already be too late.

The exterior bolts that secured the gate to the wall offered the best foothold to hoist himself high enough to grab the top of the decorative spikes. If he didn't impale himself, maybe he could drag his body over to the other side. The light in the guard shack was on, but no one sat in the chair. The security guy might be one of Reggie's victims, or he might be taking a turn around the property. Angelo didn't know how much time he'd have before the guard returned and sounded the alarm.

Angelo had grabbed the bars and placed his foot on the first bolt when he saw her and nearly fell as he jumped down again and tried to back away from the light. A woman in a white nightgown was walking up the driveway toward him. Angelo immediately thought of Magdalene.

"Jimmy, Mr. McCarthy, is that you?" Susan Goldberg shouted. Her voice from a distance was thin and anxious.

Angelo knew he should have disappeared into the shadows, run to his car, and returned home. No one would know he'd been there. Reggie was screwed anyway. Instead he felt himself step back into the light and stand where she could clearly see him.

"No, it's me, Nino Angelo."

She came closer to the wrought iron gate and grasped the bars with both hands, staring at him for several seconds.

"I thought you were the guard," she said, and shaking her head, added, "Why are you here, Mr. Angelo?"

"I thought my friend was here," he said, thinking he might as well tell the truth because in a few hours the whole world would know what Reggie had done or was about to do.

"There's no one," she said, glancing back at the guard shack. "I can't find David. I thought Mr. McCarthy might help me."

"Let me in, Mrs. Goldberg."

She shook her head. "I don't know." She crossed her arms trying to warm herself. She was barefoot.

"I can help. It's too cold out here for you."

She stared at him for several seconds and then reached over and pressed a button inside the gate.

"I heard a terrible sound," she said, stepping aside as the gate opened. "A loud noise, then a scream like a wild animal. It woke me. David wasn't in bed." Angelo saw little resemblance to the self-assured, strong-willed woman he had met with a few weeks ago.

"Did you check on Jennifer?" he asked.

She nodded. "As soon as I got up. She's asleep. I woke one of the maids to sit with her. Where's Mr. McCarthy?" she asked, becoming more agitated.

"Did you search the house?"

"Of course, look at it." She pointed at the mansion as they approached. The lights were on in every window, making the exterior as bright as the middle of the day. "He's not here, but all the cars are in the garage."

"Wait inside. I'll look around. If you see Mr. McCarthy, tell him I'm here," Angelo said. He didn't want a frightened security guard hitting him with a nightstick or worse.

She didn't answer, but went inside the house and peered out at him from the window closest to the door.

He went through the garage and all the exterior buildings with no sign of Reggie or Goldberg. There was only one place left to look. He crossed the gravel driveway and found the footpath that led to the lake and Magdalene's cottage. Fifty yards into the thicket, he heard the rustling of branches behind him. Afraid the security guard had seen and followed him into the woods, Angelo stepped off the path and stood quietly in the darkness. His eyes had adjusted enough to see her white nightgown before she turned the flashlight in his direction.

"Mrs. Goldberg," he said softly, trying not to frighten her. She jumped back and dropped the flashlight before he could make her understand who he was. He picked it up and turned it off. "You should wait at the house with Jennifer." He touched her hand to return the flashlight. Her skin was cold and trembling.

She shook her head and backed away from him. "Something's happened," she said, and he could hear the quiver in her voice. "I'm going with you." He didn't argue, but took the flashlight and started walking again with her trailing behind him. He didn't understand her concern for a man she didn't seem to love or respect.

Angelo's only objective was finding Reggie and doing as much damage control as possible before the police had to be called. Her motivation might not be very different from his. With the light, he moved faster now, but made no attempt to allow her to keep up. She didn't say anything, but he could hear her heavy footsteps and grunts as she tried to navigate the potholes, large rocks, and fallen tree branches that obstructed the path. He didn't notice if she was wearing her shoes now, but her bulky frame wasn't suited to this hike under the best conditions.

It took about fifteen minutes for Angelo to reach the clearing where Matt's book bag had been found. The sound of Susan Goldberg's heavy breathing and the movement behind him had stopped. He easily found the narrow trail around the lake. Hesitating for just a moment, he was tempted to wait for her to catch up. Instead he left the flashlight turned on and threw it on the ground where she was certain to see it. He could find the cottage now with his eyes closed, and he didn't want any harm to come to her if she tried to walk near the water in the dark.

After a few hundred yards, he saw the lights. The boards had been removed from the cottage windows. Someone was there. Looking for signs of movement in the distance, he stumbled and fell, hitting his knee on the rocky ground. His right pants leg was torn, and he could feel dampness, bleeding, around the tear. He had landed hard and his knee ached when he put his weight on it. There wasn't any sign of the light behind him yet, so he walked slower and tried to ignore the pain.

He followed the same route he and Reggie had taken the night they met with Magdalene. Poor Magdalene, in her hopeless state of mind, she had given him reason to believe he could find his son alive.

He stood outside the window, watched, and listened for several seconds, but saw nothing. There was no one in the sitting room outside the bedroom. He ducked under that window and tried to look into the bedroom through the french doors. The shades had been drawn, so he had no choice but to go inside. Fortunately the doors were unlocked. He opened them and cautiously stepped into the room.

David Goldberg was curled up on Magdalene's white comforter with his back to the door and appeared to be sleeping. He was dressed in a gray business suit and wore his polished burgundy shoes. Angelo walked around the bed. Two pools of blood saturated the space in front of him, one where the man's face should have been and the other in the general vicinity of his crotch.

Even without the unmistakable odor of a freshly fired weapon, Angelo recognized the work of a double-barreled shotgun. David Goldberg had spent his last few minutes on earth looking at the instrument of his death. His mutilated, bloody hands were outstretched in a defensive manner. He had died pleading for his life, and that gave Angelo a peculiar instant of satisfaction he'd never felt around such violence. Usually he'd pity even the worst criminal if his death was this terrible. Goldberg had been dispatched to hell with no time to prepare his soul, no penance, no atonement for his sins. His eternal fate had been sealed.

Angelo heard a woman crying in the front of the house and a man talking to her. He inched open the door to the hallway and saw a shotgun leaning against the wall. His first instinct was to pick it up, but he didn't. His fingerprints on the murder weapon with his overwhelming and frequently expressed desire for Goldberg's death would make a pretty good circumstantial criminal case against him. He would face whatever was in the living room without a gun.

Reggie standing in front of the fireplace was the first thing he saw, but his friend didn't seem concerned that he was there.

Mrs. Pike was sitting on the couch behind him, crying like a baby. She looked up at Angelo as he cautiously approached Reggie; she wiped her eyes and nose on the sleeve of her coat and stopped crying immediately. Apparently it was okay to blubber in front of Reggie but not him.

"Stop looking like that. It wasn't me," Reggie said, nodding toward the bedroom. "She did it." His voice was clear and strong with no indication that he had been drinking or that he hadn't slept.

Angelo caught a glimpse of the dining area off the kitchen. Blood smeared on the floor and splatters on the counters and the cupboards created a gruesome scene. Mrs. Pike slid back on the couch and her long black coat opened, revealing a blood-caked white work apron. Dried red splotches covered her legs and shoes. She had most likely picked up the little man and put him on the bed. Angelo couldn't help thinking like an investigator and moved around the couch to follow the telltale trail to confirm his suspicions.

"I'm not sorry," Harriet Pike said, trying not to cry and seeming very sorry.

Reggie tapped Angelo on the arm and handed him a couple of Polaroid pictures. They both depicted a pretty, little, pale-skinned girl, about two or three years old. She was naked except for a string of pink pearls around her neck and was posed with her chubby legs spread in a very disconcerting way.

"She found these pictures of her daughter . . . hers and Father Daly's, that is," Reggie said.

Angelo gave the pictures back to Reggie.

"He tells me my Mary's been taken in by a good family . . . then those bastards did that," she said, pointing at the pictures. "They abused and drowned my baby." Mrs. Pike stopped crying, and her voice grew stronger as if she suddenly remembered all the good reasons she had for killing David Goldberg.

She had found the sordid pictures and efficiently solved a homicide that had baffled police for months. She'd held her own trial in the cottage kitchen, and retribution was swift if not painless.

"She says that kid in the lake is hers," Reggie said.

Of course it was, Angelo thought, remembering the eerie image on the monitor. It all made sense now. Magdalene wasn't talking about her baby. She was describing the housekeeper's child. The priest was the father Magdalene had described. The poor girl somehow had discovered what her perverted father and the priest had done. The terrible secret they'd hidden from Mrs. Pike for so many years.

"I cleaned their toilets, lied for them, because I believed they found my Mary a decent home and saved me from shame." She was looking up at the ceiling, talking to no one. Tears rolled down the sides of her face, off the tip of her nose. "All the while, they were laughing at me, doing terrible sick things to my baby."

"What happened to my son," Angelo said.

She stopped and stared at him, shook her head. "No," she said.

"Tell me," he gently insisted.

Her expression hardened and her posture changed. She sat up and seemed to be steeling herself.

"The bastard promised to drive your boy home," she said quickly. "Hours later, he come back with dirt all over him, his expensive suit ruined, and says he fell." She wiped her eyes with both hands and dabbed under her nose with her coat sleeve. "When the boy went missing, I knew he'd done something awful."

It was strange. Angelo didn't derive satisfaction or comfort in hearing confirmation of what he already knew. Details didn't make the loss any more bearable. There was a hunger in him that nothing would satisfy, especially the death of a pitiful speck of dirt like David Goldberg.

"Have you called this in?" he asked Reggie.

"I tried. The phone's out."

The front door creaked open slightly as soon as Angelo punched 911 on his cell phone. Reggie reached inside his shirt near his waistband and put his hand on his Glock. The weapon was out and pointed at the door before Susan Goldberg stepped into the room. She gasped and froze until she noticed Angelo. The old security guard they had antagonized a few days earlier was a step behind her. He dawdled shamelessly and didn't appear anxious to expose himself to any real danger on her behalf. Her white nightgown was streaked with dirt and ripped in several places. The hem had a perfect ring of mud several inches above the ground. She looked at Angelo's bloody pants leg, and he thought he saw her smirk.

"What's going on here, Mrs. Pike?" she asked, and turned to Reggie. "Who are you?"

"You'd better sit," Angelo said, and directed her to a chair as far from Mrs. Pike as possible. She stopped and stepped back when she saw the kitchen. He decided that he'd better tell her now. Her arms stiffened by her sides as he nudged her toward the sitting room outside the bedroom. In those deceptively peaceful surroundings, Angelo told her that her husband, David Goldberg, was dead, and his body lay in the next room. She insisted on knowing how it happened. He told her but refused to let her in the bedroom when she demanded to see him. She didn't cry.

"Was it Mrs. Pike?" she asked and Angelo nodded. "Did she say why?" Angelo nodded again. She breathed deeply, more resigned than sad, he thought. "Have you called the police?" she asked.

"I was calling when you got here."

She stood, dusted off her filthy nightgown. It was busy work. The garment was a total loss.

"I'm going back to my house. Is that all right?" she asked.

"Mr. McCarthy can help you get back," he said, attempting to hold her arm and escort her to the living room, but she shrugged him away.

She stared at Mrs. Pike but didn't speak to her. Mrs. Pike looked up and watched silently as Susan Goldberg walked across the room and whispered a few words to Mr. McCarthy. They had almost reached the front door when Mrs. Pike stood.

"You can't protect him. The whole world will know he was evil. I have proof," Mrs. Pike shouted, as McCarthy pulled the door closed behind them.

Reggie and Angelo exchanged glances as Mrs. Pike began crying again and covered her face with her hands.

"What proof do you have?" Reggie asked when her sobbing ebbed.

"Pictures," she whispered. "I know where he hid his smutty pictures."

"Where?" Angelo demanded.

Her eyes narrowed and her jaw was rigid as she glared at him. "No, everyone protects him."

"He killed my son, Harriett. Why would I protect him?" Angelo asked and waited while she nervously tugged at her hair, battling the demons that now controlled her mind. She struggled to understand how Angelo fit into her revenge.

Angelo had instructed McCarthy to leave Mrs. Goldberg at the mansion and escort arriving police to the cottage. It was nearly half an hour before the first uniformed officers arrived and several hours more before the detectives looked at the body of David Goldberg and began their investigation of the murder scene.

While they waited, Angelo and Reggie pestered and cajoled Mrs. Pike to reveal the location of the pictures. She stubbornly refused until confused and tired she finally told them. Mr. Goldberg had hidden the pictures in the stables. There was a false bottom in the bin where the oat hay was stored.

Before he met Charley, Angelo wouldn't have known oat hay from Bermuda grass but she had educated him. She expected him to care for Ramona because he rode the horse. He was certain Ramona was part quarterhorse and part pig. She ate constantly, and oat hay was her favorite.

As soon as the detectives were satisfied that he and Reggie were nothing more than witnesses, they were allowed to leave. Because David Goldberg was a very important person, several high-ranking law enforcement officials showed up at the crime scene. They caused enough confusion that no one thoroughly pursued the fact that a retired cop and an SIS detective were visiting a family they barely knew in the middle of the night and had discovered the body. Detectives had a suspect and a confession. The rest could be sorted out later.

They left the cottage and walked as quickly as they could back to the main house and the stables. Reggie had a flashlight and led the way. The mansion was nearly dark now, but Angelo went directly to the large structure behind it. He turned on the neon overhead lights and stood for a second surprised by the size and lavishness of the barn. Although every stall had a magnificent head peering out at him, the place didn't smell of horses.

He described the texture and appearance of oat hay to Reggie, and they started searching at opposite ends of the building. Of course there was more than a single bin, and on the third try, Angelo located the one with the false bottom. It was the only one with a false bottom, and it was empty. Angelo let the lid drop closed and kicked the side of the wooden box. Goldberg was dead, but no one would know what a sleazebag he was. If it ever existed, the proof was gone.

When they returned to the stable door, Susan Goldberg was sitting there at a small desk. Her hair had been washed, and she smelled of lilacs. She was wearing brocade slippers now, had disposed of her ruined gown, and was dressed in a long silky lounging dress.

"Shit," Reggie said. He understood a second before Angelo figured it out.

"You took them," Angelo said, not expecting her to admit anything.

She stood and turned off the light. They followed her outside to the gravel road where she waited while Reggie shut off the exterior lights and pulled the gate shut.

"I warned you my family would never be involved in a scandal. That deranged woman murdered my husband. It's over. As soon as this investigation is finished and both of you are off my property, it would be best for me and my children if you never came back."

After she spoke, Susan Goldberg followed the bright security lights back to her mansion. Angelo watched until she was inside. She'd get her way, but in the bigger game, he figured, like him, she'd already lost.

TWENTY-EIGHT

Love is compromise. Angelo didn't want to sell his house, but he put it on the market before the wedding. Charley loved her Burbank retreat, but agreed to lease the property to strangers after she and Angelo were married. They would take the money from the sale of his home and buy another house big enough for her horses and his workshop. The money from the lease would help make the payments and pay the taxes. Conciliation meant change, a little discomfort, and the promise of a new life for both of them.

Angelo was surprised how much his property was worth. The real estate woman was certain it would sell faster if it were vacant. That wasn't a problem because he wanted to pack his tools and empty the house before it was shown. He hoped the family ghosts and residual sadness would disappear if the furniture and memories were removed and placed in storage for a while.

The most difficult chore was dismantling the basement. Each picture had to be taken down and carefully wrapped for protection during the move. Packing his friends' images felt like losing them again. Whenever Angelo lingered in this place, he could feel their presence. The spirits gathered in the wine cellar to share a few quiet moments together. Those memories comforted and energized him.

Angelo had resisted for a while, but a few days after the funeral, he'd hung Matt's picture on the wall beside the others. It was the only photo Angelo had of his son where the boy was laughing. Reggie had taken the picture shortly before Matt disappeared. It made Angelo smile every time he looked at it. This picture would go with him. The new house would necessitate a wine cellar, but Angelo wasn't certain his gallery of ghosts would ever come out of their boxes again. He had Charley.

His wine was stored in crates to be moved to Burbank until they found a new home, but he kept out a bottle of cabernet for a farewell drink. He cleaned off his chair and sat facing the empty wall. Faded rectangles marked the places where pictures had been. He didn't need to see them. After years of staring at the same photos, he could recall the faces as clearly as if they were still hanging there. He sipped from the bottle, toasting dead partners and friends. Finally he looked at the empty nail where Matt's picture had been. He reached beside the chair, picked up the photo, and took a long swallow from the bottle. Sometimes there isn't a way to say good-bye.

When he opened the door from the cellar to the kitchen, Reggie was sitting at the pine table drinking a can of Pepsi.

"I like yours better," Reggie said, looking at the half-empty bottle of wine in Angelo's hand.

Angelo opened an empty cupboard before remembering all the glasses had been packed. He wiped the rim and handed the bottle to Reggie who took a quick swallow and put it on the table.

"What are you doing here?" Angelo asked.

"Thought you might want to know. DNA from the kid in the lake matched Harriett Pike and the good Father Daly."

"Was there any doubt?"

"Nope," Reggie said, taking another gulp of wine. "But they still have nothing to link Goldberg to Daly and Hill. Harriet Pike kind of ruined her credibility after the cottage massacre."

"Doesn't matter," Angelo said and meant it. "But I've got to ask you something."

Reggie smiled. "Okay."

"That night, if Mrs. Pike hadn't done it first, could you have blown the little weasel's brains out?"

Reggie stopped smiling and sat back. The pale blue eyes were clear and serious. "We both know I could have, Angie. The real question is would I throw away my life to kill vermin that needed killing."

"Well?"

Reggie tossed the empty Pepsi can in the trash box. "Charley's in the attic," he said. "She's got most of it packed up but sent me down to find you."

Angelo didn't push for an answer. He had learned a lot about Reggie Madison during their time together. If he didn't want to talk about something, he wouldn't. It was comfortable to believe his friend wasn't capable of an execution, but Angelo understood the truth might be different. He couldn't say he was sorry Goldberg was dead or that the punishment didn't fit the crime, but Angelo would always wonder where Reggie was when the shots were fired and how much encouragement the distraught Mrs. Pike actually received.

"I gotta go," Reggie said, standing. He hesitated a moment, then turned and opened the kitchen door. He stopped again and faced Angelo. "Yes," he said, and was gone.

TWENTY-NINE

Charley was on her knees taping a box for the movers. Angelo hated this attic and hadn't been up there for years. Spider webs and mice had claimed the space, and he willingly abandoned it. Angelo had loved his mother and father but had no desire to rummage through the leftovers from their lives. On the other hand, he couldn't bear to throw the junky memories away, so Charley agreed to pack them. He had decided that everything in this room would remain in storage until eventually he had the guts to destroy most of it.

He kissed the top of her head after she looked up and smiled at him, and she continued to wrap the box.

"Reggie said you were looking for me," he said, sitting on an empty crate beside her.

"Uh huh, that's true. I wanted to show you something."

"Oh, God, Charley, you didn't find my baby pictures, did you?" He was such a dorky-looking, hairy kid. It was scary.

"Better," she said and held up a white, crocheted, baby dress. "I think it was your baptismal gown. Lucy described it to me."

"She would know." He took the dress and touched the pink ribbon threaded around the neckline. It looked new, but had a musty smell. "Want to keep it as a memento?"

"No, I thought I'd use it."

"For what?" he asked.

"Our baby's baptism." She looked up at him.

It took a minute for his brain to engage. "You can't have babies," Angelo said. He stopped and for the first time noticed her slightly rounded belly. In the last few weeks, he hadn't really looked at her. No, he looked, but never really saw her. She was tired a lot and had put on a few pounds that he thought were attractive and sexy. He had been consumed with revenge and never noticed the life growing inside her. He kissed her and said, "You're pregnant."

"I didn't want to tell you until I was certain my body wouldn't reject it. I shouldn't be pregnant, Angie. The doctors told me I couldn't have another baby."

"Two full-blooded Sicilians? Our people can't even hug without getting pregnant," he said.

"We did more than hug, honey."

"You don't think I'm too old?"

"Apparently not," she said, laughing.

He touched her stomach and thought for an instant about Matt, the awful pain of his loss, and the anxiety he would feel every minute of this baby's life. But it was a gift. He had been given a miracle, another chance. This time would be different. He would be a real father, a protector. Angelo slid onto the floor and on his knees he hugged Charley.

"You're okay with it?" she asked.

He nodded. "I'll be a good father."

Charley laughed. "You'll be a great father." She was serious again. "This baby will live a long life. I promise."

"I know," Angelo said and relaxed. He gently placed the christening dress on her lap. The baby would be baptized and he would ask Reggie to be the godfather.